THE Alpha's SEDUCTION

by

MARLOWE ROY

Content Advisory

This is a work of omegaverse fiction. It contains adult themes, mature language, and explicit sexual content. Reader discretion is advised.

Table of Contents

DEDICATION

For all the women of a certain age who absolutely deserve to get railed against a tree.

CHAPTER 1

Della

Della hated parties. No, that wasn't quite right. She abhorred parties. Not the idea of them (a gathering to celebrate or socialize was banal enough), but the memories they evoked. Memories of a different world and a different life: sophisticated crowds glittering with power, prestige, strategy, and, most important of all, ambition. A reminder that once upon a very different time, basking in the endlessness of "what if," stood a woman she barely remembered but whose skin she inhabited.

Her own skin, which felt less like a vital organ and more like a living shroud relegated to contain the remains of Adeline Cabrese, whose star rose right before the world fell.

Della, as she was now known, blinked back to the present. She grounded herself in the sharp pops of the bonfire, the sting of wood smoke in her eyes, and the loud guffaws of large men. Known as Alphas in this upside-down reality, they replaced the glitterati to claim all the power in this new world. Nursing a cup of what passed for liquor, Della bided her time at the impromptu party, thrown together to welcome half of the Pack back home from their three-month trading trip.

The Alphas clustered in jovial groups of varying degrees of intoxication. Some new faces mixed with the familiar, as the group had picked up several new "brothers," as they referred to each other, like members of some weird dystopian frat. Della hadn't caught the names of the new ones and, frankly, didn't care. Like every Alpha who'd trickled into the Pack, they would inevitably cross her path with some uncouth comment or obnoxious behavior. In short, she'd learn their names when they pissed her off.

In her early forties at the start of the apocalypse, Della had lived through the century following the collapse. Millions died while massive radiation and environmental disruption fundamentally altered those who remained. Beyond creating the new Alpha and Omega dynamics, the resultant mutations also disrupted normal aging in some who survived. Della included.

So, now, when she looked into the cracked mirror in her humble cabin, she didn't see a withered centenarian crone. She saw the face of a distinguished, older woman. A woman who'd lived through it all and abandoned all of her grandiose goals for one overarching imperative: survival.

Never one to back down from a challenge, Della'd ticked that checkbox. She'd survived. And that's exactly how she felt. She'd survived for so fucking long, she couldn't even remember what it was like to actually… just… live?

Around the bonfire, someone plucked a guitar to the forlorn strains of an old folksong about a woman named Jolene, while the few Alpha and Omega parents in the settlement began herding children to their beds. Yawns dotted the faces of kids and their parents alike, and Della fought one of her own. With the Alphas' return, the day had become unexpectedly busy unloading the horses, sorting the supplies to their various storage areas, and situating the new Alphas in the community. The caravan bore goods and supplies and sweets for the children, but the only thing Della coveted from the haul was the story of how the one new Omega who'd arrived with them, a pretty woman named Kess, had bonded with Hunter, the leader of this Pack, the Alpha of Alphas they called him, and Della's oldest (and only) living friend.

If anyone had asked, Della would've disbelieved it was even possible for Hunter to mate and bond with an Omega in the way these younger, newer Alphas did. Like her, he'd lived through the cascading geopolitical, environmental, and social crises of TheEnd and on into the next age, now called the AfterEnd. Also, like her, his aging had slowed to a snail's pace.

She'd come to the party wanting to hear the story from him directly before bending his ear about a pressing concern that had arisen while he'd been gone, along with her proposed solution. Yet all evening, he'd stood glued to Kess's side, laughing and enjoying himself like never before in their twenty-year friendship. Unable, in good taste, to interrupt a party with an agenda item, Della set it aside till tomorrow.

Exhaustion asserted its sluggish weight on her eyelids, and another yawn snuck out of her mouth.

Before the Alphas appeared and precipitated a flurry of activity, Della had already been awake since before dawn for her daily five-mile run. Now, well past sundown, she'd accumulated enough fatigue to ease her always-rocky passage into slumber. At least, she hoped so.

With a toss of the high-proof-low-enjoyment alcohol down her throat—one advantage of losing her sense of smell was not being able to taste the disgusting brew—it was time to head home. She winced until her eyes watered, letting the harsh burn steer her away from memories of expensive aged whiskey, bespoke cocktails, and a working nose to appreciate them.

Leaving the cup in a wash bin, she turned her feet toward her cabin and her cozy, snug bed.

"Hey, Del," Hunter's voice reached out as she attempted to skirt unnoticed past the gathered group of Alphas surrounding Hunter and his mate. "Come here for a sec. We're talking about your favorite thing, infrastructure."

Della halted. A dozen Alpha eyes pivoted to her, some more alcohol-glassy than others, and her ears tingled with excitement. Infrastructure had been precisely what she wanted to speak with Hunter about. Perhaps now was a good time to make her pitch after all.

"Thinking about building a bathhouse." Hunter's craggy face lit with a wholly atypical expression of excitement. "With a water heater and a big ole bathtub. What do you think?"

The wind dribbled from her sails, but she quickly regrouped. Tilting her head, she considered it. A bathhouse with indoor plumbing and hot water wasn't the worst idea. They had nothing so sophisticated in Morris Hill, nor any way she knew to construct it. Even if they could scavenge the necessary piping, heat required energy capture. But the idea would be popular with the Alphas because it benefited everyone, whereas her proposal only benefited a few.

Della took a stab at imagining Hunter's vision. "You want to use the solar panels?"

"Possibly."

"Don't have enough," she said simply. They'd been down this road before and had never been able to make much use of the salvaged panels.

His eyes sparkled. "Have a tip on finding more."

The Alphas voiced excitement at Hunter's announcement, rushing to talk over one another about where he'd heard about more and how soon they could organize to investigate. Della bit the inside of her cheek to keep her immediate opposition in check. A bathhouse would be nice, sure, but it was a luxury when the settlement had more important, basic needs to be met.

First and foremost, the new, unmated Omegas needed a bunkhouse of their own. The two unmated Omegas who had recently joined the settlement were too new and timid to advocate for themselves. The other female residents of Morris Hill were all *mated* Omegas, most of them preoccupied with their growing broods and swelling bellies and no space to think about larger village issues. That left Della to raise the issue and lead the charge.

But after long years in the AfterEnd trying to organize rebuilding efforts, Della had learned her lesson: Alphas couldn't be led anywhere. Not by a woman, and *especially* not by a relic woman from a former era who didn't fit in their tidy boxes of Alpha, Omega, or Beta.

No, Alphas had to be *influenced* to do the right thing. And right now? She had no patience or tolerance to do any influencing in a mixed group of half-drunk man-beasts.

She made eye contact with Hunter. "It's a nice idea," she said diplomatically. "We should revisit it when you've got the panels in hand. If you'll excuse me…" Not waiting for a response, Della spun on her heel and continued down the path to her cabin.

A rude response? Possibly.

Probably.

But Hunter knew her well enough not to take offense, and she had a reputation as the Pack harpy to live up to. Hunter was grumpy—or he *had* been—but the Pack tolerated his crankiness because they loved him and respected him.

Della, they tolerated. Or avoided.

She passed by the largest building in the settlement, quiet and cool after the evening meal had been eaten and cleaned up. The combination mess hall/cookhouse served as a central hub. Beyond it, further toward the perimeter, lived the quieter sections of family cabins, the Alpha bunkhouse, and her own small domicile. Hopefully, Rue would be asleep so they wouldn't have to interact as Della got ready for bed. She empathized with the quiet Omega, obviously traumatized beyond comprehension, yet Della longed to have her cabin back to herself.

"There you are."

The deep male voice oozed with a familiarity that stopped Della in her tracks. To her left, coming down the darkened path that led to the Alpha bunkhouse, strode a tall, languid shadow.

"Pardon?" Della asked, purely on instinct. A hundred years in a coarse civilization and she hadn't yet been able to relinquish all of her hard-wired etiquette.

The man approached, his gait smooth and easy and exceedingly fluid. Arms swinging at his sides, there was a looseness about him, a nonchalance. It lent him an air of sophisticated confidence so unlike the typical Alpha hulking assuredness. If they were fe-fi-fo-fum giants, he moved with a feline grace, complete with the wide, self-satisfied, Cheshire cat grin aimed at her from where he stopped, a mere foot between them.

"Been looking all over for you." His voice tumbled down from his height, saturating her with its thick, luxuriant twang. Parts of her brain, unused for decades, sprang into action, dissecting the broadness of the vowels and the drag of the consonants. She hadn't heard anything like it for a very long time. Oklahoman? Texan? Those places no longer existed, yet here this accent was, hugging her eardrums like a long-lost friend. "You aren't headed home now, are you?"

The inquiry snapped her back to the moment and the stranger in her path. "I am," she said decisively, deploying the crisp Della tone that even the densest of these Alpha creatures never failed to understand as not-fucking-interested. But instead of marching off on her way, she lingered, her brain snagging on the mystery of what he'd said. "What do you mean you've been looking for me?" she demanded, disliking how the presumption grabbed her attention and derailed her path to her bed.

Stray light from the bonfire touched his face, confirming his identity as one of the new Alphas whose names she hadn't bothered to learn. He canted forward a few inches, close enough that Della recognized the blank air where his scent should've whispered across her nose. Unlike the Alphas and Omegas, who evolved to survive in the AfterEnd with their heightened sense of smell, hers had only diminished. The fires that robbed Della of everything she loved had also scorched her airways and stolen her olfaction in a last, final insult.

Nostrils flaring, the man inhaled audibly before grinning even wider. "That's good stuff right there," he murmured, more to himself than to her.

"I beg your pardon," Della sniffed with her nonfunctioning nose. "It's not polite to comment on someone's…" She silently balked at the word scent, with its primal, intimate connotations she didn't care to reference in front of this stranger. Problem was, all the other words that came to mind (fragrance, perfume, bouquet, aroma) were no better, possibly even worse.

"Scent?" he supplied, a big smile tucked into the small syllable as if mocking her hesitation to say the word out loud. "How polite is it to smell the way you do and run anywhere except into my arms?"

A whooshing heat roared up Della's neck and blasted onto her cheeks, quickly followed by a cooling stream of sharp annoyance. It had been a while since she'd fended one off, but Della was no stranger to Alpha propositions. Yet an Alpha's clumsy attempts for her attention had never resulted in such an immediate and assertive bodily reaction. "Wh—what did you say?"

"You heard me just fine." He rocked back on his heels, giving her some much-needed breathing room. "I've been catching traces of you since we rolled up this morning. A little here, a little there, but never enough to be satisfying. I'd heard there were a few unmated Omegas here, but—"

"You're mistaken," Della interrupted. "I'm not an unmated Omega."

The Alpha's grin extinguished like a blown-out candle. "You're mated then?" He jerked his chin back toward the party. "Which Alpha is yours?"

Della shook her head, her flustered tongue tripping over itself to get the words out. "I don't have an Alpha, and I'm not an Omega. That's all I was trying to say."

Two thick brows popped halfway up his forehead. "Well, darlin', you ain't no Beta."

Della sighed an exasperated huff. Setting aside the fact he'd called her *darlin'*, which was ridiculous and over-the-top, even for an Alpha, she despised this discussion and the hundreds of times she'd been mired in it. What was the fucking obsession with labels? It was like the human race forgot about every other distinction that used to divide people and went all in on this business with dynamics. Alphas as the "new" version of men, Omegas as the "new" version of women, and Betas as everyone else who hadn't changed in some biologically improbable way. Everyone had to be categorized and put in their proper place, and, god forbid, if you didn't fit into one, you'd never hear the end of it.

What was she? Della wanted to snarl. *How about a twenty-first-century feminist living in some caveman-adjacent post-apocalyptic society witnessing the simultaneous evolution and devolution of the entire fucking human race?*

"It doesn't matter what I am," she snapped, her good manners finally giving up the ghost, "and even if it did, it's none of your business. Now, if you'll excuse me..." Pressing the back of her hand to an unyielding bicep, Della moved to swipe the Alpha out of her way. More of a symbolic gesture, really, but she was making a point.

The man relented, feinting to the side to let her pass, but as she slipped past the arm in question, she found herself spinning off her path and pinned against his solid chest. Before she could protest with anything more than an undignified squeak, he'd backed her up against the rough side of the mess hall.

Instinct tallied up the danger in her situation. She was alone, in the dark, trapped against a solid structure by an Alpha she didn't know while the rest of the settlement partied the night away at least a dozen yards from where she stood. Alpha hearing being what it was, someone would hear her scream and come to her rescue. That is, if they weren't all too plastered or rendered blind from Lars's most recent batch.

Della opened her mouth to test her theory but hesitated as more data points notched onto the opposing tally. Her heart thumped at an accelerated clip, but not with the skidding, hurtling scramble of fear. Her breasts tingled, awake and interested in a situation that did not involve them in the least. And her belly whirred with a dirty, restless tickle that signified something else entirely.

She wasn't actually afraid.

As if he read the thoughts on her face, the Alpha's broad grin reasserted itself. "My apologies for surprising you," he said in his soothing drawl, "I ain't gonna hurt you, you see?" He slid his palm from around her waist and coasted it up the length of her arm and then back down again. Despite her clothes and the warm night air, Della shivered at the touch. Strong, determined fingers hooked around her own, then raised her hand in a loose grip she could easily break, yet didn't.

The Alpha brought her hand to his lips, sliding her knuckles across them in a slow, seductive movement. Shadowy eyes locked on hers and Della's breath caught in her throat, as if time were suspended along with all her bodily functions.

Well, not all of them.

"You can explain it all to me later,"—his low, soothing voice cascaded down her spine like a physical touch—"what you are and what you're not. Where you're from, where you've been, and how you got here, and I'm gonna listen to all of it and anything else you gotta tell me, all right?" He flipped her hand over to press a slow, humid kiss to her palm. "But I can't have you brushing me off like some unfortunate gnat who crossed your path. That ain't how this is gonna go."

Della swallowed, her entire body buzzing like someone carbonated her blood. She floated in her body, unable to look away from the faint bonfire flickers that offered enticing glimpses of his face while withholding the complete picture. Unmoored, yet unable to ignore the sultry, hypnotizing gusts of his breath on her palm or the luscious strength in his muscled chest as her nipples hardened against it.

Nothing in her life resembled this dizzying acceleration. Maybe the vile alcohol had finally gone to her head? Who was she, again?

Outside of this moment, she wasn't exactly sure.

"How what's gonna go?" The words rasped through her throat, dry from the open-mouthed heavy breathing she hadn't been aware of.

"You don't run from me." Even in shadow, his eyes simmered with an intensity that sent a warning shudder over her skin. "I take care of what's mine, and from now on, that includes you."

Alarm sounded from somewhere deep in Della's brain. Some invisible line had been crossed. What had been intriguing the moment before turned threatening with the implication of claiming and possession.

"I'm… I'm not… *yours*." Della removed her hand from his grip. He didn't attempt to restrain her, only letting his long fingers trail over hers on the release.

The corner of his lip quivered like that Cheshire cat smile itched to come out and play. "No?" He stepped back, taking his solid heat and searing strength with him. Della glued her feet in place, fighting an urge to cross the space and hurl herself back against his powerful body, derailing the departure she'd initiated the moment before. She had no business rubbing herself against this unknown Alpha, this stranger. And he had no business making declarations about who belonged to whom based on nothing more than his highly suspect inclinations.

What was *wrong* with her tonight?

"No," she said, palm outstretched like a traffic cop. "I don't know who you think you are cornering me like this." She thrust a pointer finger toward the party. "But ask anyone here. Della lives alone and takes care of herself." That finger swiveled to jab at her own chest as she hissed, "I don't belong to anyone."

"That your name? Della?" He backed up another step, shoving his hands in his pockets as that slow smile slid back into place. "All right. You go on home. I'm gonna head back to the party and ask the kind residents of Morris Hill to tell me everything they know about Miz Della, who takes care of herself."

Della threw up her hands. "Do whatever the fuck you want. Just leave me out of it."

Scooting around him, she took off at a pace somewhere between dignified rush and rattled scurry, trying to still the crashing waves of confusion pounding down around her head. Who the hell did he think he was?

And why did she desperately need to know?

CHAPTER TWO

Cal

Cal watched his Omega disappear into the darkness, her long hair flapping against her back like a retreating flag. He'd let her go, for now, thinking she had the upper hand. It was a strategic withdrawal, not a surrender.

Body drumming with the barely-leashed desire to chase her down and claim her right there and then, his thoughts centered on what he did have: a name and a face to match the scent. As soon as he'd come in range of this place, her aroma had invaded his senses and crippled him with lust. Rich and sweet, it sang to him of luscious black currants stewed with hints of sharp anise or juniper. All day, he'd caught whiffs here and there, stronger and then fading, like chasing a ghost in the corner of his vision.

A childlike giddiness lightened his steps, and, lungs filled with her, he ambled back toward the party in a strangely philosophical mood. Maybe some supernatural force had herded him to this place, where an Omega waited for him. His decision to come to Morris Hill, driven by instinct and impulse rather than any deep, thoughtful consideration, suddenly became much more interesting. Not since he'd come of age, when Pa began to hand over more of the Pack responsibilities, had he experienced such wide-open possibility. Back when he'd overflowed with duty and responsibility for his future as Alpha of Alphas.

Only none of that had come to pass. The memory of those early ambitions, what followed, and all his terrible regrets diluted his cheer. He'd strayed too close to the edge of things he tried hard to forget. His booted toe sent a rock sailing off the path, underwhelmed as it launched and spun off, swallowed by the night. How much easier would life be if regrets could be kicked into the abyss?

Predictable guilt followed that sentiment. Was he complaining about living with memories of what had happened? At least he had lived. Thanks to him, several members of his Pack could no longer make that claim.

"Cal!" Matteo's voice jarred him from his morose reverie. Simon and Matteo, the two Alphas he'd joined the Morris Hill Pack with, lounged on the far side of the fire, chatting with another Alpha sprawled on the ground. Raising a hand, Cal headed toward them, trying to recall the other Alpha's name. Was it Rodrick? Or Rennik? He'd met so many today, he couldn't remember. Matteo handed Cal a battered metal cup half-full of strong-smelling liquor. "Where'd you go?"

Cal balked as the powerful smell evicted Della's delicious fragrance from his nose. But he nodded his thanks with a lift of the cup, sinking down to take a seat on the log bench next to Matteo. "That poor pup, Heck, got too deep in the drink. Took him back to his bunk to sleep it off."

Matteo snorted. "He'll be hurting in the morning." Not concerned for himself, his party-animal friend took another hearty glug from his cup. "Riddick here says Hunt's gonna put us all to work at the ass crack of dawn."

Riddick—*Riddick was his name*—a tall, lanky fellow with a shock of wild curly hair, chuckled bitterly and raised his glass. "Our fearless leader likes to make a point about not overdoing it."

Matteo wiped his mouth on a tattered sleeve. "Nah, he took off with Kess a few minutes ago. He's gonna be lost to the Rut, and we aren't gonna see him again for a week at least."

Riddick raised a brow. "You wanna wager on that, new guy? I'll take that bet."

"Maybe we should get a pool going," Matteo said excitedly, eliciting a dramatic scoff from the quieter Simon seated on his other side. "How long everyone thinks they'll stay shacked up before coming up for air."

"Why're you always inventing new ways to lose money?" Simon said into his cup, earning a dirty look from Matteo in turn.

"You underestimate the Alpha's strictness about this place." Riddick circled his chin to indicate all of Morris Hill. "He's a right bastard when he wants to be."

"Listen." Matteo leaned forward, delighted to have stumbled into his favorite thing: a pointless argument with someone new. "We've been on the road for over a week, and he's been eye-fucking her—"

"And regular fucking her," Simon added under his breath. Cal cringed recalling the long nights pretending he wasn't half-hard from hearing some other Alpha's Omega come.

"—the entire trip. Ain't no fucking way we're gonna see him tomorrow." Matteo's voice boomed louder with each offensive sentence. "He's gonna be crawled so far up her—"

"All right, brother, that's enough," Cal warned and knocked his shoulder into Matteo's, sloshing alcohol from Matteo's cup and onto his pants. Cal didn't usually rush to exert dominance over his friends, but he didn't want Matteo speaking disrespectfully about the Alpha of Alphas on their first night in their new home. He wasn't a paranoid type, and, for the most part, he liked the Morris Hill Alphas he'd traveled with, but Pack dynamics and loyalties could be a tricky thing.

"Oh hell, man." Matteo wiped at his damp pants and looked mournfully into his cup.

Cal flashed a glance at Simon, a silent inquiry of *"how drunk is he?"* Simon responded with a subtle, sideways head bob, which Cal took to mean *"not great but not as bad as it could be,"* and Cal trusted the assessment. Simon and Matteo grew up in the same Pack until, as often happened, they'd left their home when their full Alpha natures emerged. Cal had met up with the pair when he'd been traveling through the plains country as part of his self-imposed purgatory of transience. Their work ethic and sense of honor mirrored his own, and the three banded together. By that point in time, Cal'd been Pack-less for twenty-five years, and while he'd hoped to eventually shake off the longing for the safety and security of a Pack, he'd craved it with a desperation both pathetic and inescapable. Eventually, the three of them made their way across what was once the Western US and came to Old Tacoma to look for Omegas and work, in that order of priority. They found little of each, but it was there Cal met Hunter during a frenzied search for a kidnapped Kess.

He'd liked the crusty Alpha immediately, identifying him as one of the Old Ones, like his Pa, and someone Cal wouldn't hate himself for bending the neck to. His acceptance in Hunter's Pack was more than he deserved after what he'd done, but no one knew that but him.

Simon and Matteo, without any other prospects, simply followed his lead and came along, although sometimes Cal suspected the two of them only stuck around so he could break up their bickering and frequent fights. Younger than Cal, thirties to his fifties, they deferred to his judgment and dominance without him ever making a point to demand it. But if there was a leader to their little trio, it was him.

Rolling with Cal's correction, Matteo righted himself, sighing wistfully. "That's what I'd do if I had an Omega of my own." He raised a toast to his fictional Omega. "You wouldn't see my ass for a fucking *month*."

"Got no problem with that," Simon drawled. "I've seen enough of your ass to last me a lifetime."

Riddick snickered into his drink, Cal hid a smile behind his fist, and Matteo blew Simon a sarcastic kiss. "Don't pretend you don't love it, brother."

"Oh, for fuck's sake," Simon groused.

"It's a shame, though"—Matteo swirled his cup, apparently having drunk enough to be unfazed by Simon's ribbing—"that there are only two unmated Omegas here. I'd thought there might be more in a place like this."

Riddick shot Matteo a regretful glance, his curls waving at the slight movement. "We had none before Zorah and Rue, and I'd count Rue off limits, unless you'd like to get your head bashed in by Sloan."

Matteo visibly deflated. "Well, shit."

Someone tossed a fresh log on the bonfire, and a flurry of sparks exploded into the night sky, as numerous as the questions Riddick's comment sparked in Cal's mind. The embers flamed out, one by one, as he waded through the confusing and conflicting information. Riddick didn't include Della among the unmated Omegas; Della herself denied her Omega status, yet every ounce of his Alpha nature had come to the exact opposite conclusion. None of it made a lick of sense.

Most infuriatingly, if Cal wanted to know more about her, he had to ask, even if it meant disclosing his interest in the prickly woman. An interest that could be used against him, or even worse, might be used against *her* in some unknown way. Sure, Hunter had accepted him into the Pack, and he'd fought his way in fair and square, but did that mean he could trust every Alpha here, especially when it came to something as important as his newly discovered Omega? Absolutely not.

Then again, he needed to clear up the mystery of this Omega. If he could take their conversation thus far as any indication, Riddick seemed as affable and lacking in deceit as Matteo. Taking a deep breath, Cal shifted his wary attention to Riddick and strove for a casual, disaffected tone. "What about Della?"

"Who?" Simon asked.

Riddick scoffed and flashed a single gold tooth that glinted in the firelight. "Sorry, brother, but Della ain't no Omega."

"Who's this?" Matteo pressed, leaning in and refusing to be left behind in a conversation about a woman no matter who she turned out to be.

Riddick sipped from his cup. "Old lady Del."

Cal angled his chin down in consternation. Old lady? Granted, even in the dark, he could tell she wasn't a fresh-faced youngster, but tucked against his chest, she felt alive, spirited, and soft in all the right places. She felt *perfect*.

"She's at least as old as Hunter," Riddick continued, "maybe more. She tries to impose some civilization on this place. Hunt said once that she was someone important in the before times, so I guess that's why." He lifted a shoulder and dropped it. "Usually, she looks out for the Omegas. A lot of them are too shy to bring stuff up, so Del does it for them. Rubs some Alphas the wrong way, but I don't mind her."

Cal scraped a palm over his stubbled chin, carefully stowing the information away. "And she's not Omega? I could've sworn she scented like one…"

Planting his palms behind him, Riddick leaned back, looking Cal over with a new, appraising shine in his eyes. "Is that right? You sure you weren't picking up on Zorah? She's been all over this party tonight, meeting and greeting all the new potentials."

"Gonna be a fucking throw down over that one," Matteo grumbled.

Riddick's expression stilled. "Remember, though: no one claims an unwilling Omega. You try any shit like that, and you'll be lucky to leave with your precious ass still attached to your body."

"He knows," Simon said, gaze narrowed on Matteo.

The insistence on Omega consent was a unique innovation in the Morris Hill Pack. Cal wished he knew the origin of it, but didn't anticipate it being a problem for him or his friends. It wasn't in him to take an unwilling woman, Omega or not, and Della was no different. Besides, she had no idea how persuasive he could be or how enjoyable said persuasion could be.

"But she's unmated? Della?" Cal pressed, not yet willing to let the topic go now that he'd taken the risk.

"Oh, yeah." Riddick reached for and drained his cup. "Hunt talks to her. They go way back, I think." He pitched his voice low to evade any eavesdropping Alpha ears. "Some brothers like to call them Mommy and Daddy when they got an itch to bitch and moan." He affected the speech of a bemoaning Alpha. "'Mommy says we gotta get the poison ivy cleared off the path before the young 'uns get into it.' 'Daddy's not happy about the state of the east pasture.' Shit like that."

Matteo guffawed. "Too bad for her, there's a new mommy sleeping in daddy's bed now."

"This daddy would be more than happy with two mommies." Riddick laughed, stretching his arm out to clink cups with Matteo.

Cal's spine seized up in instinctive, jealous alert. Mommy and Daddy? What did that mean? They went way back? Had Della been *involved* with Hunter? Since when? And for how long? And if she'd been with Hunter, was he the only one? Or were there others?

Disgust pulsed in his temple at the visual his brain vomited up of Della being passed around like the Pack whore. Not that he had anything against whores—if that's what they wanted to do, who was he to judge?— but he did object to sharing, *especially* when it came to what was his. Suspicious, he scanned the party, looking for the dozens of Della's former lovers hunched in the shadows.

He tugged his collar to the side, trying to coax some cool air on his heated neck and return to the land of reason rather than paranoid fantasy. When they'd been close, not a single whiff of Alpha musk tainted her heavenly scent. No one had touched her any time recently. Granted, half the Pack had been away for the last three months, so if she had a lover, maybe they hadn't yet—Cal grit his teeth—reconvened.

But no, that couldn't be it. If he'd been fucking an Omega, and he'd been away for three months, he sure as shit wouldn't be sitting at a bonfire socializing and calmly waiting to make sweet, tender love to her in the quiet of the night. No. He'd be railing her up against the nearest building at the first available opportunity. For *starters*.

Somewhat mollified, Cal tuned back into the conversation between Matteo and Riddick, unsurprised to discover it had strayed in a decidedly more vulgar direction. Simon sat looking quietly amused, but their laughs grated across Cal's eardrums like a chorus of braying donkeys. He knew they were fucking around, getting drunk, shit-talking, and bonding, but he didn't like any of it. Not the suggestion Della had been sleeping in Hunt's bed, not the idea she'd been rejected and replaced by Kess, and especially not Della being the inspiration for Riddick's dirty threesome fantasy.

Cal hungered for more information, but held his tongue. Plenty of time to sort it all out because, while his decision to join this Pack and try to make a home here for himself and his friends was so far a good one, he now had another, much more important reason to make this work: he had a reluctant Omega to woo.

CHAPTER THREE

Della

Morning frost crusted the newly sprouted grass, crunching and scrunching under Della's feet on her cooldown walk back to her cabin. Cheeks still warm from her run, she turned her appreciative face into the chilled wind. The crisp, piney scent grounded her in her surroundings, reaffirming that she'd left the fires and droughts and destruction of her native California long behind. Even now, a century later, a longing for home sometimes ate at her. She'd loved her state, but after TheEnd, it ceased to be hers. Now, she took comfort from the rich, dense evergreen forests, their strangeness calmly reminding her that not everything beautiful had burned.

As she cut across the grass at a brisk pace, her joints moved like well-oiled machine parts. Despite a night of restless, poor sleep, the run energized her body. Despite being twice their age, none of the aches and pains of advanced age had ever plagued her in the way they plagued her grandmothers once they entered their elder years. In some ways, her current health surpassed her life before TheEnd, when she spent her days dashing from one meeting to the next, surviving on coffee and cocktails and the occasional greasy slice of pizza consumed in three heartburn-inducing bites.

Running wasn't her favorite activity, but she'd taken it up after years of an inability to fall back asleep after one of her many flaming nightmares. Only nightmares hadn't deprived her of sleep the night before—it had been him. She hadn't forgotten—how could she when her body buzzed for hours after their impromptu meeting?—but she'd filed the episode away as the drunken misadventure of an Alpha not yet assimilated to their community. Nothing unusual and certainly nothing to lose any more sleep over.

Movement caught the corner of her eye, and she turned to see Hunter striding across the settlement at a fair clip. Alone.

The excitement of opportunity whizzed through her veins. She hadn't expected to see him out and about in the village, especially without his Omega, so soon after his return. As leader of the Pack, his presence was always in high demand, and she'd secretly feared that private conversations would be impossible with his new mate added to his long list of obligations. Catching him alone gave her hope that maybe he hadn't changed all that much in his time away and even greater hope that he might be sympathetic to her pitch.

"Hey!" Della yelled, jogging to catch up. Acknowledging her with a chin tip, Hunter slowed his pace, but only barely. "Where's the fire?" she said through puffing breaths.

"Got a few things to take care of, then I need to get back to Kess." His voice, always abrupt and to the point, sounded like it had been scratched over sandpaper on its way out of his throat. His hair pitched a fit in a wiry, tangled mess on top of his head, accompanied by the tiny, fresh claw marks that snaked up his neck.

Was all Alpha-Omega lovemaking that intense? And, if so... *yikes*.

Della frowned, annoyance prodding her guts. Of course, he needed to get back to Kess. Stretching her hips to match his long strides, she crushed the inconvenient resentment under her heel. She didn't need to worry about that now. She needed to focus. "Anything I can help with?"

He glanced down over his shoulder and paused, hands on hips. "Maybe. Logan said there's been some trouble with the food stores, things going missing. Have you seen anything suspicious?"

Della's chin jerked back. This was news to her as well, and disturbing news at that. The settlement's head cook, Logan, was a good cook and an excellent manager. If he said things were missing, things were missing.

She wiped a bead of sweat from her hairline. "We've never kept the basement locked," she said thoughtfully. "Never had to." Hunter gave her a knowing look, an acknowledgment they were thinking along the same lines. If someone was stealing food, then something somewhere in the settlement was off.

Some problem they weren't aware of. Some need going unmet. She dropped her hand to her side. "I'll ask around the Omegas, see if anyone has been taking extra for some reason. I think Marie is expecting again, but I don't understand why anyone would feel the need to steal..."

Across the central clearing, Della's gaze fixed on the steady stream of Alphas, Omegas, and children (affectionally called pups) trickling into the mess hall for breakfast. Morris Hill boasted a dozen children, ranging in ages from newborn to fifteen, an impressive number of offspring considering they all came from only three Omegas.

After the nuclear devastation of a brief but cataclysmic world war, environmental catastrophes mounted. With each new disaster, more was lost. Disease spread, violence surged, and lack of infrastructure made medical care a distant memory. If the hospitals weren't flooded, burned, or razed by earthquakes, then no medical staff showed up to work, or too few did. On top of that, no sterile supplies were available, and the staff was attacked by violent, roving gangs who wanted nothing other than to sow more chaos in their failed society.

Children died, women miscarried, and those who managed to carry pregnancies to full term barely survived delivery or postpartum. Della passed a hand over her cobwebbed womb. It had emptied its precious contents shortly after the fires, erasing the last trace of her husband left in the world. She'd barely even grieved for the child she'd never have. Not that the loss didn't carve out the last piece of her heart, but back then, grief was a luxury no one could afford. Not when the world crumbled and the screams of orphaned children and the sobs of aggrieved families drowned out her pain, leaving her with the worst thing of all, her utter and total helplessness.

So, even after almost twenty years in Morris Hill, it was bewildering to walk around and see happy, thriving families. Even more astonishing to witness Omegas give birth year after year and not suffer birth complications or any ill health effects either. More than once, she and Hunter marveled over it in low, hushed conversation, speculating on the rhyme and reason of it all. However it happened, their population grew every year, and now with two new, unmated Omegas in the Pack, more children might be on the way by next summer.

Except, in the interim, they presented a different challenge.

When Rue and Zorah, whom the Pack had discovered during their travels, were escorted to Morris Hill, Della deduced the oversight in the community plan immediately. Without anywhere to put them, Zorah had been housed with a mated Alpha-Omega pair and to help out with their brood of pups, which turned out to be a fair solution.

But when Rue had been situated similarly, proximity to an Alpha had triggered some sort of trauma response in her that set the settlement on its ear. Hence her emergency relocation to Della's house as a temporary measure. That had been over a month ago, and no one had bothered to explain how it was temporary if no other alternative arrangements were being made.

"I'll let you know if I find anything out," Della promised, closing the door on the food discussion. Now that she had his attention, she seized the moment. "Hey, listen, something I wanted to run by you. Those two unmated Omegas you took in last month?" Hunter nodded. "They need somewhere to live that isn't in the corner of someone else's cabin. What do you think about building an Omega bunkhouse?"

Hunter grimaced. "I was hoping they might be mated by the time we got back. Once they're claimed, the newly mated pair gets their own cabin built. Problem solved."

"Yes," she agreed, her mind flipping through the arguments she'd prepared for this objection. "That has historically been the case, but Rue is not likely to be mated any time soon. And Zorah?" They both pulled a face at the mention of the flirtatious little Omega. "Hard to say what she'll do. Or when. It could be a year or more before they're claimed. Don't you think they deserve their own space in the interim?"

Hunter peered down his nose. "You want Rue out of your house."

She ignored the accusation and pulled her best wheedling smile out of cold storage, her blood thrumming with the old energy of bringing someone around to her way of thinking. "You came back with what? Four? Five new Alphas? We've got work enough for them, but how many will stay if they have no chance at finding an Omega of their own?"

Hunter folded his arms over his broad chest. "Omegas are rare, Del, you know that."

"Right, and because of that, they're pursued, and threatened, and endangered everywhere they go." She took a half-step forward, tilting her chin to account for his height. "If we build a safe place where Omegas could be free of unwanted Alpha attention, where they had a space all to themselves, in a community where Alphas are prohibited from nonconsensual claiming, don't you think that might entice more Omegas to come live here?"

She paused to let the argument sink in and considered her father's tried-and-true advice: find what they want and give it to them in a way that gets you what you want.

"You have big plans for this place," she continued. "A bathhouse, running water, more varied crops… but to do any of that, we need good Alphas. If we build an Omega bunkhouse, the word will quietly spread that Morris Hill is a safe place for Omegas, and more will come here without you having to go out and beat the bushes to find them. And where Omegas are, Alphas follow, and soon you have all the men you need to scavenge every working solar panel in the Pacific Northwest"—her lip curled with mischief—"and get your damn bathhouse."

The creases alongside Hunter's eyes pinched, his tell for soft amusement. "I get into trouble when I forget how persuasive you are, Senator Cabrese." Della smiled at hearing her old title on her friend's lips. Once, those words evoked gravitas and a sense of accomplishment. Now, they sounded like a side character in a film franchise, someone she recognized but who would never get their own feature film.

She appreciated Hunter's use of them as a compliment, but more than anything, she cherished the way she could deal with Hunter directly, as an equal. They'd come from the same time, had lived through the same era, and as such, he treated her like a valued colleague and friend, not an annoyance. Other Alphas required a soft-peddling finesse she found exhausting and tedious. With Hunter, she could state her ideas plainly and not be dismissed out of hand simply because she wasn't Alpha.

After a moment, Hunter's expression smoothed to a careful blandness except for a muscle jumping in his cheek. "I'm going to miss talking to you. I hope you understand."

Della's smile faltered a split second before she hoisted it back up into place. "Yeah, of course," she said, her tone chipper and agreeable. "You'll be busy settling in with Kess and getting her used to this place. Maybe in a few weeks we'll have time to catch up, but in the meantime, the bunkh—"

"No." Frowning, he looked off into the distance, not meeting Della's eyes. "Kess wouldn't appreciate me spending time with another woman. I can't risk doing anything to hurt her."

Static invaded Della's head. Hunter was her friend. Despite working beside the man, forging Morris Hill into a thriving community, they'd never crossed the line into a romantic interest or even a physical one. Not even once.

Della's frozen smile lost its grip on her face. "But why would..." She huffed uncomfortably. "We're *friends*, you and I. That's not a threat to Kess in any way. Rakesh had loads of women friends when—"

"It's not the same," he said softly but firmly. "I can't explain it, but it's not the same. I'm sorry."

"Hunter..." She tried again for a placating tone, laying a gentle hand on his arm. "You can't be serious. What is this? The third-grade playground? You have a new girlfriend so you can't talk to me? We're grown-ups," she argued, then barked a bitter laugh. "Hell, we're the most grown-up people alive!"

He didn't react to her attempt at a joke, simply removing her hand from his body like it was something diseased, his face solemn and serious. Della nearly toppled backward, the force of the gentle but decisive rejection of her touch landing like a blow to her chest.

"Kess saved my life," he replied, his face urging an understanding of something important, something profound, yet beyond her comprehension.

Della spoke with care. "What do you mean she saved your life?"

The space between them emptied like a vacuum, the very air molecules stepping aside to make room for an ominous confession as icy blue eyes locked on hers. "She saved me from harming myself. I owe her everything, and I won't do anything to jeopardize that."

The spiraling vortex in Della's head accelerated, whirring high winds that screeched in her ears like a thousand tornadoes. "You never told me you were considering *that*," she whispered, her sinuses burning. "I would've stopped you."

He shook his head slowly. "You couldn't have."

The unspoken implication rang out clear: *she*, his friend for twenty years, couldn't have stopped him from taking his life, but Kess did. Della felt sick. And empty. And alone.

"I suppose,"—she blinked furiously, not wanting to cry and show weakness as the horror morphed to fury—"in your mind, you unilaterally planned to opt out of our friendship months ago, and since I would have to get used to *that*, this isn't any different. Right? Only"—she waved sarcastic jazz-hands—"lucky me, I don't have to deal with your fucking *death*—because there hasn't been enough of *that* in my stupid fucking life—I only have to deal with getting friend dumped by my only friend." She staggered a few steps back, holding up a palm when he opened his mouth. "Did you ever consider what effect your death would have on us? On the settlement? How selfish and cruel and fucking stupid that would've been?"

"Della, honey—"

"Don't *Della honey* me." Drips of hot, salty anger slipped over her bottom lids. Della swallowed and swallowed again, trying to keep her giant junk drawer mess of emotions from scattering out on the ground.

Not far away, the low hum of voices and activity surrounding the mess hall ceased, and dozens of pairs of curious heads roved in their direction. Della turned her head away from the crowd, staring into the surrounding woods as she battled her feelings into submission.

Hunter pushed a hand through his salt -and -pepper hair. "I don't know what to say to help you understand. Kess—"

"This has *nothing* to do with you and Kess." Della's voice was tight. "This has to do with you and me." She cut a glance at him, noting the distress lines on his face with some grim satisfaction and then feeling like shit about that. Grief, anger, and frustration burned an acid hole in her chest. The sensation so acute and painful she checked her shirtfront to reassure herself it wasn't real.

Except that it was. It was all too real, an all too real reminder of the lesson she'd learned decades ago: caring now equals pain later. She'd let her guard down with Hunter; they'd become friends, and here's where it brought her. Twenty years of working together to build Morris Hill from a run-down, abandoned vacation venue to a beautiful, healthy, thriving community, only to discover he'd secretly planned on *killing himself*? Without even mentioning it to her or saying goodbye?

"You're right. I don't understand," she finally said, her tone steady and under control. "I'm sorry you didn't feel like you could talk to me about whatever you were going through. And I'm sorry you're choosing to cut me loose, for both of our sake's."

Footsteps rustled through the grass, someone approaching at a rapid clip. Della dashed her shameful tears with a vicious swipe.

"Hey, thought you were out of commission for the day." Colt's familiar voice announced his unwelcome and inopportune presence.

"I am," Hunter replied without any hint of emotion. "Need a word with you and Logan, though."

Feeling marginally under control, Della backed up a few steps to prime her escape. There was nothing else she needed to say to Hunter today. Or maybe ever.

Colt's attention flicked between the two of them like a worried parent. "Everything okay over here?"

"Yes." She pivoted into brusque senator mode. "Hunter and I were discussing building a bunkhouse for the unmated Omegas. He'll fill you in on the details, but we should get started this summer. I'd love to chat with you about it sometime. Not right now, though. I have… things to do."

Like an automaton, her legs pumped stiff and jerky as she retraced the path back to her cabin. *God dammit.* It was all too much. Too much to assimilate with her feelings pulled in all directions like she was being actively drawn and quartered. Less than an hour out of her cabin and all she wanted was to lock herself inside, curl up in her bed, and try to remember a time when a fallout with a friend didn't feel like the end of the world all over again.

CHAPTER FOUR

Cal

Ignoring the shouting coming from the stable behind him, Cal rolled his shoulders, impatient to get started with his first official Morris Hill work assignment: patrol duty. Despite the rocky start to the day, patrol duty suited him. His protective instincts always ran deep, but even more so now that he had something precious to protect.

Unfortunately, a delay ensued as Sloan, the stable manager, worked himself up into a full-on meltdown about the state of the stables upon his return. He loudly and fervently insisted on personally inspecting all the horses before "allowing" any of them to be taken out. Silas, the Alpha paired with Cal for patrol, requested an estimate of the time required for two mounts, only to be met with ear-splitting wrath.

Already hard at work shoveling shit in the stable, Simon flashed Cal a look that said *if I were you, I'd get the hell out of here.* He didn't need to be told twice. Leaving Silas to negotiate with the volatile Sloan, Cal took the opportunity to stroll around the large, well-kept corral.

Shaking off his impatience, he stretched his neck to the sky and sucked in a deep, cleansing lungful of the pine-scented air. Mid-morning sunshine stole through some fluffy clouds but, thankfully, none of them appeared to hold rain. With luck, they'd have a nice, dry ride checking the northern perimeter of the Morris Hill Pack's territory. Having grown up on the opposite side of the continent, he itched to explore this lush, green part of the world, particularly since it appeared he'd be staying for a while. From the stables, the sound of a bucket crashing against the wall punctuated the latest burst of curses. Cal grimaced. That is, if they ever got going.

Movement on the north side of the paddock drew his notice. A slight figure slung blankets over the fencing as a breeze whooshed by and delivered a trace of black currants to his nose.

Della.

Heart tapping a driving rhythm against his breastbone, Cal prowled closer.

Unbound hair poured down her back and swished over her straight spine. It shimmered in shades of faded copper, white, and gray, like a feline calico. Signs of her age contoured her face in ways that set her apart from younger Omegas: fine lines that feathered from her eyes and a certain delicate texture to her skin. But, somehow, all of that only confirmed his interest. Here was a woman who'd survived on her own merit, who didn't cower to Alphas or make compromises to her honor even when caught alone in dark corners.

Fully entranced, he moved closer, drinking in her proud, fine-boned profile, rare in hearty Omega stock. Her deep-set eyes were clear, honest, and entirely focused on her task. High cheekbones and stubborn chin gave her an aloof, queenly air that called to him like a beautiful thing he wanted to meticulously savor before ravaging completely. How firmly rooted was that lofty composure? How much digging would it take to find her hidden reservoir of passion?

Because, surely, no woman with a mouth like Della's was as indifferent as she fronted last night. Full lips, the color of the evening primroses that grew near his childhood home, pursed, and puffed, and flexed as she worked, as if carrying on a silent, one-sided conversation with herself. Every subtle muscle twitch, expressive and seductive, provided all the evidence he needed of thwarted sensuality beneath all the earnest dignity he burned to upset.

Cal inhaled, letting the traces of her zesty-sweet scent filter in and stir him from the inside out. A sharp note, like junipers, cut through the floral part of her aroma and made him desperate to know what tangy flavor he'd lap from between her thighs. In the broad light of day, he wanted all that and more. He wanted her body pinned under his, his knot thrust deep in her cunt, his name pleading on her lips, and his claiming mark blazing on her neck.

Corralling that impulse back in check, he turned his attention to her activity. From yards away, he spotted the slight shaking in her muscles and the laboring heave of her chest as she worked alone, dragging thick, unwieldy blankets up and over the fence. Horse blankets, it looked like, heavy and sodden from a recent bath, taxed the Omega's arms. As he cleared the final few yards between them, the potent animal smell confirmed this fact.

Della stooped for another load, and Cal bent to help. Surprised, blue eyes snapped to his face and then quickly away, shoulders immediately stiffening as she wrestled with the opposite side of the blanket. "I can handle it," she sniffed.

"Not arguing that point," he said mildly, continuing to help her hoist the dripping thing over the fence. *Christ, hadn't anyone bothered to wring these damn things out?* "But since I'm here…"

Blanket arranged over the top rail, Cal squeezed excess water from the freely hanging folds as Della stepped back with her hands on her hips.

For the first time in their short acquaintance, she stood still and looked him fully in the face, chest open and chin raised, defiant and confident. Unable to resist, Cal skated a glance down the front of her body. She wore a practical button-down shirt, transparent from laundry water soaking her from slim shoulders down to her rounded thighs—a good sign this Pack had enough resources to keep their Omegas pleasantly plump, which he appreciated.

A stiff breeze blew past, not enough to agitate the heavy blankets but enough to pebble her nipples beneath her soggy shirt. Large and pronounced, the sight made his mouth water. In the dark, he'd gotten an all-too-brief feel of her, but the desire to map her completely, to outline her particular shape in every nuanced dip and rise, drummed deep inside him with an urgency like nothing else he'd ever experienced.

"I said"—fire smoldered in her features as she made note of his blatant perusal—"I had it handled."

Like a trouble-making pup who finally got a reaction from an annoyed parent, her irritation delighted him. Not because he wanted her to be pissed off, but because he liked seeing all that moxie on frank display. She wasn't submissive or deferential like so many Omegas, nor coy and flirtatious like others. Refreshing and unexpected, the directness of her response drew him in and only enhanced the overall appeal.

Undeterred, Cal propped a shoulder against a fencepost and slid his hands in his pockets. "I'm sure you can, but I'm here, and I'm offering to help. No need to cut off your nose to spite your face."

Nostrils flaring, her narrowed look would strike fear into any young Alpha's heart. Good thing he wasn't a young Alpha. "My granddad used to say that."

"So you've been stubborn for a long time, then." A grin tickled his cheek, but he kept it in check. "I figured as much."

"I didn't say he said it about me," she shot back.

Cal raised a deliberate, disbelieving brow. "Didn't he?" At that, she shifted her gaze elsewhere, a confirmation he'd hit a bullseye if he'd ever seen one. "What else did your granddad say about you, Della Mae?"

Her shoulders flinched at his use of her name, and she fussed with a lock of hair, pushing it behind her ear with a slender hand in a flustered gesture. "Della Mae isn't my name."

"It's pretty, though, ain't it?" A smile edged into his voice. "Why don't you tell me your whole name, then, so I get it right next time?" If she was one of the Old Ones, as Riddick hinted last night and Cal was inclined to believe, she would've possessed more than one simple moniker. Back when the population stretched the limits of resources and people were too numerous to only go by one name, as they did now.

Somehow, her scowl deepened. Adorably. "Don't you have a work assignment?"

He inclined his head, silently promising to revisit the name discussion at a later time. "Patrol duty with Silas, but"—he paused, opening up the space for more of Sloan's bellowing to fill—"as you might infer, we're having some trouble getting horses for the job."

Her lips pursed in an expression of royal disdain. "I'd appreciated how much quieter it was while he was gone."

Cal snickered. "There's one in every Pack."

"A *Sloan*?" Despite her reluctance to engage, curiosity twinkled in her blue eyes.

"A hotheaded mini-tyrant."

"And I suppose that's not you?" she said with an unladylike snort.

"Me?" He grinned. "Not even close."

Stubborn chin lifted, she folded her arms over her chest and studied him. Cal leaned into the experience, enjoying the feel of her eyes on him, reveling in her pointed, exacting examination. Liking that, concealed deep in that careful regard, Cal detected the flicker of something else he liked even more: *interest*.

"You came on pretty strong last night," she finally said, voice ever-so-slightly hoarse.

"Going after something I want is not the same as being a hothead," he said slowly. "A fact a smart woman like you knows as well as I do."

Her steady gaze never wavered. "I don't know anything about you."

"But you'd like to."

"I didn't say that."

"You didn't have to." Cal advanced a half step and slid the basket out of the way with the side of his boot, removing the obstruction but not coming any closer. She watched him do it, her expression guarded but permissive, and his eyes clung to hers, unwilling to let the moment go or to advance it further.

Time tautened like a bowstring, the space between them saturated with a low, thrumming pulse that swayed back and forth like waves lapping against a shore. "*You'll know when you know*," Pa had explained all those years ago. "*When you find your Omega, there won't be any space for doubt.*"

Cal had no doubt, but he studied her upturned face, wanting to know, *needing* to know if the unseen power hooked her the way it did him. Did a similar rhythm beat in her breast; did she feel an answering tug on the other side of this unmistakable pull?

He got his answer as, bit by bit, the lines and curves of her body let go, as her strained posture relaxed into a placidity so unlike her combative default. Muscles that seized up from the moment of his approach unknotted. Shoulders slackened. Fingers uncurled. Lips went lax. Long, pale lashes fluttered weakly, as if experiencing the first longed-for touch against a sensitive body part.

Triumph warmed his chest. She did feel it, then.

"Tell me something," his voice dipped low and gravely. "How long did you lie awake in your bed last night, thinking about our little introduction?"

The words dangled in the air for a slow breath. And then two, and then, like the slamming of a door, any softness in her countenance disappeared between one blink and the next. Her chest lifted, and a barrier snapped into place like the raising of a shield.

"Listen, whatever-your-name-is,"—her barbed tone lacked any trace of gentleness—"I appreciate the predicament you're in here. You joined this Pack thinking there were oodles of Omegas breathlessly waiting for a big, strong Alpha like you to come and claim them." She bent and, in an obvious provocation, dragged the basket back into the space between them and to the next empty rail while continuing to talk. "Only to discover you assumed incorrectly. So now you're trying to cut your losses and settle for me." She smiled up at him—a cold, patronizing flash of white teeth—and heaved the next blanket off the pile. "And while I appreciate your strategy of coming out swinging, I'll save you the trouble." She jerked her chin in his direction. "I'm not looking for an Alpha, I don't need an Alpha, nor am I interested in any kind of casual arrangement with one, and if you can't accept that, maybe Morris Hill isn't the place for you. In which case, I'd suggest you head back to wherever you came from."

Cal held back, hiding his flaring impatience as best he could. Truth be told, he needed the moment to figure out how to respond to the spew of insanity she'd rained down on him. Meant to be a dismissal or a barely polite brush-off, he couldn't react because, for such an obviously intelligent woman, her understanding of his intentions completely missed the mark.

Did she honestly believe he wanted her as some sort of... *consolation prize*? Tension gripped his spine in a vice. Was that the way she was treated in this place? As some sort of second-class citizen?

With a frustrated huff at his nonresponse, Della bent to the basket as if to return to her chore. Breaking his inertia, Cal charged forward until his shins touched the basket rim. "The name's Cal. Guess I forgot to mention that."

Standing, she rubbed a palm down her face. "Did you hear anything else I said?" The question held no anger or malice, only a sad, tired resignation.

"I heard it." He flashed her a quelling look as her mouth opened to argue. "Don't agree with it, got a lot of questions about it, but, as I said last night, I'm gonna listen to whatever it is you have to say, whenever you want to say it." His feet decided what to do next, kicking the laundry basket out of his way to get to her, this time with more force.

Della angled her upper body away from him but held her ground. Toe to toe, the top of her head reached his chin, and it took every lick of self-possession he'd learned over his fifty-odd years to stop himself from delving a hand into her hair and tilting those rosy lips up to meet his own. This close, a mere inch from the angry points of her nipples that jutted out and begged for his attention, the damp heat rising from her skin beat against his chest. It seeped directly into his blood, making his heart skip faster, harder, pounding out the words *she's yours, she's yours.*

"If you heard me," she rasped, "then why're you still here?"

He curled his lips. "Your basket's empty, why're you still here?"

Her lashes drooped to half-mast, the only sign of fluster in her otherwise locked-down face. But, despite her obvious efforts, the Omega couldn't hide everything. Like the smallest ripple in a deep, still lake, the sound of her galloping, excitable pulse fluttered in his ears. He savored that smallest of responses, rejoiced in it, and craved even more.

Reddish brows inched upward. "You're in my way."

It was a lie, and they both knew it. Hands in his pockets, he had her constrained in no way at all; she could easily step aside and evade him. If she wanted to.

Instead, her steady regard faltered, tripping down his face and landing on his mouth as he mouthed the question, "Am I?"

"Cal!" An Alpha voice barked from the opposite side of the corral. "Time to go!"

Tamping down a curse at the inconvenient timing, he acknowledged the summons with a wave, his eyes never leaving Della's face. "One clarification before I go, Omega: ain't nothing about you that is settling. I ain't cutting my losses"—he tipped forward, hovering his lips over hers—"and I ain't going nowhere. Not without you, you got me?"

A slight tremble in her exhale whisked over his chin. It wasn't much, but it was enough. Maybe Della wasn't as affected by him as he was by her, but she *was* affected, and that, he could work with.

Satisfied, Cal straightened and backed a step away, taking a luxuriously decadent parting sweep up and down her body as he did so. *Goddamn*, once he got his hands on her… A bolt of lightning stirred his dick at the mere thought, but he battened it down for the time being.

"Like I said, I'm on patrol duty"—his eyes slid back to hers—"but I expect we'll be back by supper. If you're not in the mess hall, I'll come for you."

Della's back stiffened, which only served to push her nipples further against her damp shirt. Cal clamped down on his tongue to extinguish a groan and took a few more backward steps. "Is that a threat?" she said in a hoarse whisper.

"Only if you consider a good time to be a threat." He winked. "I understand it might be a shock to your system, seeing as you spend your days hanging up soggy horse blankets. Alone."

Translucent pink colored her cheeks. "What if I'm not interested in having a good time with you?"

He shrugged as if to say, *yeah, so?* before turning and striding away with a spring in his step, throwing, "You're not that good of an actress, darlin'," over his shoulder.

CHAPTER FIVE

Cal

"We'll break for lunch up there." Silas's voice startled Cal from his thoughts. Not that he'd had the opportunity to have any *new* thoughts since riding out of Morris Hill, and, to be honest, he'd tired of the same Della-related looping. Half a dozen times, he'd parted his lips, a question for Silas on the tip of his tongue, only to slam his jaw shut, reminding himself that his courtship of her involved no one but the two of them.

"Alphas don't court, Alphas claim."

Another extremely relevant quote from Pa excavated itself from his memories. That was Pa's take on the Alpha-Omega relationship dynamic in a nutshell: once you knew, you knew, and once you knew, you claimed.

Wild frustration thrashed in Cal's chest at the inconvenient reminder. In the twenty-four hours since he'd arrived in Morris Hill and first sampled Della's intoxicating scent, he'd done exactly zero claiming. In fact, riding out of the settlement, away from her, implanted an irritating burr under his skin that worsened with every clip-clop of the mare's hooves. His base, animal mind, compelled him to turn the horse around, find the Omega, bend her to his will, and be done with it.

After their conversation, he refused to believe she persisted, unaware of the energy that sizzled and popped between them, so vibrant he swore it scintillated in the air. His presence affected her, as hers affected him, and only stubbornness held her from submitting to its inevitability.

It perplexed him. Omegas *wanted* their Alphas. They *wanted* to be claimed. Didn't they?

Then again, for whatever reason, Della maintained she was not Omega, an assertion he had no evidence to counter other than his own experience. In fact, from what Riddick reported, no one else in the settlement picked up on what he did when it came to Della, either. If he had to guess, he would speculate it had something to do with her status as one of the Old Ones, the ones, like Hunter and Pa, who survived from before TheEnd. Those that weren't born Alpha or Omega but who *became* them in some mysterious, unexplained way.

An idea percolated around his thoughts, exhilarating as much as befuddling: was Della's Omega transformation invisible to everyone but him? Excitement flared to life at the base of his spine. If that was true, then she was his, *truly his*, as if created for him by some divine hand.

"Let's stop here," Silas said over his shoulder, already halfway out of his saddle as Cal's horse pulled up to the stopping point.

Cal swung a leg out of the saddle, feeling the ache as his thighs and backside adjusted to the solid ground. Silas secured his horse near a small patch of early spring grass, grabbed his saddlebag, and jogged down a barely-visible trail.

"What's the damn rush?" Cal muttered, going through the same process before chasing to catch up. "Hey, where're you going?"

Silas beckoned him to follow. A short walk later, the sound of water tinkled in Cal's ears, and the air thickened with damp humidity and a faint sulfurous sting. They popped into a clearing with a small hot spring tucked into the rocky side of a ridge. Smiling, Silas stripped off his shirt. "The secret benefit of being on patrol." He bent to unlace his boots, groaning theatrically. "My back hurts like hell, and my head isn't much better. I need a damn rest."

Trees rustled in soft accompaniment to the spring's bubbling drips as Cal took stock of the clearing. A secluded, peaceful spot, the clear pool with a dusting of rising steam skating the surface. It spanned about eight feet in diameter, plenty of room for two Alpha-sized bodies. Admittedly, he wouldn't mind a soak himself, but they also needed to complete their assigned task and make it back before nightfall.

Cal glanced at the sun's position, estimating the time as late afternoon. Frowning, he cleared his throat as Silas eased into the water with a dramatic sigh.

"How long will it take to finish the patrol route? We got a late start and—"

"Stop bitching," Silas said from behind closed lids, "this is the halfway point. We hang out here for a while and then head back in time for supper. We'll do the rest of the route tomorrow."

Creeping unease slithered into Cal's belly. A good, solid, reliable patrol protected the settlement and everyone in it, and Silas was asking him to cut corners on the first day? Did Silas not understand the point of a patrol? That being to identify problems before they progressed to threats, to catch hostile parties unawares before *they* were caught unawares, and to keep any danger well away from the more vulnerable members of their community. Pups, Omegas, Della... all would be in jeopardy if an unwelcome presence stole onto their lands.

Danger encroached on all sides in the AfterEnd: animals, weather, accidents, disease, violence, starvation. Every way one turned, something new lurked and waited, gauging the right moment, cultivating the precise amount of vulnerability, biding its time to strike. One small mistake, one too many overlooked warnings, and entire lives could be ruined. That scenic fresh-water stream? Half-mile upstream, a decomposing body could be poisoning the water. That abandoned house? Could be overrun by rabid raccoons. That cement bridge that easily supported one horse and rider? Could crumble like stale bread under the weight of anything more.

A cavernous pit of shame yawned open inside of him, exposing yet another hidden danger: memory. This particular hazard he'd sequestered with a thin membrane of time and distance and pure, white-knuckled suppression. A necessary barrier that made it possible for Cal to put one foot in front of the other, to keep moving through space and time, always seeking a new home for himself, a new purpose for his life. Which, after decades of scratching out a lonely existence, maybe he'd found in Morris Hill and Della.

And this moron wanted to jeopardize all of it by failing to complete the simplest of tasks. Cal ground his molars, anger roiling his guts.

"Get in," Silas lolled his head back against the edge, clearly settling in for an extended soak. "It's fucking amazing."

Cal stared at his lazy guide for a long, hard minute, deciding on an approach to deal with this joker. Silas hadn't been part of the group Cal had met in OT, so he didn't have enough of a sense of the Alpha to gauge how best to bring him around to the *correct* perspective on their responsibilities.

Maybe he could concede to a short break and then finish the route. After a week on the road, he wouldn't mind a chance to get clean, but they didn't need to spend all afternoon boiling like eggs. As a conciliatory gesture, Cal toed off one boot and worked on the other. "Yeah, okay, but let's keep it quick and try to do the full circuit at least once before we go back. If we push the horses, it shouldn't take—"

"Nah, fuck that." Silas lifted a shoulder, scratching his back on the rock wall. "Like I said, we'll do it tomorrow."

Cal smothered a snarl. He'd traveled with Pack members for the last week, and none of them shirked duties, let alone have the audacity to suggest another Alpha laze about with them. What the fuck was wrong with this Alpha?

"Listen, man," Cal began, keeping his voice even and conversational, "I'm new here, and I don't need anyone pissed off at me for half-assing this. How about you show me the whole route today, and then tomorrow, you can hang out here, and I'll go by myself?"

Slits of Silas's eyes squinted across the steaming pool. "No one's gonna know, dude. We'll do the whole thing tomorrow, no worries." He scooped a handful of water and dribbled it over his face. "Besides, if Hunt finds out, we can blame Sloan for being a giant dick about the horses and making us get a late start." His head lolled back to rest on the ledge. "Now, can you shut up? I'm trying to heal a hangover over here."

Asshole.

Controlling his resentment, Cal lowered himself into the steaming water, shooting a glare at his companion and considering what other means of persuasion would be required to get them back on track.

An hour later, Cal had bathed, eaten, and dressed while Silas's lazy hide only managed to relocate from the pool to the ground, where he snoozed in open defiance of Cal's mounting impatience. Cal pushed his hands through his hair, aggravation and agitation making him itchy and restless. Stomping back along the path, he checked on the horses, who barely lifted their heads from their contented munching. They weren't too keen on finishing patrol either.

He didn't like it, but what to do... *what to do?*

He could take his horse, leave Silas, and ride back to the settlement alone. But then what? Report the situation like a child tattling to his mother? Not to mention, with Hunter occupied with Kess, Cal would likely be reporting to Colt, a prospect he didn't relish in the slightest.

Not that he had anything in particular against the Pack's Second, but Cal strongly suspected Colt harbored an unnamed problem with him. As tradition dictated, new Alphas joined a Pack by fighting an existing Pack member of their choice for membership. Alpha instinct spurred all of them to take on the biggest and baddest of the available options, no matter one's size or strength or the chances of getting their jaw broken.

Having worked with Hunter the day prior when they'd rescued Kess from a drug-addled wreck of an Alpha, Cal didn't feel like challenging him directly. But he didn't want to choose an unimpressive, middle-of-the Pack Alpha to prove himself, either. He'd lived in the free-range world long enough to know he needed to stake his claim as someone not to be fucked with.

So that left Colt.

When it came to it, they were equally matched. Colt managed to blacken Cal's eye and even landed a few stomach shots that winded him before Cal's fist found Colt's nose in a spray of blood. Afterward, they'd shaken hands, and Colt stiffly welcomed him to the Pack. Their subsequent dealings were cordial but far from friendly.

Riding back and reporting this situation to Colt held no appeal. Alternatively, he could take his horse and keep heading west, follow the ridgeline, and hope he picked his way along the border, approximating the Pack's territory line. But he didn't know this terrain at all. He'd grown up in the flat, dry plains of what had once been Laredo, the opposite of this lush, evergreen wilderness in every possible way. Common sense dictated he stick with a "buddy," given his unfamiliarity with the land. Night would arrive soon enough, and to go off on his own courted disaster. Given Silas's obvious lack of concern for Pack safety in general, if anything happened to him, Cal'd be left to die, no question. He shook his head in disgust. Some fucking *buddy* Silas turned out to be.

The most obvious answer remained: march right back up to that asshole and kick his ass till he got off it and finished their job. That idea had a definite appeal. Physically, Silas had an inch or so on him but, by his own admission, wasn't in top shape due to his hangover. Cal could easily beat him into submission. At this point, he was so worked up that he couldn't be sure he wouldn't kill the fucker outright.

God dammit. This was *not* how he wanted to spend his first day, and, *god dammit*, he really didn't want to return to Della with bloodied and bruised knuckles like a brawling barbarian. But it was either give in and put the settlement at risk or force the issue with his fists.

He'd let Silas have his little nap, and then they were finishing this shit, dark or no dark.

Too agitated to just wait and stare daggers into his companion's skull, Cal stomped off the path and deeper into the woods. A hike might work off some of this aggravation.

A short distance from the hot springs, the scent of fresh water laced the air. He followed his nose to a creek bed carved between the rock and then picked along the widening stream. The water suggested a natural boundary to the Pack's land, but without Silas's confirmation, he couldn't be sure. He walked on, letting the woods soothe him. It hummed with a vibrant, peaceful rhythm all its own. Bird calls, some he recognized and many he didn't, drifted on the breeze. Scents of animals—squirrels, foxes, deer—brushed over his nose, but none hinted of any human presence other than his own.

After filling his canteen, a full bladder sent him deeper into the trees, seeking a spot to relieve himself when his boot tip nicked something hard and rattling. He knelt and pushed aside the vined ground cover to unveil a rusted steel-jaw animal trap. A horrified shudder walked down his spine at the sight, which only worsened when he noticed the bone shards pinned between the hideous teeth. The trap had been triggered shut, and by the looks of it, something small like a fox had been its unlucky victim. The fur had long since blown away or decomposed, but chillingly, no further remains of the animal's skeleton rested beside the device: only a shard of leg bone, half in and half out of the grisly metal jaw.

The poor little thing gnawed its leg off.

His heart sunk at the deduction. If the animal had been retrieved by whatever human set the trap, the hunter would've collected their trap to reuse it. The fact that it had been left implied it had been entirely forgotten by whoever set it. Not that it saved the poor bugger who unluckily stumbled into it.

No stranger to hunting and trapping, Cal understood the need if one wasn't able to raise animals for food. But to force an animal to self-amputate in a final, desperate attempt at freedom struck him as an unnecessarily cruel and sad ending to this creature's life. Cal couldn't blame the little critter, he would've done the same.

With a grim sigh, he set the trap upright against the tree trunk and then took care of his personal needs. Feeling saddened and once again out of sorts, he trudged back to the flowing water and spied something interesting on the opposite rise. About twelve or fifteen feet above the ground, an irregular shadow interrupted the otherwise ragged limestone wall. As he examined it, a beam of sunlight parted the clouds and got swallowed up by what he now confirmed was a definite break in the rock. Curiosity poked through his sour mood. What the hell was that? He cast a look back in the direction of the hot springs, as if he could check on Silas's lazy ass from this far away, before deciding a few minutes of exploration wouldn't derail the afternoon any more than the pit stop already had.

After crossing the water, he grasped two rocky handholds, hopefully strong enough to support his weight. With a small surge of boyish adventurousness, he heaved himself up and scaled a path toward the shadow. Reaching it would be easier from above, but to do that, he'd have to backtrack and follow the water from the other side of the gully, which would take more time than he wanted to invest in this spontaneous side quest. Climbing proved a much swifter, if effortful, path. Plus, there was something oddly satisfying about the scrape of the roughened limestone against his palms and the gentle radiating heat of the sun-warmed rock wall on his belly. Muscles he hadn't used in days woke up, propelling him step by step and grasp by grasp toward his destination.

The final heave upward onto a narrow ledge confirmed his suspicions: it was a cave. Bordered by mossy overgrowth, the ghost of an opening (large enough for him to pass through in a stoop) gave way to a much larger chamber. Dampness hung in the air, and his nostrils flared at the tainted scent of stale animals. Maybe raccoons or foxes had once made their home here, but nothing fresh.

Hefting a rock, he tossed it inside, sending up a racket of noise to disturb any nocturnal friends, such as bats, who might be concealed by the shadows. When nothing moved or squealed, Cal slipped inside, finding the opening spacious enough that he could stand upright. With the shaded entrance, the late afternoon sun failed to penetrate very deep, so he tossed another rock into the inky darkness, nodding thoughtfully when the crashing echo answered from well beyond where his vision ended. Further exploration required a torch or a lamp, neither of which he had.

He paced in a slow circle, kicking a rock that rattled over the stone floor. Looking down, he saw his foot had inadvertently walked through an old fire pit and disturbed the circle of rocks someone had left. Bending down, he reseated the rock into its vacant divot, taking a closer look. Dust covered the rocks, and any ash that had once been in the middle had long since blown away or been scattered by animal traffic. Only faded scorch marks indicated the pit had ever been used for an actual fire. Cal breathed deeply again, a closer search for traces of people, and found none.

No, this cave was abandoned. His head circled around the space again. All things considered, it was quite a nice cave: dry, hidden, secluded, and close to fresh water. Hard to get to but convenient for a hunting party to overnight or utilize as shelter in a storm. Was he still on Morris Hill territory? Did the Alphas of Morris Hill know about it? Or know about it but never utilized it? Or had known about it at some point and then forgotten?

He'd ask Silas, but at that moment, exchanging more words with Silas was about the last thing he wanted to do. Cal ran a hand through his damp hair, faintly amused by the irreverent thought of hiding Silas's dead body in here. He wasn't a murderer by any stretch, even if Silas's behavior acutely tested that particular ethic.

Buoyed by the unexpected discovery, Cal slipped back through the entrance and began a reluctant descent down the rock face. The cave intrigued him, but he had other things to take care of today. First off, he needed to convince the wayward Silas to finish their task. Because one thing was certain, he wouldn't be returning without ensuring Della's safety and that of everyone else in Morris Hill.

CHAPTER SIX

Della

Tugging her blanket tight around her shoulders, Della poked at the small fire in her hearth and reassured herself she wasn't being a coward. She simply didn't feel like going to dinner. Besides that, Rue had gone to the mess hall for once, and Della would be foolish to miss this opportunity for some alone time. She had an apple and some cheese left over from lunch that would suffice if she got hungry. Others, nursing Omegas and their young, for example, needed the calories more than her. So, see? She was being considerate of her community and definitely was not hiding from that Alpha, who managed to be both challenging and unflappable at the same time.

Cal.

His name rang in her memory, the brevity of the syllable offset by the drawling twang of his delivery, punctuated by the shivering fascination that skated over her skin in some kind of visceral acknowledgment. As much as she hated to admit it, he *affected* her. Last night in the dark, with his sudden appearance and unbelievable gall, she hadn't attributed the way her heart kicked against her breast and her breath snagged in her throat to his presence. Sure, she'd gone to her bed feeling squirmy and restless. She'd chalked that up to the stress of the entire day, not her fleeting interaction with him, even if her thoughts orbited around him into the wee hours of the morning.

Today, though… today he sauntered like he had nothing else in the entire world he wanted to do than lick her up like she was a melting ice cream cone. His focused scan ran over every last detail of her figure, immobilizing her without exchanging a single word. Chemical reactions and the memory of his strength pressed against her in that darkened, secret corner of the night flooded her wide-awake body. Yet, she'd stilled under his review, afraid that the slightest fidget of her hand against her leg or the merest roll of her lips against her teeth would unintentionally reveal something she'd rather keep private.

It was dizzying, being the focus of that kind of intensity.

Given his distinctive (and wholly seductive, she grudgingly admitted) accent, she'd speculated he'd grown up close to the former southern border. But, in the daylight, the traces of likely Mexican heritage came to the fore. Glowing, golden russet skin, a bold, handsome nose, and hair as dark as wet slate completed the breathtaking picture. Unlike hers, his face was unlined, yet he carried none of the immature air of a younger Alpha. He looked, to her, to be in his early thirties, but with the strangeness in human aging after TheEnd, he could be anywhere from forty to eighty, and she wouldn't know the difference.

But the one feature she did recognize, the smile he'd flashed in the star-speckled darkness, stopped her heart in the full light. Deep dimples bracketed his wide grin, which added a boyish charm to the overall effect. How he managed to look both innocent and degenerate, she couldn't explain if she tried.

Staring into the fire, Della fiddled with the book in her lap, the brittle plastic edges snapping against each other. Every few weeks, she revisited the photo album and confronted the memory of a life so distant that she sometimes wondered if it was all a dream. But with Rue sharing her home, she'd forgone the ritual, not wanting to explain or describe her past life to her roommate. Tonight, Rue's absence presented an opportunity she hadn't had all summer, and perhaps it would also take her mind off the Alpha. With a sigh, she flipped open to the first yellowed picture.

The first photo elicited the usual dull, lifeless recognition. Every detail, highlight, and shadow of the image had long ago been imprinted in her memory. Closing her eyes, she could describe each white-edged crease and every minute discoloration. The picture was an old friend, but the woman in the picture was a stranger. Was that truly *her*? Smiling bright and beautiful in the exquisitely designed wedding dress? Laughing at the camera, her hand lovingly resting on Rakesh's tux-clad arm as his dark eyes sparkled in the soft, chandelier light?

As she'd done thousands of times, she admired the contours of her dead husband's chest, trying to remember the feel of it beneath her fingertips, to recall the rasp of his chest hair or the texture of his skin. His jacket's tailoring sculpted to his shoulders, every stitch a work of art, every seam flattering the dashing billionaire who'd once upon a time stolen her heart.

A flick of her fingernail opened the next page: a wide shot of both their families lined up in a massive, blended herd of white and brown faces. There was her father, with his silvering, leonine head and his movie star good looks, the senior senator from the great state of California. And her brother, standing between her parents, an adult child buffer between divorced adults. A proto-Alpha, if there ever was one, in the stiff dress whites of his Naval Captain uniform, tall and straight and strong as a California redwood. Her big brother had been so handsome and capable.

In some ways, Hunter reminded her of him, in the serious, decisive practicality and no-nonsense attitude. Hurt resurfaced as her thoughts tripped too close to their stupid confrontation earlier in the day. She'd resolved to put it aside. It's not like she would beg him to salvage their friendship. If it meant so little to him, perhaps she didn't need it anyway. Or maybe time would soften this wall, and they could start over. If not, she'd survive. She always did.

But the sting of that fresh wound highlighted something even worse: the dull, lifeless memories of older wounds that went much, much deeper.

Her eyes glided to her mother, zeroing in on the ghastly bones of her hand clutching her brother's sturdy arm. His strength and vitality morbidly contrasted with the sickly frailty of her mom's wasted body. When Mom died not three months later, it was the worst tragedy of Della's life. In retrospect, it shattered her heart, yet it was only a preview of what was to come.

Then there were Rakesh's parents, grinning broadly, and all his sisters with their colorful saris and glossy black hair. And next to Rakesh, sitting in a place of honor, his beloved grandmother, his *Amma*. Amma, who'd pressed this very book into Della's hands with an admonishment to *"keep it with you, and if your house burns, you know what to grab first."*

"Amma," Rakesh had laughed as Della flipped through the glossy wedding photos in the palm-sized album, *"all the photos are safe in the cloud."*

"Pssh," Amma scoffed, *"the* cloud. *Have you ever seen anything less permanent than a cloud?"*

Della's cheek quivered, remembering the elderly woman chiding her tech mogul husband. Amma had been right in the end, hadn't she? Maybe the cloud existed somewhere, in some secret server farm that hadn't been blasted to smithereens, in some place where electricity flowed unbroken... but she doubted it. In a strange and sadly poetic way, it mirrored her relationship with her own fraught memories: the emotions existed somewhere, but remained largely inaccessible. Unplugged and devoid of power, they languished in permanent statis, a part of her and forever separated from her.

Tired of reminiscing, Della flipped past the rest of the wedding photos, past her honeymoon and a few others tucked in from other adventures, saying another silent thank you to Amma and another silent prayer that she had died peacefully and unaffected by the end of the world.

That was one of the cruelest things, the *unknowing* of it all. Once communications went down and failsafe after failsafe failed, everything was cut off from everything else. The only situation you knew was your immediate environment; your only sources of information were the people you spoke with and the rumors and lies they passed along as truth. When things went wrong, as everything did, there was no one to call for help.

No one to call when wildfires raced through your beautiful town and ate up the houses like a ravenous beast of mythical proportions. No one to call when a tree fell, blocking the escape route and splitting your fleeing group in two. No one to call when you screamed goodbyes to your husband over the roaring flames as your neighbors dragged you away.

No one to call when the things she'd believed in, worked for, devoted her life to amounted to nothing more than fanciful, quaint notions of a pseudo-civilization. Government's responsibility to its citizens, its ability to guide a traumatized populace through a catastrophe, the ability of leadership to provide a steadying hand in a time of crisis, the social contract and citizens' commitments to each other for the good of all... all of it gone in a frenzy of panic and a rapid descent into everyone out for themselves.

Della sighed, letting the photo book flutter closed on her lap. She reached for her now-cold tea, taking a slow sip of the bitter liquid. What, precisely, drove her back to the album? What was the value in revisiting this again and again? To remember? To grieve? To honor?

No. Nothing so sympathetic as all that. In the deepest recesses of her heart, Della could admit she did it to recall a time when feelings zipped and swooped inside of her, when emotions were something more than abstract concepts, something more than the dulled wash of vague recognition. Della would never utter that trite colloquialism, to say a part of her died at TheEnd. She hadn't died with Rakesh and her father and her brother and millions of others. She'd lived through it all. Each successive year wore her thinner and thinner, yet life never fully relinquished its hold. Her aging slowed, she lived well past human life expectancy, and then kept on living. But each year, more and more of Adeline Cabrese washed away.

She hadn't died. She'd *eroded*.

All of her edges worn smooth, a twenty-first-century woman in a world dominated by beastly

Alphas, she'd accepted her position of relative unimportance in Morris Hill. She'd accepted her status as neither Alpha, nor Beta, nor Omega, but *Other*. She'd accepted her dreary reality, the dull monotony of subsistence farming, the endless laundry, and reading and rereading the same books. In the time after TheEnd, she'd lived through far more dangerous situations, so she accepted the boredom of the relative safety of Morris Hill and blended into the background like a smooth river rock, unfeeling and inert. Yet she returned to the photos again and again, dissected her most poignant memories, compelled to locate a trace of her once-powerful emotions in the wreckage of her life, only to come up empty.

A shuffling noise at the door kicked Della's pulse up into her throat as Cal's vow whispered across her mind, *"If you're not in the mess hall, I'll come for you."* He wouldn't barge in her cabin, would he?

The door opened, and Rue skittered in like a frightened squirrel, giving a timid little head dip in greeting. Della leaned back in her chair as her heart rate settled. An odd, wistful feeling took the momentary excitement's place as if, for absolutely no good reason whatsoever, she'd *hoped* it was Cal for one split second.

"Did you have a nice dinner?" Della asked, mostly to distract herself from the disquieting disappointment.

"Yeah, some kinda stew. Rabbit, maybe?" Rue scratched absently at her stubbled head. When the slight Omega had first arrived, someone explained to Della *sotto voce* that the Alphas had shaved her head because she was infested with lice and it was the only way not to introduce it to the entire Pack. Several weeks later, defiant black stubble sprouted all over, sticking straight up like a constantly surprised cat. It would be months before it fully returned.

Della downed the rest of her tea. "Did you get enough?"

"Uh-huh. I had seconds..." Rue screwed up her face as if thinking hard, the expression making her appear not much older than a teen when Della knew her to be older than that. "And thirds." A wide yawn contorted the woman's mouth, revealing several black holes of missing teeth. She bent to remove her shoes. "I ate so much it made me tired, so I came back."

Intrusively, her thoughts strayed back to Cal and his uttered promise to find her. "Was... uh..." Della cleared her throat. "Were the new Alphas at dinner? Did you by any chance see Cal?"

His name stole past her lips. She hadn't yet spoken it aloud, but her tongue curled around the spare three letters, and the tip of her tongue brushed the roof of her mouth like a caress. Silently repeating the syllable, the sensuous dance of her lips and tongue had awareness crackling along her nerves.

Wait. What *the hell* was going on with her?

Rue crossed the room and sat heavily on her bed, puckering her brow. "Which one is he?"

Della stood from the chair and moved to her bed, automatically tucking the small photo album beneath her mattress. She reached for her pillow, fluffing it simply to do something with her hands. "He's… uh… tall… dark hair, has an accent, and uh…"—she cleared another sudden catch from her throat—"smiles a lot?"

She cringed as the paltry and unremarkable description blundered out of her mouth. But how to describe the sheer overwhelming *presence* of him?

If she wanted to describe him in truth, she'd describe the fluttery expectancy in her belly as he loped his way over to her along the corral. She'd detail how his inspection turned her insides into a melty, gooey pool. She'd explain the heart-stopping allure that held her in its grip whenever he stood near, leaving her unable to do anything more than sputter out wholly ineffective snubs.

Rue crawled under her blankets, no trace of recognition on her face. "Not sure I've met him, so I couldn't really say." She snuggled down with another wide yawn. "They were talking about how the Alphas that went out on north patrol hadn't come back."

An uncomfortable ringing filled Della's ears, and a highly suspect concern condensed in her belly. Immediately followed by an attempt to reassure herself with all the reasons Cal's misadventures on patrol didn't concern her in the least. No doubt Colt would be all over this. Hadn't they gotten a late start anyway? Surely a very logical, sensible explanation for their delayed return existed. Maybe one of the horses threw a shoe, or maybe they got lost or were being extra thorough since it was Cal's first day.

And, most importantly, *why did she care*? He was nothing to her, absolutely nothing.

Throwing her pillow on the bed, she grabbed another, fluffing with more exuberance than necessary, trying to dislodge the discomfort caused by lying to herself. Okay, *fine*, she was nosy and wanted to know what was going on. But also… Cal declared his unambiguous intent to find her and, even with what little she knew of him, he wasn't someone who made commitments and didn't see them through. So, if he hadn't been at dinner and hadn't come to find her, that meant something delayed him, or something had happened. Not to mention, the purpose of patrol was to patrol, so their absence could very well signal danger for the entire settlement. In which case, maybe there would need to be some leadership response, and Della might be needed to help organize the Omegas and pups.

That settled it. In two steps, Della ditched the pillow and crammed her feet into shoes. Grabbing her wrap from the hook beside the door, she was ready to go in under twenty seconds.

"I'm going to go check in with Colt and see if they've returned," she said to Rue as she opened the door. A blast of night air hit her in the face, and she pulled her wrap tighter. "It'll be easier for you to sleep if I'm not here making noise."

"Okay…" Rue said in a voice already clogged with sleep. "Good night."

"Sleep well." Ignoring the puzzlement on the Omega's face, Della breached the threshold and charged into the deep, dark night.

CHAPTER SEVEN

Della

Summer solstice approached, gradually lengthening the days, yet the nights remained black-hole black. It was just so. Goddamn. *Dark.*

Nighttime always reeked of barely concealed malice. A city girl born and bred, she'd never adjusted to feeling comfortable once the sun sunk below the horizon. In the turbulent years following TheEnd, when deplorables banded together to steal from, rape, and terrorize those weaker than them, her fear only intensified. She'd endured more than one nighttime ambush as she'd sought some remedial sense of safety for herself and others like her. Maybe the Alphas and Omegas tolerated the night better with their improved vision, but Della never stopped wishing for floodlights to illuminate her path. In truth, this uneasiness kept her inside her cabin as much as her antisocial tendencies did.

Ducking her head against the reticence, she hurried along the cracked pavement walkway toward the stables. Once upon a time, no doubt as a let's-be-rustic-but-not-get-ourselves-sued-when-grandma-falls-down-and-breaks-a-hip safety measure, track lights lined the footpaths between the family lodgings and the main buildings. Those lights had long since gone out.

Twenty years prior, Hunter had staked out the area as the site of a new community. He'd somehow known about the abandoned wilderness resort and predicted that its remoteness in the British Colombian wilderness might've spared it the worst of the destruction. His hunch turned out to be correct, and on one of his many trips to gather building supplies for the rehabilitation, he'd invited Della to join in the efforts.

At the time, she'd been living in a fishing village not far from Old Tacoma. They'd met a few times over the years and established an easy kinship via their shared, but unspoken, history of having lived before TheEnd. Compared to the years she'd spent running from violence and evading the worst elements of the human race, the fishing village wasn't a bad life, but Hunter's invitation proved to be irresistible. He'd promised a place where Alphas protected those weaker than themselves, one where Beta and Omega women would be free from brutal claimings and forced matings. After decades of watchfulness, paranoia, and too many close calls to even count, the allure of being able to live without constantly looking over her shoulder made up her mind in an instant.

In the early days, that safety came with the price tag of rehabbing the dilapidated campgrounds. Della had tackled the main office building and excavated the bureaucratic remains of the once-posh resort. Yellowing invoices, decaying activities schedules, and stained inventories all crammed together in dusty, aluminum filing cabinets. Among the paperwork, she'd uncovered glossy marketing pamphlets that showcased the camp in its full glory. Originally built as an escape from the constraints of modern life, it was one of those retreats where the more you paid, the less you got. The restroom and showers were communal, and the cabins sported electricity but little else in the way of amenities. As the pamphlet expounded, guests hiked the surrounding trails, fished in the well-stocked lake, and roasted free-range, organic hotdogs and vegan marshmallows around the central firepit. A pantomime of survival sold at a premium price. The kind of place Rakesh would've loved and she would've hated. Vacations, according to her younger self, were best spent on a yacht with a colorful drink in hand, not off the grid checking her socks for ticks.

The irony was not lost on her.

Stepping off the pavement, she beelined toward the stable as the well-trod dirt muffled her steps. If and when the patrol returned, the stables would be their first destination. As she tracked alongside the corral, the horse blankets swayed on the line. Their undulations needled her, as if their gentle waving singsonged, *you can lie to yourself, but* we *saw you flirting with him.*

A streak of chagrin slowed her determined feet. What was she even doing out here? Honestly, they were probably already back, and the errand would be for nothing. No. Resuming her pace, she blinked the hesitation away. Checking on the patrol didn't mean anything. She was simply looking out for the settlement, that's all. Once she ensured everything was fine, she'd return home. No fuss, no muss.

Deep Alpha voices spilled from the barn. Lamps were fully lit inside, making it easy to slip through the propped-open door. Yet as soon as she stepped inside, the Alpha conversation ceased and four pairs of eyes swung expectantly in her direction. As anticipated, Colt was one of them, giving her a look of bemused curiosity.

She addressed him directly. "I heard the north patrol was still out. Is everything okay?"

"We're talking it over now." He angled his chin toward the group, which included Sloan, Lars, and a new Alpha she hadn't yet met. Although, of the four of them, the look from the unknown Alpha gave her the disconcerting impression *he* knew *her*. She ignored it and refocused on Colt, taking a few steps farther inside, leaving the creepy night to keep its own company for a while.

"Could something have happened with the horses?" Lars asked, dismissing her and resuming their conversation.

"I already said," Sloan said with an added edge to his always-edgy voice, "I checked them both over, and they were in fine shape before they left."

Della gave him a scrutinizing once-over. *Hotheaded mini-tyrant* Cal had called him. Now that she compared the remarkably astute assessment to the Alpha himself, a giggle birthed in her chest. Sidling out of the way, she passed a palm over her mouth to hide her curling lips. Alphas were a sensitive bunch.

Colt slapped a friendly hand on Sloan's shoulder. "We believe you, we're going over the possibilities before we send out a search—"

Colt cocked his head. The Alphas stilled, their faces taking on dreamy far-away looks as they listened for something their superior hearing alone could discern. The only sounds Della could pick out were the snuffling and shuffling of the horses in their stalls and the faint drip of water somewhere in the barn.

After a moment, Colt's shoulders slumped, and the rest of the Alpha's postures visibly relaxed. "They're coming now. Quarter mile away," he said to Della by way of an explanation.

Relief trickled over her for one comforting instant before awkwardness replaced the tension her shoulders released. Her toes itched in her boots, her body's reminder that she planned to leave as soon as she ensured everything was fine. If she didn't go now, what would she do when *he* strode through those doors?

Rewrapping herself tighter, she bounced her chin in a series of nods. "Oh, that's good. No cause for concern in that case." Fresh worry streaked Colt's face, and Della took a step forward. "What is it? What's wrong?"

"There's some blood..." Colt admitted, "not much..." He exchanged a significant look with Lars as Della reviewed all the myriad reasons for this development. None of them particularly good, the conclusion rooted her to the spot.

"Yeah," Lars added, a wry tilt to his lips. "Some blood, the animals are sweating, and... no one's particularly *happy*."

Tense minutes passed. The Alphas scuffed their boots on the ground and dug hands in pockets, awaiting the arrival of the errant patrol with patience. All except for the Alpha unknown to her, who slinked closer to the stable doors as if he wanted to be the first to intercept the pair. His dark eyes snagged on Della's in the process and held them, an inscrutable message hidden in their depths. He didn't exude nefarious intent, yet the deliberate positioning and extended eye contact suggested that whatever he feared would walk through the door had something to do with him *and* her.

Hoofbeats broke the hushed nighttime quiet, followed by the squeaks and jangles of large bodies dismounting outside the stable doors. Fresh nerves rattled around her chest as she wrung her hands together, cursing herself for even coming here. She'd told the man to fuck off, so why was she now deliberately putting herself in his path? *Such an idiot move, Della*!

The barn door slid open and Silas entered—leading his horse by the reins with one hand and bracing his other against his ribs. Sloan stomped toward the horse, scowling at Silas and wasting no time laying into him. "Where the fuck have you two been? You've got Gus all lathered up, and there's a goddamn chill in the air."

Silas muttered some shitty retort, which Della barely heard because Cal appeared in the doorway with a wide bruise discoloring his jaw and a vicious split in his bottom lip. Her eyes swept over the rest of his body, top to toe, searching for other injuries. Mid-perusal, she chanced on his enigmatic expression, and the world around her shifted into slow motion.

His dimple winked and lips parted as if to speak, but the unfamiliar Alpha strode forward and relieved Cal of his horse's reins. They exchanged some quiet words, but Cal's gaze never wavered. His bright, hazel eyes sparkled as if he'd uncovered the best possible secret.

Heat simmered low in Della's pelvis, the pulsing vibration wheedling lower and lower with each passing second. She froze, transfixed and immobilized by the sensation as Cal took a decided stride in her direction. Alarm freed her, and mirroring his action, she took one step back, preserving the spare few feet between them. Hazel amusement and the additional appearance of a second dimple taunted her, mocking her assumption that a few spare feet would save her.

"So, are you two gonna explain what happened out there?" Colt's harsh question disrupted the nonverbal dance.

"Ask that asshole." Silas hiked his thumb over his shoulder at Cal. "He attacked me out of nowhere. We need to send him packing." Silas's glower shifted between Cal and the unfamiliar Alpha. "Him *and* his trouble-making friends."

"That's not what happened." Cal turned away from Della, his tone soft and studiously even. "I'd suggest you reconsider the story you're peddling."

"Hey, fuck you," Silas snarled before tucking his shoulders and launching into Cal like an enraged bull.

Everything smeared in one fast-moving blur. One second, Cal stood a few feet away, and the next, his enormous body rammed into hers. The crack of her head against the stall door punched the air like a starter pistol. Agony rattled her skull, her vision blurred, and her ass ached as she slumped on the cold, hay-strewn floor. Discomfort spread from her head to her neck to her arm to her back, all of it like one giant throbbing bruise.

Noises crashed through the barn: Alpha shouting, big bodies slamming together, and the sloppy sound of blows landing on flesh. Behind her, horses snorted and whinnied and pranced in agitation. All of it congealed into one muffled mash jamming into her ear canals. Taking a deep breath, she blinked and blinked, trying to clear the cloudy red film that obscured her vision. Oh. Red? Huh. Was she bleeding?

"Keep this fucker away from me!" someone roared, and then a hazy face materialized in front of her. She knew this face, but there was something off about it. Blood trickled from his split lip and ran down the rivet in his sculpted chin. Did he have a cleft chin? A mysterious, handsome man with a strong jaw, a sexy accent, and perfectly cleft chin. What a cliché!

A laugh fizzed in her chest, but she ignored it because that would be wrong. You didn't laugh at someone when they were bleeding.

"Della, oh shit. Della!" the man said, his frantic tone perplexing her. Why was he so upset? "Can you hear me?" He barked over his shoulder, "Get some water and a clean cloth."

"Hey." A second head floated next to the handsome man's. This one she knew, too, with his glossy hair and kind eyes. His name came easily: Colt. "Let's get you off the floor, all right?"

"Don't touch her," the handsome man barked, easing Della upright and propping her against the stable door. "Why don't you get your Pack under control, *Second*."

"What're you gonna do, Cal, fight everyone?"

"If need be."

"He says you attacked him first."

"Yeah? Well, you saw him jump me and catch the Omega in the crossfire, so you make your own judgment."

"She's not Omega, and what business is she of yours?" Words ping-ponged back and forth, too fast to follow all the subtexts and implications. Colt glared at the handsome man, and distantly, Della opened her mouth to tell them their bickering was pummeling her tired brain.

A cloth appeared in the handsome man's hand *Cal*, she latched onto the name with some satisfaction. Cal with the drawl that poured over her like melted chocolate. God, it had been so long since she had chocolate. What she wouldn't give for some chocolate...

Taking her chin in his palm, he dabbed her forehead, creasing his brow in concentration. The sting startled her awake, and a small whimper slipped out of her throat in protest.

"Hush now, darlin', I got you." His voice soothed soft and low, accompanied by a gentle rumble that seemed to start in his chest and end in hers. "How's that? Better?"

She blinked some more, nodding as her vision improved, although her head still throbbed, and she swore her skull shrank three sizes too small.

"She might have a concussion," someone said, their words coming clearer now. "We should get Hunter, he's a doctor."

Despite her confused haze, an amused snort ripped out of Della. "What's he going to do? Order a CT scan?"

Two puzzled Alpha faces stared back at her as if she'd uttered a foreign language. Maybe she had. Her mistake—alluding to life before TheEnd always made everyone uncomfortable. Whoops. She knew better than that.

Cal nodded, his hazel eyes twinkling again, mesmerizing her with their pretty green-gray-gold sheen. "No need to disturb Hunt. I'll keep an eye on her. You can go deal with..." He jerked his head over his right shoulder, where some ruckus continued in the barn, only now between Sloan and Silas as Lars wedged himself between them, commanding each to cool down.

"This is a problem for you, you know that, right?" Colt frowned. "Morris Hill is a peaceful village. No place here for violent Alphas." Cal began to interrupt, but Colt spoke over him with authority. "We'll convene the entire Pack tomorrow and go over what happened. You'll get a chance to tell your side of the story. But you should know, if the fault lands on you, you'll be expelled from the Pack. Immediately."

Cal's body hardened. Rigid, not like a statue, but like a coiled viper lying in wait. "Is that how it's gonna be?" he said with the slightest of sneers.

Colt gave one short, decisive nod. "Listen. You're not in a great position here, being new and all, but if you're honest, that will help."

A lengthy pause sizzled in the air, neither of them giving up a single molecule of resolve. "Somehow, I doubt that." Cal murmured, turning back to her with worry in his eyes.

Colt said her name, and reluctantly, Della dragged her attention to him. Deep frown lines bracketed his lips, his usual placid countenance marred with annoyance. "You feel well enough to get up? I'll carry you home if not."

"Like hell you will." Cal's body shifted like a viper strike, lightning-fast and smooth, caging around her and blocking out Colt and everyone else. Heat from his nearness blasted through her sluggish senses, bowling her over with a new awareness of the powerful lines of his body and a lovely, answering softening in hers.

A memory fought to the foreground in her bleary thoughts: she'd been close to him before and hadn't liked it, but she couldn't remember *why*. Right now, it was rather pleasant, inspiring a powerful urge to act like a rag doll and collapse into him completely.

Cal spoke over his shoulder to Colt. "You go on and deal with the rest of this mess. I'll take care of her."

"Della?" Ignoring Cal, Colt addressed her again. "You gonna be all right with him? I can still go get Hunt—"

"No." She shook her head and immediately regretted the small movement as dizziness scrambled her vision. "Don't bother. I'll be okay."

The taut line of Cal's shoulder eased the tiniest of degrees, and when her eyes steadied on his face, the left corner of his lip lifted in the hint of an approving smile.

"Okay then." Slowly, Colt rose to his feet. "Tomorrow morning, Cal, there'll be questions for you to answer."

Cal didn't appear concerned, his hand once again cradling her face and staring deep into her eyes. Della's stomach pooled liquid and gooey, which could've been from the maybe concussion or possibly the touch of his skin upon hers.

His mouth kicked up another notch closer to a smile, the dimples out in full force. "Don't worry. I got you now. Everything's gonna be fine."

Lost in his seductive pull, she found herself nodding and, even more remarkably, discovering she meant it.

91

CHAPTER EIGHT

Cal

Della's lips curled in a slight, dreamy smile that settled his jittery nerves, at least related to concern for his injured Omega.

No question, though, inside he pulsed with cold, seething fury. At Silas. At Colt. At the entire stupid lot of them. At himself for not expecting Silas's retaliatory attack. *His* flying body knocked Della into the wall, and for that, he wanted to drown that motherfucker Silas in the nearest water trough. It was too much to ask for that asshole to take his beating by the hot springs and leave it at that. No, that coward had to start shit up once he had his protective brothers to back him up. Naturally, their loyalties would be with Silas rather than a newcomer like him. That prick plotted it the entire trip back, along with whatever pack of lies he'd vomit up when questioned.

Fucking ridiculous.

Worst of all, anger at himself festered like a gangrenous wound. Like a moron, he'd convinced himself Morris Hill would be a place where he could find some measure of community and justice. A foolish, naïve hope; he should've known better.

"Hey. She okay?" Simon appeared on his left, eyeing Della. "Sloan says there's a cot in the little room to lay her down."

"She'll be fine," Cal said with false confidence, as if he could will it so.

"I'm not tired." Her words slurred as her eyelids drooped. "I'm thirsty."

Glancing down, Cal examined his bloody and swollen knuckles. He had enough strength to carry her back to the hot springs if needed, but he only wished he could be less of a mess when he laid his hands on her for the first time. The moment grew with significance in his mind, something that warranted more care and reverence than he was able to provide with his filthy body and throbbing face.

She deserved better.

"All right, darlin'." Shaking himself loose, he accepted the moment fate offered and gathered her up, taking care to handle her sure-to-be-bruised body as gingerly as he could. Her shape, soft but pleasingly solid, slumped against him, her small head nuzzling into his chest with an adorable little sigh. If he needed confirmation of a concussion, her transformation from a bristling hellcat into a sleepy kitten made one helluva strong case. "We'll get you some water. Are you hurting?"

She shook her head, her nose knocking into him, which apparently inspired her to take a long, exaggerated inhale. Cal's chest swelled in response. *That's it, Omega. Scent me, breathe me in.* She babbled a pleased little noise he didn't understand but enjoyed nonetheless.

Lifting her from the ground, Cal jerked his chin at Simon. "Get my canteen and meet me in there." He cut a glance around the room. Sloan and Lars tended the horses while Colt bent his head to have a quiet word with Silas. Satisfied they weren't being watched, he nonetheless kept his volume so low anyone other than his friend wouldn't hear. "We need to talk, and I need these guys out of here before we do."

"Let me see what I can do." Frowning with understanding, Simon bobbed a discrete nod and then strode away. Later, Cal would ask his companion how he ended up being in the stable tonight, but for now, he was grateful it was Simon and not Matteo here to help him execute his rapidly forming plan. Matteo was useful in a scrap, but he needed Simon's level-headedness right about now.

Located at the other end of the stable, the small room looked to have once been an office of some variety, complete with a rusted metal desk and tattered, dusty curtains on the windows. A cot rested against the back wall, looking a touch less filthy than the rest of the office. A quick sniff determined the linens to be relatively fresh.

"Easy now. There you go." He laid Della down, savoring the way her arms clung to his neck, as if not wanting to let go till the last possible moment. Crouching at her side, he stroked the length of her supple thigh, and, amazingly, she didn't protest, only regarded him with a peaceful serenity.

Immediately, he became all too conscious of the two of them, in a room, alone, with a bed. Not that he'd take advantage of her in a compromised state, but explicit imaginings strolled through his thoughts uninvited. Detaching from her with some effort, he pulled over the dusty metal chair and took a seat next to the bed, pressing her nearest hand between his own. A smile lit her face, and, if such a thing was possible, his heart thumped in acknowledgment.

"Why're you being so nice to me?" she asked.

He turned her slim palm over and traced the lines with his rough, blunt finger pad. "Why wouldn't I be?"

The elegant arcs of her eyebrows nudged together. "I don't think I've been very nice to you, have I?"

He huffed a weak laugh and brought her palm to his lips, placing a kiss in the center. "Not yet. But I ain't giving up."

At that, she looked even more confused before sinking her head deeper into the old, flat pillow. "I wanna go home. My head hurts."

"Soon," he said, adding a rumbling purr to the words. The purr settled her as it had earlier out in the barn. Another confirmation, as if he needed one, she was Omega.

Simon returned, handing off a full canteen. "Up you go." With an arm under her shoulders, Cal hoisted Della and lifted the canteen to her lips. Thankfully, she grasped it for herself and took several long, slow gulps. "Not too fast now, don't make yourself sick."

She drained half the container and screwed it shut, immediately flopping back and clearly ready to drift off to sleep. Cal addressed Simon, speaking low and under his breath, "You reckon I oughta keep her awake?"

Simon tilted his head. "Nah, let her sleep for now, but wake her up every few hours to check. Although…" He paused, shooting Cal an anxious glance. "Not sure what we'll do if she has a serious brain injury, anyway."

Saying a silent prayer, he watched Della slide into unconsciousness, hoping this wouldn't be the last time he'd ever see her awake. He couldn't lose her as soon as he'd found her. Before he'd made her his. "She'll be fine," he said, voice roughened.

Outside the small room, the stable noises, Alpha and animal, had quieted. "They gone?" he asked Simon, easing his back against the chair and pouring the rest of the water down his parched throat.

"Yeah. I offered to finish brushing the horses and cleaning the tack. Told 'em it was only fair since I'm new and needed to pay my dues." His mouth formed an ironic quirk. "They took off, all except Sloan. He damn near made me recite an entire manual of horse care to him before he agreed." Simon glugged from his own canteen and then spit a mouthful on the floor. "But, whatever, he's gone. What're you thinking?"

Cal took a breath, wrangling his thoughts into something resembling order. All his instincts screamed at him to take his Omega and run, but he had to be smart about it. He couldn't tear off into an unfamiliar forest and hope for the best, especially with Della in a compromised state. "You heard what Colt said. Tomorrow there's gonna be some kinda trial where I have to explain my actions, and there's a high possibility I'll be exiled. I need to leave. Tonight. And I'm taking her."

Simon's chin dipped with slow comprehension. "Where're you gonna go?"

He swept a length of Della's hair off her neck, the silken, multihued strands sifting through his fingers. "Got a place in mind, but I need supplies: bedding, cooking gear, a change of clothes, a lamp or two, and at least a week's worth of food. I'll need my pack and whatever else you can get your hands on without raising suspicion."

Simon rubbed a hand over his brow. "It'll take me a minute," he said slowly, "but I got some supplies set by, and I'll check with Matteo. Between us, probably enough to get you started."

Cal released a relieved breath, the enormity of this undertaking descending on him. He'd planned journeys before, many of them, but never this slapdash, never when the stakes were so high, and never when he had an injured Omega to care for in the process. It edged uncomfortably close to a retreat, like skulking out of town in the night like a dog who'd stolen a chicken from the coop. Except instead of chowing down on the chicken and consuming the evidence, he'd be leaving their scents as a breadcrumb trail that could potentially be followed.

But he didn't reckon he had much of a choice. Now that he had an entire night to think of one, Silas would lie and make up some story to implicate Cal in some dubious plot. He'd no doubt announce it for the entire Pack to hear at this tribunal or whatever the fuck would happen in the morning. Cal didn't like lying, and he didn't like sneaking, but he wasn't dumb enough not to notice the clear warning in Colt's words, and that fucker didn't even like him.

Fuck. He'd thought this Pack, with a solid Alpha like Hunter at the helm, stood as good a chance as any of being somewhere he could find a purpose, have a home, be part of a community, and make a life for himself. Somewhere he hadn't yet tainted with his bumbling incompetence. But where the fuck was

Hunter in all of this? Snugged up in a Rut with his Omega, and who could blame him?

But it left Cal out to dry.

Even if reason prevailed and Cal stayed, in the next day or so, Della's mental clarity would improve, and then she'd be back to her irritable self, refusing to have anything to do with him. Then how would he spend enough time with her to induce a Heat? With the wildly inconvenient "rule" about Omegas consenting to being claimed, would she hold out long enough for him to lose his fucking mind from not having her?

No, there was no choice; plenty of reasons to go and none to hesitate. It would have to be the cave. He'd take her there, watch her for a few days to make sure she was all right, get her bonded to him, then they'd leave and find somewhere else to live. In Old Tacoma, he'd heard talk about places further inland with consistent electricity and more developed civilization. He'd take her there, and they'd start over, together.

Slapping his hands on his thighs, Cal rose from the chair. "While you gather supplies, I'll finish up with the horses and saddle a fresh one to carry us. Figure I'll get to the spot, unload, and then set the horse free to find her way home. If you can keep a look out tonight and put her away when she returns, no one has to know."

"Let's pray she makes it back by morning. If not, there's no way I'll be able to hide it from Sloan."

Simon grinned an evil grin. "Half suspect he's a horse fucker for how protective he is of 'em."

Despite himself, Cal barked a laugh. "Go on and see what you can find. The sooner I leave, the better." With one last lingering caress of Della's cheek, he strode from the room, intent on his plan. Simon followed, heading toward the exit, when Cal stopped him with a hand on his arm. "Me disappearing is going to put you two in the hot seat. You and Matteo need to lay low."

"Cal..." Simon darted a glance back at the office where Della slept. "What happens when they find out she's missing? They're gonna come looking."

He winced, sucking air between his teeth. "I know it, but I think she keeps to herself. If anyone asks you, tell them you saw me carrying her." He lifted a shoulder, acknowledging it wasn't a full-on lie as he had carried her into the side room. "They'll assume I took her to her cabin, and if we're lucky, that'll buy us some time."

"They'll track your scent."

"Maybe, maybe not." He made a disgusted gesture toward himself. "I'll wash as soon as I can, and I've got Silas's fucking filthy BO all over me, which might throw 'em off. If they don't catch a fresh trail, it'll be lost within a day."

A dark cloud passed over Simon's face. "I hope so, man. If they catch you running off with one of their women..."

Cal's jaw tightened. "Once we're bonded, they won't be able to do shit without hurting her too."

Simon didn't look convinced, squinting one eye at Cal. "You reckon they give a shit about that?"

"Let's hope we never find out." Cal rubbed the back of his neck. "You and Matteo gonna be able to keep yourselves in check without me? I know I'm running off on you both."

Simon held out his hand, and they locked arms for a quick, solid embrace. "It is what it is, brother. You'd do the same for me."

Cal gave his friend one final slap on the back. "Go on now, we got work to do."

CHAPTER NINE

Della

Dripping water plunked in an unrelenting pattern, luring Della into unwilling consciousness. Water was a problem. Was there a leak in her cabin? Had the framing of the door settled again? Or was it the roof this time?

She'd been dreaming. Dreams about a breakneck horse ride through the dark, snugged up tight against a man's chest, the smell of coffee and cinnamon tickling her nose. Slowly, the dream remnants released their sticky hold, and glimmers of bright light assaulted her barely--slitted eyes. Her eyelids trudged the rest of the way open, only to be greeted by a window of midday sun that blinded her with its intensity yet failed to illuminate the shadowed corners of...

Della shot upright, her head spinning with the sudden movement. *Where the fuck* was *she?*

Her stiffened, sluggish neck swiveled around her surroundings as she grappled for pieces to put together. Was she... in a *cave?*

Turbulence crowded her head, her last memories fuzzy and uncooperative. She'd been at home, looking at her photos. Rue came in, but something was wrong. The patrol hadn't returned, and Della'd gone to investigate. Snoop, maybe more accurately. Shouting Alphas, a fight, and then her head throbbing with overstuffed misery.

A deep male groan ricocheted around the stone walls before being swallowed by the cavernous space. To her right, a large man sprawled on the ground. Not next to her but a mere arm's length away. Della ran a panicked hand over her shirt and underneath the blankets that covered her. Her boots were off, but otherwise, she was fully dressed, everything in place as it had been since she got up yesterday morning. Had it been yesterday? Or had she been asleep for days? Had she been drugged?

The man smacked his lips, a pink tongue darting out to wet them as the arm slung over his brow slid off and fell to his side, revealing his face.

Cal.

That face, *his* face, full of hovering concern, came back to her in foggy snapshots. Cleaning blood from her forehead. Checking her for broken bones. Carrying her across the stable. Laying her gently in a bed. The dreams took on a new significance, turning her queasy stomach into a solid block of ice.

The dreams, the ride on the horse... those weren't dreams at all! In her confusion, he'd packed her up and taken her... *somewhere.* Advice from her old life floated up from her memory like a taunt: "*Never go to a second location. Your chance of survival drastically drops when you're taken to a second location."*

Another quick perusal of the cave confirmed that "second location" was the absolute best spin on her current situation. She needed to get out of here and fast.

Quickly, too quickly, Della rolled and staggered to her feet. Her insides sloshed like she was aboard an unsteady ship, and shadows flirted on the edges of her vision. Hands outstretched, she wobbled to the nearest wall, the cool rock rough and indifferent under her fingers but blessedly unmoving. Shit. What was wrong with her head? Was she *concussed*? That wouldn't make this any easier. Hand on the wall, she tested her unsteady gait with a few tentative steps. Ignoring her heaving stomach, she shuffled toward the opening and peered outside, her heart immediately leaping into her throat at what she found.

Squinting into the sun, fifteen feet of stone stretched between the cave and a briskly flowing stream below. Too far to jump, scaling the wall would be dicey even if she weren't woozy and on the verge of passing out. Sweat misted her forehead, and a surge of dizziness had her drooping to position with her head between her knees.

Her sinuses burned with desperate tears. No. No crying. Her dad's voice chided in her memory, *"Solve the problem, Adeline."*

A sudden longing for her father reared up like a rampant lion, threatening to grind her to dust beneath its giant paws. Six years old, ringed by the scattered remains of a block tower, cheeks streaked with tears as her dad's patient face brimmed with love. His deep voice rumbled, "Cry *for a minute, Adeline; then solve the problem.*" Nineteen years old, her college-aged self raged against the latest injustice or bigotry. The clear blue eyes he passed onto her peered over his spectacles as he softly chided, *"Rant for a minute, Adeline; then get to work and solve the problem."*

No single person shaped Della's existence more than her father, Senator Michael Anthony Cabrese. They were people of action, she and her father, yet Della never took for granted the privilege of being a senator's wealthy daughter. Being a person of action only worked insofar as you possessed sufficient power to actually make things happen. Yet none of the privilege of her former life helped her when TheEnd came, and it wouldn't help her now.

Taken to a cave in the middle of nowhere with a strange Alpha who'd already made his intentions crystal clear, she longed not for her father's wisdom or guidance but a far more basic, primitive need: protection. That feeling of being a small child scooped up and held tight with one arm while he waved with the other to the roaring crowd of amped-up supporters, secure in the knowledge that as loud, frightening, and intimidating as all those faces looking at her family was, she was utterly, completely safe.

Despair cut through her nausea. Her father, long dead, couldn't protect her. Rakesh, long dead, couldn't protect her. This was the AfterEnd, and she hadn't been safe since civilization fell. Within the confines of Morris Hill, she'd believed Hunter and his Alphas offered a reprieve from the constant threat of lawlessness. Yet, somehow, right under their noses, she'd been spirited away, cut off from the security she'd taken for granted. Della hung her throbbing head, wrestling her emotions back from the brink and failing miserably as tears drenched her cheeks.

"Cry for a minute, Adeline; then solve the problem."

Solve the problem. Solve the problem. But...she *couldn't*. Not this problem. Not right now. Not like this. Breaths, fast and shallow, wheezed between her lips. Her lungs begged for a deeper, purifying inhale, but an iron band confined her chest and imprisoned the air inside. Her mind refused to settle, spiraling into a full-on panic like a child hurtling down a hill on an out-of-control bicycle.

"Hey, now." A deep voice crashed through her hysteria, startling her and upsetting her precarious footing. Her body jerked, her vision reeled, and the steep, stony precipice teetered in and out of focus as if beckoning her toward the headfirst plunge. Maybe Hunter had the right idea after all: it would take nothing to pitch over the edge and leave the rest up to fate. What was the point of pretending she had anything resembling freedom and choice in this stupid, backward world, anyway?

"Woah, woah, woah." A sturdy force encircled her waist and eased her back from the brink. Bare feet sliding on the pebbled entrance, Della wanted to resist, to fight back and tell him to get the hell away from her, but she didn't get a chance before sleep-warmed arms bundled her against a broad, firm chest. He tightly secured her trembling body, a broad palm soothing up and down her back. Slumped against him in desolate resignation, utter helplessness suffused her limbs, and a sob ripped from her throat.

"C'mon now. I promise it ain't as bad as all that. What're you trying to do, give me a heart attack?" he whispered into her hair. "Trying to catch a little shut-eye, and the next thing I know, you're stumbling around on the edge. 'Bout scared me half to death."

His hands ran along her back, a steady up and down, as if erasing her fear like chalk from an old-fashioned chalkboard. The rhythmic flex of strong fingers lured her thoughts from the careening panic. They wove a spell that satisfied, in some sick way, the protection she'd longed for moments before.

"What're you going to do with me?" she murmured into his shirtfront.

He didn't answer. Or, at least, not with words. His hands continued to work their magic up and down her neck and spine. Tension sloughed from Della's neck and shoulders, and her head relaxed into his working palm, so large it cradled her skull like a newborn's.

With a throaty sigh, he tucked her face into his neck. "Ain't gonna hurt you," he rumbled against her skin.

Not an answer to her question, but strangely, she wanted to believe him. No doubt, it was stupid, and she'd no doubt regret it later. She wanted to believe this unknown Alpha was different from all the dangerous, volatile ones she'd encountered in the AfterEnd.

Sense and pragmatism revolted, pounding on the door of her reasonable mind to try to wake it up, reviewing argument after argument for the intrinsic savagery of their kind, reminding herself of all the violence she'd witnessed and run from before she'd come to Morris Hill. So many years of fighting tooth and nail to maintain some degree of autonomy, some semblance of choice, some right of self-determination, only to be abducted in the night and hidden away God-knows-where in a fucking *cave*?

How could she believe his intentions were anything but vile?

And yet.

The warmth of his body seeped into her cheek and quieted her sobs. Della drew in a long, hiccupping breath, filling her lungs with air seasoned by her tears and the heat of his skin. Soothing, rich coffee flavor and the toasted zing of cinnamon spice worked its way into her nostrils, recalling more scent memories of the horseback ride dream.

Only the scent tickling her nose wasn't a dream. Her heart stutter-stopped. It was *real*. She was truly smelling something.

She was smelling *him*.

A surprised noise popped out, and she pulled in another breath, greedy for more. And more she got. Despite her tear-clogged sinuses and stuffed-up nose, the pure notes of the spicy, wholesome aroma shuddered down her spine. Overcome, Della gorged on breath after greedy breath, afraid it was a hallucination. Afraid it would disappear and plunge her back into the blunted olfactory wasteland of the last hundred years.

Unable to hold back, she yanked at his shirt, exposing more golden skin in which to bury her nose and shamelessly indulge. Inside the confines of his clothes, the scent built up steam, becoming richer and more complex, infused with a provocative, masculine tang. It arrowed directly into her, prompting a small, helpless whimper as it struck her pelvis with a deep and powerful thrum. Sensations she hadn't experienced for literal decades zoomed around her insides, and none more powerful than an anguished neediness in her sex.

With some difficulty, Della yanked herself away and confronted a pair of smoldering hazel eyes. "It's you," she whispered, heart thundering in her ears. "I..." She swallowed. "I can smell you."

CHAPTER TEN

Della

"You don't… you don't…"—too shocked to do anything more than stammer, Della gaped into Cal's confused face—"understand. I haven't been able to smell anything since…" The fires, the destruction, the end of the world as she knew it. Della squeezed her eyes shut, strong-arming those memories back into the darkness where they belonged. "For a very long time," she finished lamely.

She opened her eyes, only to find Cal's attention fastened on her lips like she was the last sip of water in a desert. The lust already crashing through Della's body crested in one heaving crush, exploding out in an alarming release of fluid between her legs. With a gasp, she looked down, dampness spreading over her crotch like she'd wet herself. "What the fuck?"

Cal groaned, a deep, powerful sound that prompted a second humiliating gush. "That's your slick." He pulled her closer, his chest heaving in great, sawing breaths. His hands flexed and released, aggressively kneading her hips as Della recognized a definite thickening hardness against her belly. "You scented me, and now you're responding the way an Omega responds to an Alpha."

"No." Shaking her head, Della angled her body away from him, unable to back away farther because of the hands that moved to cup her bottom. "I'm not Omega."

Something dangerous flared in his eyes, and his huge body—how hadn't she noticed before how *huge* he was? — curved over hers, his posture suddenly looming.

This is where you ought to be afraid. Her rational mind argued like a distant voice calling up from the bottom of a well. Except fear wasn't shooting pleasurable trills deep in her pelvis. And it certainly wasn't fear that decided his enormous, deliciously fragrant body wasn't scary but, rather, quite *stimulating*.

"Whatever you are, you're mine now. *Fuck,* you smell so good." He made the noise again, that groan, that gruff grumble, that guttural *growl.* Overflowing with potency and raw sexual force, Della's core spasmed around nothing, and a shallow climax rippled through her and nearly knocked her off her feet again. A shocked cry sailed out of her at the sudden wash of unexpected bliss.

Cal moaned as if in pain. "*Fuck me*, did you come?" His hand wiggled between them, cupping her sex over her sopping pants. "Did this pussy come for my Alpha growl?"

His scent awakened something inside her, but his words made her lose her mind completely. Without a thought, without a single stitch of hesitation, Della's pelvis tilted into his palm, angling closer to that possessive grip. If he took his hand away now, she'd go insane.

"What's happening to me?" she demanded, yanking on his shirt, wanting more of something, more of everything, more of *him*.

Pity tinged the flaring heat in his eyes. "Come on, Della, you know what this is," he chided gently, detaching her hands from his clothes before bending his knees to scoop her up and carry her back into the gray darkness of the cave.

With trembling, scrabbling hands, she circled his neck and fisted in his hair for something to hold on to, determined to anchor her spiraling acceleration. This wasn't *her*. Adeline Cabrese didn't writhe and pant and grind against Alphas she barely knew.

And yet, she couldn't stop.

Gently, he lowered them back to the improvised sleeping area, cradling her head so as not to knock it against the stone, exhibiting a perplexing and altogether surprising degree of consideration from a body vibrating with pent-up excitement. But she didn't have time to process that incongruence because, with a few deft movements of his fingers, he'd undone her pants and whipped them off her legs. Damp thighs and swollen sex exposed, she gasped as the chilled air hit her heated flesh. More rough sounds rumbled in Cal's throat. Hooking her knees, he hiked her legs up and spread them wide, wider than her shoulders, displaying everything to his ravenous regard. He'd made his intentions plain in his insouciant, unhurried way, but the full force of those desires now sprang to the surface.

"You have a needy Omega cunt that's been neglected for far too fucking long." The coarse words, highlighted by the gritty restraint cutting through his usual silken drawl, made her head spin and not from concussion. Each word stoked the blaze higher. Taking her hand, he tucked it behind her knee, in the same place his own had been. "Keep that there," he said with the unmistakable tone of an order, and Della's body lit on *fire*.

Positioning her other hand on her other knee, he nodded in approval, soaking up the picture he'd composed. Some distant part of her wondered if she should be appalled, embarrassed, or disgusted with herself and her unprotested, unresisted submission. Maybe she ought to be, but she had no space in her mind for that, not when Cal once again laid his palm on her sex, this time, his bare flesh against her most intimate spot for the first time. She whined, an agonized sound, feeling the building need for another, *better*, release.

"Look at you." His eyes touched on hers briefly before returning to her core. Slipping his fingers along her slit, he nudged inside her outer lips, and Della whimpered with this gentle first breaching and again when one strong finger grazed alongside her clit. Then, with his fingers rubbing and circling and slipping and sliding in her extraordinary juiciness, he *growled*, louder and stronger and somehow deeper than the first time. And again, Della's pussy clenched, another climax making her arch and squirm and wail as his clever fingers coaxed her to an even greater height.

He swore again, staring with open-mouthed awe. Slowly, he withdrew his hand, glossy with her arousal, and smeared the slick across his lips and chin. A bright, yellow ray of sunshine streaked into the cave, illuminating the erotic tableau of Cal sucking two long fingers in his mouth with a tortured groan. A single drop of slick caught the light, running down his wrist and sparkling like a drop of honey. Della watched, transfixed, as he scooped up that stray drop with a quick flick of his tongue, his expression incandescent.

"So fucking beautiful." A flicker of a smile lodged in his dimples, and Della's emotions shattered into a thousand million pieces at the sight. She barely knew anything: her birthday, her history, her *fucking name*, but she knew she wanted this man. In every single way she could have him.

Still boneless and floaty but filled with newfound purpose, Della launched herself upright, the need propelling her toward the source of this insanity inside her. Her head swam at the sudden change in position, queasiness and dizziness and nausea asserting themselves in no uncertain terms. Della reeled, her head bobbing as the room rotated around her.

"Woah, *woah*." Large palms braced her shoulders, keeping her upright as she swayed backward. "Easy there now."

He steadied her movements, yet the acceleration in her brain didn't ease up at all. Feeling her stomach revolt with a sickening lurch, Della covered her mouth with her palm and shook her head, trying to indicate she couldn't talk but only succeeding in making herself even sicker. She let out a little muffled wail but didn't protest as Cal dragged her a few feet away and propped her against the nearest wall.

The stone's chill permeated through her shirt, the contrast in temperature distracting her from the whirling agony in her brain. Her head fell back, and she rocked it gently against the stone, battling to reestablish equilibrium.

"Here," Cal said, his voice close and strangely soothing. "Have some water."

She accepted the canteen, taking a small, careful sip, followed by another. Now that she sat still and upright, the dizziness abated enough she didn't feel on the verge of vomiting. Fingers fidgeting with the dangling cap, she avoided looking at the man crouched by her side. The man whose easy, comforting essence soothed her from the inside out despite her churning guts. The man whose fingers had, not minutes before, helped himself to the most intimate parts of her as if he had every right to be there while she splayed her legs like a cat in heat.

She'd never been so hungry for sex in her entire life. Flinging herself upright with the intent to rip his clothes off? This wasn't her.

Blinking, she tested her vertigo against the light that continued to pour in through the cave opening. Once assured the room had stopped whirling, Della fastened Cal with an accusatory stare. "What happened to me?"

"You hit your head yesterday in the barn. Do you remember? Silas rammed into me, and I..." He swallowed as if fighting his own wave of nausea. "I knocked you face-first into the stable door. I think you have a concussion." He paused. Stern, unhappy frown lines carved into his handsome face as he gestured toward the makeshift pallet where they'd engaged in their scandalous activities. "You weren't ready for all that just yet. I shouldn't have let you get carried away."

"*Let me?*" Della's voice rose, the unexpected volume causing a sharp stab of pain in her brain. A concussion? Sure. Fine. That made sense, but it ranked as a secondary concern to why in the hell she could suddenly smell and lust rampaged through her body. "*Come on, Della, you know what this is,*" he'd said moments before. Yeah, she'd heard all about Heats and slick and Omegas coming into their natures, and all of that would make perfect fucking sense *if* she was an actual Omega. Which she *wasn't*.

She glared and flung a disgusted hand at her lower body, her knees still flagrantly spread and moisture running down the inside of her thighs. "*You* did something to me. You drugged me. What is it? Some kind of black-market Omega pheromone concoction? Some variant of a drug, like scratch?"

Even to her sluggish brain, the far-fetched hypothesis strained credulity. No mention of such a drug ever fell from the lips of even the juiciest of gossips. Yet Della clung to it like a life raft. She wasn't suddenly an Omega. There had to be another explanation.

"Della." Cal's luminous green-gray-gold eyes hardened like blades. "I'm only going to tell you this once, so listen up." Snagging her chin, he tipped her face toward his to better harness her with his solemn expression. "I did not drug you, and I am not lying to you. Not now. Not ever."

Ignoring the unexpected warmth coursing through her at his touch, Della pressed her advantage. "Then tell me where we are."

"About a half -day's ride from the settlement," he answered simply, notably not disclosing in which direction.

"That's not a full answer."

"It's the truth."

Scowling, she tried again. "Why did you bring me here?"

At this, he reached for one of the blankets she'd slept under. "I'll tell you the whole story, but not right now." He draped the cloth over her naked lower half. "You need to finish that water, then you need to eat, and then rest. Your poor little head ain't quite right."

Torment and uncertainty took up residence inside her throbbing skull. "Am I your prisoner?" she asked, her voice soft and trembly.

"Prisoner?" Cal scoffed. Tucking the edge of the blanket around her feet, he rubbed each of the bottoms in his quick, confident hands, warming them when she hadn't even realized they were cold. Glancing up, he shot her an incredulous look. "I keep telling you, Della, and eventually, you're gonna believe me: you're not my prisoner, you're my *mate*."

A worrying sprig of doubt unfurled between the cracks in her certainty. What if he was telling the truth? After a century, and against all expectations, she'd inexplicably regained her sense of smell. How could she explain that? Was it any more preposterous than some Alpha showing up and proclaiming she was his? And an Omega, to boot? Reeling for reasons having nothing to do with the concussion, Della's head tipped back to rest once again on the rock wall, closing her eyes against a torrent of confusion that would not let her go.

CHAPTER ELEVEN

Cal

Cal halted, stilling his feet and his breaths so as not to disturb the sticky air. A bead of sweat dripped from the tip of his nose, the only movement on his body and one he did not endeavor to wipe away. Stock-still, his focus narrowed, and he strained his ears, searching for any indication of intruders in the area he'd staked out for this impromptu adventure.

Earlier, after leading Della outside the cave to relieve herself, he'd caught the faint whiff of Alphas on the breeze. Too distant to estimate their exact number, the danger blared in his ears nonetheless. After shuffling her safely back inside and shoving some food in her hands, he'd hid himself and waited to see if the scent heralded an approaching search party. It did not, and even more importantly, Della gave no sign she'd scented them, either.

But his high-alert state never faltered. While Della snoozed, he'd patrolled the area, gathered firewood, set some snares, shook out their bedding, took stock of food supplies, and on and on. Well aware of the risk of disclosing their location, he'd moved with stealth and stayed downwind while completing his chores. Blessedly, the woods remained pristine and untainted by any human presence but his own.

The Alpha's Seduction

Satisfied nothing stirred in the woods, he continued his trek through the trees, retracing his steps back to the hot springs. The blazing mid-summer temperature slowed his movements and added a sluggishness to his fatigue, putting him further on edge. Sweat glossed his brow and dampened his back, reminding him yet again of the risk of polluting the air with evidence of his presence. The strain of the last day had added an acrid, stress-filled reek to his usual scent and that concerned him even more. He hated to stray so far from the sleeping Omega, but the need for a bath was imminent.

A sulfurous tang on the breeze grew potent as he neared his destination. At the hot springs, thick vapor blanketed the water's surface like the sinister steam over a witch's poisonous cauldron. Hardly inviting in this kind of heat. Shrugging out of his sticky and blood-crusted clothes, Cal resigned himself to the particular torture of taking a hot bath while baking in the hot sun. It wouldn't be the first time.

Growing up, his Alpha father refused to tolerate neglect in matters of hygiene and cleanliness. One of his many, many lectures having to do with the good of their small Pack, his frequent rants about other Alphas' animalistic tendencies instilled some very particular lessons in Cal's young life. Lessons he'd fought to follow when the Pack's leadership fell to him.

Fought, and ultimately failed.

He paused again, utilizing all of his Alpha senses to probe the environment one more time before lowering his body into the scalding brew. He would make this brief. Briskly, he submerged his head and began scrubbing filth from his skin. It pained him to rinse the traces of Della's slick off his body, but safety necessitated it and, all things considered, he'd prefer to be clean when he finally claimed his Omega.

His Omega. Remembrance of what passed between them that morning renewed his barely idle lust. Nothing in his entire life had prepared him for the onslaught of Della's frantic desire. The serious, cold woman unraveled, her body ripened and her pussy swelled as her sapphire eyes overflowed with hunger. Hunger for his body. Hunger for his scent. Hunger for *him*.

It was heady, heady stuff.

Yet nothing compared to her response to his growl. He'd been with women, even a few Omegas as a much younger man, and none had ever climaxed with the merest of rumbles from his chest. He honestly wasn't sure which of them had been more surprised at this discovery. And still, Della denied the most obvious of conclusions: her status as a late-blooming, latent Omega. The confirmation of her nature trumpeted deep in his soul. He'd never heard of such a thing, but that didn't matter. He only had to make her see it for herself.

And soon, so they could move on from this area and the threat of detection. The cave suited as an emergency hiding spot. Thank happenstance, he'd discovered it when he did, but the risk of lingering this close to the Morris Hill Pack curdled his guts. Reaching for a handful of dirt, he scoured dried flecks of Silas's blood from his hands, and the bite of anger and injustice again chewed at him.

Could he have handled things differently with Silas? Should he have gone along with the half-assed patrol and simply taken it up with Hunter and Colt upon his return? His entire motivation, indeed his entire ethos, organized around ensuring the safety of the settlement and Della within it. But, in his efforts to protect her, he'd dragged her away from that safety and exposed her to the dangers of a wild, Pack-less existence. His fists curled so tight that the shallow cuts that decorated his knuckles cracked open.

He stared at the small stripes of fresh, red blood, a bitter reminder of his inescapable limitations. As long as there was breath in his body, he would protect Della, but the fact remained, a lone Alpha could only do so much. Without a Pack or even just Simon and Matteo to watch his back, he was vulnerable. And that made Della vulnerable, too. Cal plunged his hands back into the water and savored the sting of the minerals against the tiny wounds. Returning to Morris Hill now was beyond impossible. The best he could do would be to take her east and try to find another established, peaceful place where they could live safely.

To do that, she needed to heal from the concussion, accept her Omega nature, and bond with him. One thing was certain: they were not leaving that cave until she'd done all three. After witnessing her responsiveness on the dusty cave floor, he had a pretty good idea of how to make it happen.

CHAPTER TWELVE

Della

Prying her crusty eyes open, Della woke as waning daylight trickled through the cave opening. A fucking cave, for God's sake. Dragged off by an actual, honest-to-Christ caveman.

Fuck. *Fuck!*

"Damsel in fucking distress," she muttered, rolling to her back. Her eyes roved over the small stalactites pointing down at her like hundreds of accusing fingers. "*Your move*," they seemed to say as the shadows deepened with every passing minute, the night emerging as yet another jailer.

If the sun was setting, that meant she'd been gone almost a full day. Had Hunter, Colt, or any of the others noticed she'd vanished in the middle of the night? The idea of a rescue was itself galling, an affront to her independent sensibilities, but at the moment, it was all she had. Back in the barn, before the concussion... Colt had been there... Sloan... and Lars, too. Alphas could be dense, but those three weren't total idiots. What would they do? Send out a search party? Talk to Hunter?

The memory of her last conversation with Hunter stung like the sharp flick to an earlobe. In compliance with some biological imperative to conform to this fucked up new world order, the *one* person she'd been somewhat close with had cast her aside. Well, okay, then. What was the loss of one more friend when she'd lost dozens?

His withdrawal of friendship was a good reminder. For the twenty years she'd lived in Morris Hill, she'd largely kept to herself. Sparing the others her incomprehensible status as neither an Alpha nor Omega nor Beta, she'd sat back as they lived out their best Alpha-Omega lives. Mating, bonding, going through Heats, cranking out the pups without serious Della around to cast judgment on the sexist gender norms Alphas and Omegas gravitated toward. Like with the Omega bunkhouse proposal, she checked in with the Omegas, watched out for them, and advocated for them, yet considered none her friends.

She told herself it was easier for everyone this way, but there were darker, more sinister reasons for her hiding-in-plain-sight isolationism: it kept her safe in a different way. Safe from the intimacy of relationships and friendships, safe from the connections that had torn her apart.

Connections, both personal and political, wove the fabric of her former life. All the colors and contrasts melded together into something exquisite, beautiful, and secure. Something she could wrap around herself and point to as evidence of "*Yes, I belong here. These are my people, my communities, my purpose, my home.*" Except TheEnd came and ripped those connections, that fabric, in two. Threads unraveled, scattered to the wind, or burned to a char as if they never existed, and Adeline Cabrese withstood every merciless tear.

Only to end up here, in the middle of who-knew-where, with an Alpha she had no reason to trust, while her hormones went absolutely berserk. No, she was quite alone in this. The stalactites were right: she'd have to save herself.

Striving for calm, Della took a long, slow inhale. Unexpected, but enticing, food smells greeted her. Onions, potatoes, and something meaty nudged her appetite, and her stomach answered with a resounding growl. Fully awake, she slowly sat up and looked around, grateful the movement failed to trigger any nausea and that, for the moment, she was alone.

On the other side of the cave, steam rose from the bubbling pot, and she indulged in another deep breath. When was the last time she'd eaten a proper meal? Even more shocking, when was the last time she'd *smelled* dinner cooking so intensely? Besides the stew, more smells wafted into her awareness: the clean damp stone walls, the grassy, woodsy moss that blanketed the rocks near the entrance, and the—

Knife. Not a smell but a *sight.* Propped on the stone-lined edge of the firepit, the blade winked in invitation. Scrabbling to her feet, Della hurried across the floor, although giddy at this change in her luck. True, Cal had exhibited no violent tendencies in their short acquaintance, but Alphas were famously impulsive and excitable. She'd seen enough turn on a dime to be wary of this one, no matter how courtly his manners. A weapon offered a modicum of protection, some semblance of control in this thoroughly out-of-fucking-control scenario. Her chance of physically overpowering an Alpha bordered on absurd, but she had to *try*.

But as her hand closed on the handle, she paused. Where was he anyway? Was the knife a trap? A test? He'd clearly left it there, in plain view, and therefore, would notice if it disappeared right out from under his nose. Forget about any element of surprise, she'd be lucky if he didn't pluck it from her hands the moment he stepped inside. And *then* what would he do? Laugh at her audacity? Or something more villainous? Tie her up? Refuse to let her eat? Punish her in some other way? All kinds of salacious scenarios stormed through her brain, sending unexpected zings straight to her core, waking up an appetite of a different kind altogether. Memories of his wide, strong hands on her tender inner thighs ripped through her mind. Spreading her wide, he'd explored her open sex with assumed dominion, and she'd not only allowed it but welcomed it, *burned* for it.

Shit, no. She had to stop this. So what if his presence triggered an olfactory awakening and unlocked some untouched well of horniness? What happened earlier couldn't happen again. But her mind refused to budge from the memories. His stupidly handsome face with his impossible eyes, winsome smile, deep dimples, and *fucking cleft chin* were bad enough. There was absolutely no fucking reason to fixate on the sizable bulge he'd sported while conjuring two orgasms out of her from thin air.

No. She needed to focus. He could return any second. *Where the fuck was he?* Abandoning the knife as too obvious to escape his notice, she cast about the cave, anxious to get her hands on something, anything, that might be of use. Maybe Omegas couldn't resist their biology, but she sure as fuck could, and resistance would be a whole lot easier with a weapon in her hand.

"Solve the problem, solve the problem," she whispered like a calming mantra.

Several knapsacks lay to the side, opened and half-unpacked. Immediately, she tore through the nearest one, shoving aside clothing, food, and whatever else, checking pockets and flaps as if her life depended on it. All while praying to a god that didn't exist. Please let her find *something* useful, something that wouldn't be so immediately noticed as missing, something that might mean the difference between staying true to herself and being mated and claimed on the dirty floor of a dreary cave like an animal.

Her nose twitched, and the faint hint of cinnamon coffee caused her eyelids to flutter involuntarily. Like a signal for her alone, his aroma billowed around her, causing a subtle but definite pliancy to the tense and stressed lines of her body. The temptation rose to sit there and wallow in it, lost to anything but that intoxicating balm.

Fuck, Della, wake up!

Shaking off the languor, she rummaged through the bottom of the final sack, her fist tightening around something small and hard and metal-cold. Yanking it free, she hastily repacked the bag and hurled herself back onto her pallet, slipping the jackknife prize under her covers as she laid down as if just wakening from her nap.

Smooth, assured footsteps crunched on the stones, and an enormous body ducked through the narrow opening, momentarily blocking out the twilight. Pulse thundering in her ears, Della raised her tired eyes, hoping against hope he couldn't hear her heart hysterically knocking against her ribs. If he did, he gave no sign of it, greeting her with a paired raise of an eyebrow and one corner of his lip that she found way too appealing.

"Feeling better?" he asked, thankfully not pausing to await her answer. Squatting fireside, he tore some greens in his hands and added them to the stewpot.

Rising, Della ran a hand through her tangled hair, partly to assess the disgusting mess it had worked itself into and partly to buy herself time to think. She had the knife, but a knife wasn't a plan. Adeline Cabrese made her living as a wheeler and dealer, a compromise-seeker, a consensus-builder. Maybe they could work out an arrangement of some sort, some sort of bargain to get her back home to Morris Hill. He had to want something. Her cheeks warmed with a sudden flush. Something other than her body, that was.

She faced him again, scrutinizing her caveman captor like a political opponent. What were his strengths? His weaknesses? His blind spots? His pressure points? She didn't know, but she'd find out.

"My headache appears to be gone," she said, opening with the most neutral statement she could find. "What are you making?"

Alphas could smell a fire on the breeze for miles, and anyone nearby would notice an orange glow at the cave entrance. Curious that he'd risk lighting one under the circumstances. She squinted into the small flame, considering. Was it stupidity? Arrogance? Or were they so far from Morris Hill that he didn't worry about a search party? Or had a search party already come and gone while she'd slept during the day? That thought chilled her to her bones.

Cal stopped stirring and began spooning out a portion into a wooden bowl. "Simple stew. Sorry, there's no fresh meat for it, only dried." He handed the bowl to her, and she took it with a nod of thanks. "I set some snares, so maybe tomorrow a rabbit will get unlucky. The creek also has some fish. Trout, I think."

Della arranged herself cross-legged on her pallet, draping a blanket over her bare bottom half. After the earlier debauchery, her trousers mysteriously disappeared, and she'd bet anything he'd squirreled them away as some sort of insurance policy against her making a run for it. A simple but compelling deterrent. Not an idiot, she had to admit. Lifting a spoonful of the fragrant dish, she blew the steam away. "You're used to living rough, then?"

"You could say that. Here." He tossed a roll into her lap, one of Logan's. Interesting. Somehow, he'd gotten his hands on Morris Hill food supplies. Had he stolen it? Did he have help? How well had this little abduction been planned?

"That's stale, but if you break it up in the stew, it'll soften right up."

"Thank you," she said softly, ignoring the weird pang in her chest. The genuine concern for her welfare that propped up that innocent comment touched some sensitive spot deep, deep in her psyche. Maybe this wasn't a man solely intent on keeping her alive to use for his own needs; for whatever reason, her comfort mattered to him.

And she didn't know how she felt about that.

As a distraction from that line of thought, she wolfed a huge bite of stew. Searing heat scorched the inside of her mouth, and she let out a closed-mouth scream, trying hastily to swallow and not spit the scalding soup back into the bowl.

Cal practically leaped across the fire, coming to her side and shoving a cool canteen in her hands. "Damn girl, are you all right?"

She gulped the fresh, cool water, feeling the burn and shock lessen. Running her blistered tongue over her gums didn't feel *great*, but nothing on par with singing the roof of her mouth with pizza cheese back in her old life. She'd be okay.

Brows creased, Cal brushed hairs away from her face, drawing her attention back to his suddenly too-near presence. His fingertips lingered to trace the shell of her ear and the underside of her jaw. This close, her skin shivered, and the burned roof of her mouth faded to inconsequential background noise.

Cal's lips quirked in that sly half-smile that had to be his trademark. "Didn't realize I had to warn you not to put boiling hot stew in your mouth." A chagrined shake of his head accompanied the teasing scold, all of it given away by the creased crow's feet crinkling happily around those hazel eyes. "Hitting your head, losing your pants, burning your mouth. What am I gonna do with you, Omega?"

Despite herself, amusement bubbled in her chest. "I don't believe *I* lost my pants. Where are they, by the way?"

He tipped forward, nuzzling his nose into her hair. Hot breath brushed against her ear when he spoke, tripping Della's stomach into a series of flip-flops.

"Wherever they ran off to, can't say I'm sorry they're gone."

With a delicate, barely-there nip of her lobe, he backed off, grinning from ear to ear like he'd stolen a plum pudding right off the queen's table, while Della's belly continued its exhilarating, terrifying free fall.

How would she get the upper hand when every little thing brought her to her knees?

CHAPTER THIRTEEN

Cal

Primitive satisfaction expanded Cal's chest. Building the fire, preparing the meal, feeding his soon-to-be mate felt deeply, perfectly *right*. Just as her body, flushed and luscious and trembling under his, felt right.

Now, sitting fireside, Della scraped up the last of her second portion of stew with only a threadbare blanket draped over her lap. It took a truly excruciating amount of willpower to keep himself from snatching it away to lose himself in her impossible softness. A few quick movements and she'd be flat on her back, writhing under him. He knew it. She knew it. Yet, here they sat, eating dinner and playing at being civilized.

"Can I ask you something?" Della's earnest face peered over the rim of her bowl. He angled his head in silent permission. "Why did you come to Morris Hill?"

Lacking any note of challenge, the straightforward question clanged a quiet alarm. "Why do you ask?"

"No particular reason." She toyed with her spoon, affecting a careful curiosity. "You implied you were used to living rough, so does that mean you prefer it?"

Cal pulled the stew pot between his legs, scooping the last few spoonfuls into his mouth and chewing through a tough piece of meat. "Wouldn't say I prefer it."

She set her bowl aside and leaned forward. "So you didn't come to Morris Hill for a roof over your head and a bed to sleep in? Were you looking to join a Pack?"

Why all the sudden interest in his life? Under other circumstances, he would've welcomed talking to his future mate about his life. But, right now, he sensed a trap. When he'd escorted Della outside the cave to relieve herself earlier, her head swiveled in all directions, but no hint of recognition passed over her face. Confirmation enough for him that she had no idea where they were, and without her pants (which he'd tucked away in the darkest part of the cave while she'd slept), any foolish escape attempt was doomed to fail.

If she endeavored to be free of him, a smart woman like Dell wouldn't give up, she'd change tactics. Donning a fake innocence and probing into his past, perhaps she sought to push him off balance and render him liable to tip his hand. It was clever. He'd give her that, but answering anticipation danced in his chest. He had another, more potent, weapon at his disposal. One that she consistently underestimated.

Meeting her questioning gaze, Cal licked his spoon clean with deliberate care, letting his lips caress every inch of the utensil. "Wasn't looking, exactly," he said as she stared, transfixed, at his mouth. "The opportunity presented itself, and we took it."

Della cleared her throat. "We?"

Shoving the dishes to the side, he unlaced and removed his boots, leaning into their little game. He'd had a bath, a full belly, and a pretty Omega to look at; they could draw this out as long as she wanted. Leaning back on his palms, Cal rolled his neck to the side, stretching out a kink and providing more opportunities to draw her attention to his physique. "Yeah. My companions, Simon and Matteo."

Pink stole across her cheeks, and her eyes dropped to her lap like a hot potato. "Which one was in the stable?"

He lifted his head. "That would be Simon."

"He helped you." Glancing up, she circled a finger around the cave. "Arrange all this." There wasn't a question in that statement, so he didn't reply. Instead, Cal flexed his shoulders, thrusting his chest in her direction and enjoying the gratifying response when her glazed focus poured down the lines of his torso. Licking her lips, she eyed him with a calculating expression. "How did you meet Hunter?"

Lazily, his eyes roamed over her figure, appreciating the graceful line of her neck, sloping down to her shoulders. The stretch of skin where her neck disappeared into her shirt beckoned to him, the future home of his mating bite. The anticipation tingled on his tongue, and he indulged in it, letting the desire flow through his body for a moment before answering.

"Kess got into a spot of trouble in OT, and I helped Hunt get her back."

Surprise lit her face. "What were you doing in OT?"

"This and that." None of their activities—drinking and whoring and coercing shopkeepers into more-than-generous trades for the animal pelts they'd trapped—were fit for Della's ears. "We'd been there a few weeks, along with some other Alphas who traveled with us," he offered, "but they weren't keen on Hunter's rules, so they set off in another direction."

Hiking one knee up, Cal flicked open the top button of his trousers and then spread his thighs, inviting her consideration of his swelling flesh as it asserted its interests. His hips rolled in a subtle, experimental thrust, one so small it would go unnoticed if her attention lay anywhere else.

Her pink cheeks darkened to scarlet. She didn't miss it.

"Turns out you're not so keen on rules either," she said with forced lightness, but Cal didn't miss the snide admonishment in her tone nor the way she boldly stared him down, daring him to argue as she pressed on. "Here's what I don't understand: why fight your way into a Pack only to turn around and betray them?"

The accusation hit him in full force. Duty and obligation to the settlement's safety drove him to clash with Silas, not any kind of sneaky impulse to disrupt the Pack's order. But she didn't know that, and right about now, he didn't really feel like explaining. She'd tipped her hand, pronouncing her judgment on him as a rule-thwarting scoundrel. That was fine; he could play that role for tonight.

"Rules are important," he said, voice gruff, "when they make sense."

Unconvinced, her eyes snapped with accusation, and *goddamn*, if the return of that sass didn't tip him right over the edge. The low, barely-there growl he'd suppressed all day erupted. It cascaded over his taut muscles and embedded deep in his groin. More importantly, it reached its intended destination. Confirmed by the tang of fresh slick that floated into the air, his Omega's automatic and involuntary response had his cock instantly alive and impatient.

Caught up in their game, she might play at defiance, but she couldn't deny the color scorching her cheeks and the racing pulse pounding at the base of her neck. Della cleared her throat. "So abducting a woman and claiming her against her will makes *sense*?"

Their eyes locked as their breathing came into unison. Yes, it did make sense. Tired of their game, he was ready to show her just how much.

Smirking, Cal peeled off his shirt, letting the cave-crisp air caress his heated skin, feeling his nipples harden in response. Shoulders hunched as if braced for a blow, Della scowled. "Aren't you going to explain yourself?"

In answer, Cal flipped to hands and knees and encroached on the trembling Omega, unable to contain her gasp of surprise. Syrupy black currant sweetness bathed him in the oh-so-incredible evidence of everything that made perfect fucking sense. Nose to nose, she stared him down—*glared* him down—losing her crusade of indifference. Delighted, he engaged in the pointless skirmish. She dared him to back down; he dared her to look away.

Another growl gathered low in his chest, its presence teetering on the edge of release. If he let the full force loose, would she climax again? Or did the arousal need to build more? The prospect of finding out, of discovering all her little secrets and tells, thrilled him beyond reason.

"What happened with Silas that caused the fight?" She hurled the question at him, her voice a delicate rasp.

Smiling, he nosed into the crook of her neck. She startled at the breach of her space, but he pressed on. He pressed so close that her face couldn't avoid the brush of contact with his shoulder when he purred, "Nothing you need worry about."

A shuddery sigh whisked out of her, and hot, female breath whispered across his naked skin like a caress. "Why did you bring me here?"

"You already know the answer to that." Mouth watering, he hungered with the need to sink his teeth deep into that tender flesh. His tongue darted out, licking a path up her throat, tasting her honeyed salt. Her suppressed moan tickled against his tongue as it fought to emerge. "You're mine, and I can take you anywhere I want."

Her spine stiffened. "Refusing to answer my questions is not an endearing quality."

"No?" His lips glided over her cheek, dotting unhurried kisses against her smooth, freckled skin before rocking back on his heels and looking her full in the face. "And what qualifies as an endearing quality to you, Della, Who Takes Care Of Herself?"

Her pink lips thinned to a blanched white. "Honesty. Integrity. Openness. Dependability."

He quirked a brow, infinitely amused at the list of virtues she rattled off like she was describing Jesus Christ himself. "Is that it?"

"Gentleness. Loyalty. Humility. Generosity. Sincerity—"

"Ah, I can see the confusion on that one."

Della's brows speared down. "What do you mean?"

Cal squeezed one eye shut. "Sometimes folks mistake a certain levity for insincerity."

She sniffed. "I suppose you fancy yourself as having the former and not the latter."

For some reason, he found her haughty displeasure adorable. "S'ppose I do."

"As far as I've seen"—breaking away from his gaze, she turned her chin toward the exit, staring out into the night—"the only amusing thing about you is how amusing you find yourself."

A surprised laugh leaped from his lips, and she flicked him a peevish glance. "See, I knew there was an intriguing woman underneath all this seriousness." His grin expanded. "She should come out and play some more."

Frowning, she pitched her torso backward, widening the distance between them. "And what makes you think she wants to play with you?"

"Oh, that's an easy one." With a smirk he knew she'd love to hate, he advanced in the face of her retreat. Prowling forward, he caged her body between his hands and knees till her back flattened on the floor. "Because I've got a few other endearing qualities she hasn't failed to notice, no matter what she'd like to pretend."

Della pasted on an indifferent smile. "I'm not going to give you the satisfaction of asking what those are."

Despite her failed attempt to hide behind a shield of aloofness, Della's bosom lifted in an unmistakable heave that sent a bolt of lust straight to his dick. Her hands laid tentatively against his pecs, but whether the touch was intended to hold him off versus appreciate one of his aforementioned endearing qualities, he couldn't say. She probably couldn't, either, and he'd be damned if that tortured ambivalence didn't make everything that much sweeter.

Slowly, he lowered his lower body to hers, letting the hard ridge of his growing erection mash against the soft cushion of her belly. Her widened pupils betrayed her awareness of its presence. Feeling her heart thudding against his chest, he turned up his smile a notch. "Well, there's no need to ask a question you already know the answer to, is there?"

She parted the plump curves of her lips as if preparing for a retort that never came. Instead, he swooped down to capture her mouth. The touch sent shockwaves through his entire body, his heart speeding with the contact. The kiss was his endeavor, but the intensity floored him nonetheless. Della's startled gasp met that first erotic touch, and he savored that too. It powered him into another and another, each one deeper, more devastating than the last, and Della met each one with a passion all her own. Whether due to his seduction plan or her emerging Omega nature, she kissed with a hunger that belied her outward indifference. Parting those perfect lips, the slide of her tongue had him groaning deep in his throat.

Intoxicated, he thrust a hand into her hair, reclaiming control as he nibbled the pillowy contour of her lower lip. The tender flesh slid between his careful teeth as he pulled away and forced a path over her jaw and down to her neck. She shuddered and moved her hands to grip his upper arms. This touch, combined with her heated kisses, destroyed the rest of his self-control. He'd waited long enough, his body screamed, and he answered. Ripping her collar aside, he dove for the meaty pouch of her trapezius, teeth clamping down but not all the way through.

Della shrieked in alarm, clutching and scrabbling against his chest. "No! Don't!"

Ignoring her cries, he nursed on the spot, pulling her iron-rich blood to the surface with a combination of gentle nips and powerful suction. Goosebumps spread over her skin, and she shimmied and wriggled and tried to get away. Every resisting, feminine twitch made his teeth ache to clamp down and finish the job.

Cal hooked an arm around her waist, hindering her escape. Saliva flowed from his gums, her scent and taste drawing him further and further under her spell. A rumbling growl built from deep in his chest, ready to explode right at the moment something cold and sharp jabbed under his jaw.

CHAPTER FOURTEEN

Cal

The sharp prick dug into his skin. Angled into the hollow where his pulse hammered, the stab rendered his body inert. A mess of confusion, instinctive fear, and disbelief drenched his lust in cold water.

What. The. *Fuck?*

Prying his teeth apart, he detached and eased away. Slender, white-knuckled fingers gripped the blade, the tip tracking his every movement. The small folding knife was his, one he'd long buried in the bottom of his knapsack. The thing likely barely held an edge, but he'd give her credit for resourcefulness. Not that she couldn't stab it into the thin skin of his neck, and, given the resolute set of her mouth, he'd wager she wouldn't hesitate to try.

Staring down his nose at his flushed and determined Omega, the initial jolt of fear withered to an abstract husk. Two minutes ago, she'd kissed him like she'd waited her entire life for the chance, and now she pulled a knife on him? What exactly did she think would happen here? One quick flick of his hand would bat the weapon away. Another twist and he'd have her wrist pinned above her head. This attempt at a physical confrontation was a farce, but he'd let her have it to discover what new game she played.

"*Don't* mark me." Her eyes hardened, and the barest of tremors touched her voice. "I don't want to be claimed."

A feral grin split his face as he swiped the blanket off her lap, exposing her lower body. She gasped, and the blade hiccupped against his throat but pressed no farther.

Braced above her on one arm, Cal trailed his other hand down her stomach and into her exposed, fragrant, dripping cleft. Sweet, tender flesh kissed the tips of his fingers, a slippery welcome that had him suppressing a pained groan when he withdrew from its humid embrace. Retracing back up her torso, he touched glossy, slick-damped fingers to her bottom lip. "You sure about that?" With his middle finger tucked inside her mouth to rest against her tongue, he asked, "Can't you taste your desire? Can't you feel it? Why fight this?"

Her lips closed around his first knuckle in an involuntary suck, and her pupils exploded outwards, the ring of dark blue eaten up by black. Cal grunted at the unexpected suction, at the picture of her hot, pillowy flesh surrounding his. Images ripped through his mind of all the other combinations and permutations of such a sight. His fingers in her cunt, his cock in her mouth, in her pussy, in her ass, her hand wrapped around his dick, her lips sucking his balls, tonguing his hole.

"You want me," he crooned, withdrawing and snaking one hand back between her legs while shifting the other to span her collarbones. Slowly, conscious of the knife still at his jugular, he tightened his hold, circling her neck. She stilled, her body now anchored in two vulnerable places, subdued but fighting her submission. "Say it, Della." He nudged his fingers through her sex, homing in on the apex as her hips began to quiver and thrust in time with his slow, steady pace. "Tell me you want this... Tell me you've wanted me since I pressed you up against the mess hall."

A slim, delicate, non-knife-holding hand dug into his forearm, and Cal smiled at the small drops of pain, feeling his cock throb harder at signs of a fight. Interesting. Had he known that about himself?

Reddish hair in a snarl, head thrashing side to side despite his grip, defiance flared in the set of her jaw. "I *don't.*"

A sinister chuckle worked its way to the surface. "Honesty is a virtue for everyone else, but not you? Is that it?" Fingers massaging her clit, he tsked. "Expected better of you."

"Don't... care..." she panted, her jaw tight as she gnashed her teeth against the climax building under his fingertips, "what... you expect."

Craning forward, he ignored the blade as it poked into his skin and brushed his nose against hers, breathing in her ragged breaths like the sweetest dessert. His circling rhythm stuttered, trailing off and then back into sync, becoming erratic and deliberately dissatisfying. Della's grip on the knife faltered. Its tip danced over his throat, more of an annoying tickle than a true threat. A pathetic, high-pitched whine squirmed past her stoic stubbornness, the hot folds of her pussy spasming in hovering release.

"Tell me you want to come."

She angled her pelvis upward, seeking out the stimulation he denied her, demanding with her body what her mouth refused. "Don't claim me."

Nuzzling his thumb against her clit, he slid two fingers inside her wet inferno, thrusting gently in and out, slow and controlled, simultaneously giving and depriving. "Ain't talking about that right now. I'm offering to get you off." He smirked. "That's what this hungry little Omega pussy wants, isn't it? Say, 'please make me come, Alpha,' and I will. See? Easy as pie."

The knife jiggled at his throat, small jabs that betrayed her moment-to-moment wavering. Had she realized she posed no threat to him but was too distracted to give it up? Or was she hanging onto this thread of control for other reasons? Reasons having to do more with herself than with him.

"Don't make me say it," she gritted out the misery-saturated words.

"All right, Omega," he said, placating, "put the knife down, and I won't make you say it."

As if remembering she still held it, Della pushed it firm to his throat. "No biting," she said through clenched teeth.

Raw emotion torched the back of his throat. How could he promise that when he'd thought of little else for the last two days? When every muscle in his jaw tingled with anticipation for this primitive act? Frustration mounting, his fingers halted their teasing thrusts, still lodged inside her, but now only a dissatisfying reminder of what she denied him. Denied herself. Denied *them*.

Because, whether she liked it or not, there would be a them. If not today, then tomorrow or the day after. This conviction settled his ire somewhat. He'd waited his whole life for this moment, for this woman, for this homecoming of sorts. What was another day in the grand scheme of his life?

Yet a powerful resistance reared up and rebelled, his inner Alpha roaring. *Alphas didn't court; Alphas claimed.* Yeah, he could wait. But why? Why did he have to? So many choices had been denied to him, so many dreams he'd abandoned. Why couldn't he take this one beautiful thing for his own? Here. Now.

Sweat sheened her brow, and turmoil flitted across Della's face, marring her refined and pristine beauty in a way both tragic and irresistible. "Promise me," she demanded, voice hoarse with arousal or emotion or desperation, or all three. Cal stroked along the base of her neck, the riot of her pulse throbbing like an accusation.

Alphas weren't only meant to claim their Omegas. They were also meant to provide for and care for and protect. And, right now, she was demanding protection from *him*. That thought seared his guts like a cattle brand, and shame flooded his bloodstream. His breaths came short and fast as the opposing needs to reassure her and possess her warred in his chest.

"You said no lies," she persisted. "Promise me. Please."

The quiet *please* was his undoing. The weight of her terror strained across the one agonizing syllable and shattered his inertia to pieces.

"All right," he heard himself say, his speech not planned or even known to him but dictated by some place deep inside his Alpha brain. Slowly, his thumb circled her swollen pearl, gratified by a fresh gush of slick against his wrist and the faint mewling sound she swallowed. "Here's what's going to happen. First, I'm going to make you come so long and so hard, you're going to soak this bed with all that beautiful slick. After that, I'm going to fuck you. Slow and deep, and you're going to come again and again and again. And when your cream is drenching my cock and running down my thighs, I'm gonna knot you right in this hot, soaking cunt, and you're going to fall asleep stuffed full." He circled faster, smirking as her breaths caught short and the knife bounced against his skin. "Later on, when I wake up, we're going to do it all over again. You understand all that?"

Her pelvis ground up hard against his hand, her answer verbal as well as non. "Yes."

His chin dipped in a solemn nod, the blade scraping a weak threat against his throat. "You do all that without a fight. You come for me like a good little Omega, and I promise I won't mark till you ask me to." A flash of shock shadowed her sex-drunk gaze before giving him an eager nod in agreement. Satisfaction buoyed his spirits, the hard-won compromise feeling like a complete victory. *Good. Good, Omega.*

"Now," he said, utilizing his Alpha command tone. "Drop the fucking knife."

CHAPTER FIFTEEN

Della

Cal was as good as his word. Before the dropped knife rattled over the stone floor, her pelvis seized in a back-arching, teeth-gnashing climax. What he'd even done to induce such a shockingly immediate response remained a mystery, one she was too discombobulated to notice. Yet as his skillful fingers worked between her legs, driving her toward the next peak, she had some idea.

"There you go," he breathed. His deep Alpha rumble felt like a caress on her distended and deprived nipples. Straining against the hand locked possessively around her throat, Della arched her chest forward, shamelessly seeking stimulation against the hard planes of his chest.

The immovable Alpha palm cuffing her neck unnerved her, not with fear or intimidation or danger, but how much she loved it. The civilized, educated, sophisticated men she'd dated before TheEnd did not make love with this element of savagery. Even in the privacy of one's bedroom, it was uncouth and unseemly.

Cal did not observe such proprieties.

One quick tug and he'd pulled her upright. With a second yank, he flipped her shirt over her head and tossed it behind him, baring her fully for the first time. A chill skittered over her naked skin, but it couldn't touch her. With his promise to leave her unmarked, fire kindled to life deep inside her belly, and a radioactive surge lit her up like the old football stadiums. Naked, panting, and covered in her arousal fluid (*slick,* her rebellious brain supplied), Della hunted through her disjointed thoughts, trying to locate her embarrassment and prudishness but came up empty-handed.

Even worse, she didn't seem to mind.

He'd promised not to place a claiming bite, and that had felt important, a strategic skirmish victory in this complicated war they waged. His nature against hers, her desire to be left alone pitted against his insistence on rearranging her life, his wants and needs versus her own. All of it complicated and confusing and unlike any other relationship she'd navigated in her overly-long life. Stolen away and taken to a remote cave by an Alpha she was moments away from fucking, she couldn't make sense of any of it.

Not that she had much time to reflect as he pressed her flat again. Bending his head, Cal pulled one of her jutting nipples straight into his hot mouth, sucking with so much force a yelp burst from her throat. Della's fingers found the curve of his neck. All his various textures collided on her fingertips: the heated skin, his damp tendrils of hair, and the carved-stone indestructible hardness of his skull. Balling one fist in his hair, she dug her nails in the perfect contour of his shoulder, all to cleave him tight to her breast, to keep him close and inseparable, any distance between them too great to tolerate.

A male grunt vibrated against her flesh, and she eased her grip on his hair, an ironic worry she'd somehow hurt him when she'd held a blade to his jugular only moments before. "I'm sorry," she whispered between panted breaths.

His mouth pulled off her tip with a loud, echoey pop. "Never apologize to me, Della." A crazed flame flickered behind his usual arrogance, and she held her breath, not daring to move as his teeth closed around her reddened nipple. After a small nip and tug, he flattened his tongue, licking and soothing the abused tissue. "Not for that. It drives me wild when you take what you want."

Rolling up off her chest, he came to his knees above her, and she drank up every inch of his golden skin, bronzed and backlit by the fire. He towered above her like an idol of pure masculine energy. Her skin fizzed with anticipation, wanting his flesh on her flesh in a way she'd never wanted anyone. Like she was dehydrated and he was IV fluids, like she was drowning and he was a life vest, like she'd been poisoned and he was the antidote.

With a quick tug of his wrist, his waistband fell open. His bulging dick popped free, consuming all her frazzled attention. Musky sharpness reached her nose, and saliva flooded her mouth, a craving for his taste loud on her tongue. It was a sizable, sturdy specimen. Not too big, not too small, a Goldilocks cock some irreverent, sex-drunk part of her brain supplied. The bulbous tip peeked out from the foreskin, and a glistening drop nuzzled in the slit like a pearl in an oyster.

With a grunt, Cal grabbed her hand and brought it to his length. Automatically curling her fingers around his girth, Della shuddered at the simultaneous soft and hard feel of him.

"*Fuck*," he said, more a ragged sigh than actual words, as his head fell back between his shoulder blades. "Yeah, like that. Work my cock, Omega."

The thick column of his throat flexed, and Della's internal mayhem accelerated further. She couldn't look away from this mesmerizing creature. Cal, the Alpha, was cocky, handsome, and undoubtedly virile. But here, in front of her, Cal, the Alpha, in the throes of sexual pleasure? Absolutely devastating.

Compelled, Della hinged to sitting, using both hands to shuttle along his rigid length in a vigorous spiral. His hips craned forward, syncing to her rhythm so he fucked into her movements. Strange how touching him like this thrilled her, how much pleasure zinged through her at the sight of his trembling thighs and rippling stomach muscles. The ruddy tip edged out further, the pearly fluid growing and spreading to her hands, adding lubrication and perfuming the air with unbridled lust.

"Do you want me to suck you?" she heard herself ask, and even stranger, she discovered she wanted to. Oral sex had never been her favorite, the giving or the receiving. But saturated with the heady cocktail of his sex and her slick and the impossibility of the entire insane situation, she didn't feel like Adeline Cabrese. She'd fallen asleep and awoken in this cave, this larger-than-life stone chrysalis, and now emerged as something entirely and uniquely new and different.

And this new her apparently salivated for Cal's cock in her mouth.

He groaned again, this one sounding tortured, as he straightened his head to stare down at her. "No," he breathed, his chest heaving like he'd run a marathon. "First, you're gonna take my knot like the sweet Omega I know you are."

Instinctively, Della shied away, anxiety snaking into her reeling senses. She'd heard all about Alpha knots, had listened to Omegas wax rapturous about the distinctive swelling at the base of an Alpha cock, yet never experienced one for herself. As much as Omegas loved the sensation, she also knew Betas had a much more conflicted relationship with this human enhancement. Some Betas found them tolerable, some even enjoyable, but many did not relish the experience.

Where that left her, she had no idea.

Standing, Cal kicked off the rest of his clothes and then slid to his knees between her legs, grabbing her ankles and hoisting them apart. His hard dick jutted out from his body, swollen and huge in the firelight. The base, a slightly darker color, remained size-congruent with the rest of his length, but she couldn't help but focus on it and wonder.

"Will it hurt?"

"Naw." He gave a single, decisive head shake. "Omegas love a thick knot. They *crave* it, you'll see." He quirked his lip, some of his usual humor peeking through the intensity of sexual need. "Now,"—he leaned forward, gathering up her hips into his large, wide hands—"get on my dick."

She didn't have time to protest even if she'd wanted to because before she took her next breath, he notched the juicy crown at her entrance and slid home. Not a fast, aggressive thrust, but a slow glide that stretched her inner walls as much as he filled them. Della cried out, not from pain but surprise and wonder at the exquisite fullness. Eyelids fluttering, he sank all the way inside, bottoming out with his pelvis nudged to her clit. Sinking down with his elbows on either side of her head, he began to fuck in earnest, his eyes growing wild with every smooth thrust in and out.

"Oh my god," she whispered. "Oh my *god*."

It had been so long—so fucking long—since she'd been fucked like this. If she ever had.

She slid her hands around his waist, clenching him to her in silent assent. Assent or surrender, Della succumbed to both the inevitable and the so-apparent-it-hurt acknowledgment that right here, right now, *this* was what she wanted.

He parted his sensuous lips, panting puffs of hot breath against her cheek. "That's good, isn't it? You're asking yourself why you've been fighting me all this time, aren't you, Della?"

The taunts drove into her with the same searing power as his cock. Even in the throes of his lust, he mustered the arrogance to needle her. But, for whatever sick reason, the mental and physical twisted together in her body and strung her along another building crest.

A broad palm found its way to her breast, kneading and pinching until pain mingled with pleasure. Mouth set in a tortured grimace, his open palm abused her tender mound in a series of sharp, forceful slaps that batted every exposed inch of her breast. The strikes zinged through her body straight to her sex, shocking, exhilarating, and close to overwhelming in the midst of all the sensations bombarding her in this crazy, unreal moment of her life.

"Nothing to say to that? No sassy retorts?" Burrowing his face in her neck, he mouthed over her skin, growling and snarling like a beast as the rhythm between her thighs slowed to a deep, deliberate punch that only served to stall her pursuit of the next much-needed peak. She ground her hips upward and clawed at his back and the hard curve of his ass, desperate to hasten the pace and bring her relief. "It's all right. You can say whatever you like with that acid tongue of yours, you don't scare me. I *like* it."

Her breath turned to cement in her lungs. While Cal feasted on her neck, shoulders, and breasts, his taunting invitation ripped her wide open. Della squeezed her eyes shut as if that would help her hide from him as he faced down the prickly facade she'd curated for decades.

Every year the mask grew more and more comfortable because it became more and more true. Her hair faded, grey mingling with copper, and lines took up permanent residence on her face. Anyone who looked at her saw not a woman but an *old woman* and, therefore, of even less consequence. Not respected as a wizened crone or wise woman, but an obsolete, expired model not worth fucking and therefore not worth anything at all. In truth, she didn't mind. Her age became another layer of protection, another way of gliding through the world unnoticed, under the radar from the worst of humanity.

Except this man, this *Alpha*, didn't give one single fuck about any of that. As he reared back and rose to his hands, his face contorted with aggressive fire, desire, and x-ray vision that blasted through all she was and laid her bare in every possible way. There was no doubt in her mind he wasn't just fucking a wet or available hole but *her*.

"I see you," he said as if he could hear her reeling thoughts, "taking my cock and loving every hard inch of it."

She formed the *yes* with her lips, but nothing emerged. Too overwhelmed to speak, his declaration invaded her soul with each powerful thrust. "*I see you... I see you... I see you.*" The hard set of his lips contrasted with the shining appreciation in his firelit face. Each punch of his hips drove the meaning deeper into her heart, making it harder and harder to escape. Like a tug-of-war between pursuit and retreat, desire drove her pelvis to lift toward his while all her finely honed survival instincts screamed caution. She couldn't hide, and what if... what if... she didn't *want* to?

"Flushed cheeks and hard nipples and your tight, soaking cunt." His guttural voice tore through her wordless moans. Grunting in pleasure, Cal accelerated his hips to a head-spinning pace, and her climax neared. After all this time, hiding from Alphas and burrowing deeper and deeper inside herself, this exposure felt good and necessary and right. Every stroke of his cock, every greedy caress, and every coarsely uttered word towed her farther out into the light, and Della basked in it the way only a woman who'd been imprisoned by fear could celebrate. Overcome, a single poignant tear breached her emotional defenses and began its insolent slide down her cheek.

Dropping down to his elbows, Cal swept it away with his wide thumb. The small act of tenderness ruined her completely. Undeterred by her emotions, he brought their lips together, his tongue snaking into her mouth and claiming it like he'd claimed every other part of her inside and out. As if to say, *Yeah, I see that too, and I'll relish whatever you want to throw at me.* She moaned from deep in her throat, the sound vibrating from his lips to hers, and he grunted in approval, pulling back to whisper, "There's no part of you I don't want, Della, and you're gonna give it all to me, y'hear?"

Not waiting for an acknowledgment, he unleashed his growl, the preview of which had crumpled her knees earlier. Now deployed against her lips and chest, it snapped her climax into existence like the strike of a whip. Convulsions shuddered out from her core to every last sinew of muscle holding her bones from blowing apart completely. Pleasure burned through her defenses, laying waste to everything she thought she knew about herself and him and their situation. She shook in his arms, a scream locked behind her teeth, as Cal held her tight and fucked her through every unending surge.

As Cal plunged deeper to find his own peak, pulsing yet pounding from her release, Della startled as an accelerating pressure built inside her entrance. His knot. Her hips wiggled as if to shy away, but that was the whole point of the knot, wasn't it? Seated behind her pubic bone, it locked them together for some indeterminate amount of time. What she didn't appreciate before this exact moment was the incredible sensation triggered by that deep swelling. Her peak crested, and the pressure grew, rubbing against and lighting up new parts of her already-sensitized canal.

Spreading her legs impossibly wider, she welcomed it, the physical sensation a blessed relief from the emotional devastation the sex had wrought. This was good. She could focus on this, on her body clenching tight around the invasion and the second, spiraling climax that skated close to the surface. Fasten herself to her physical existence and forgo the inclination to expose every last bit of her emotional core for his plundering.

Between panted breaths, his deep, twangy timbre cascaded over her eardrums. "There you go, taking my knot nice and deep like I knew you would." Voice thick and gritty, he crooned erotic approval, detonating a kink she hadn't even known existed as she reeled to find some stability in this hurtling insanity. Cal's head fell forward, his hair swishing over her brow like a kiss as he met her gaze. "That ain't so bad, is it? How 'bout a bit more?"

His hips rolled forward, wedging the knot deeper still and shoving her headfirst into another staggering, free-falling orgasm. The intensity sucked her into an undertow of ecstasy, leaving her gasping and stammering words without meaning. Covering her lips with his, Cal swallowed her delirious cries like a pleasure-fueled monster, and as Della fell completely apart, she knew that he was right about one terrifying thing: there'd be no escape.

CHAPTER SIXTEEN

Cal

Knot lodged deep, Cal collapsed to his back, dragging Della's limp body to cover him like a blanket. She nosed into his chest, stealing a taste of his scent as he let himself savor the utter perfection of the moment.

After the events of the past two days, culminating in his massive release, his body hinged on the brink of satiated exhaustion. It wasn't as if he hadn't had satisfying sex before, but fucking Della made everything that came before her look like clumsy, adolescent experimentation. Claiming bite or no, he'd come so hard he wondered if he gave himself a concussion.

Humming a quiet note, Della brushed her lips over his skin. Hard to believe this sedate kitten held a knife to his throat not one hour prior. Upon reflection, the reminder of their agreement bothered him less than he might've thought. After what just transpired, he had no doubt she belonged to him. The claiming could wait if delaying it meant something to her. A fair concession, his way of giving her some power back after she'd so bravely (yet ridiculously) tried to threaten him with his own knife, a way of apologizing for stealing her away like a thief in the night. Not that he was sorry. Fuck, no, not in the least.

Gathering her tighter in his arms, he craned his neck to press a kiss to her sweet-smelling hair before letting his heavy head fall back to the bunched-up clothing he used as a pillow, smiling. For a half second after making their bargain, he'd worried that she'd hold herself back and resist the physical attraction that sizzled between them. But, no, he'd primed her body through their elaborate dance, his deliberate machinations aided in no small part by her emerging Omega nature. Her lips espoused denial of her nature, but her body told another tale altogether. One she'd have no choice but to heed, for how could she deny the significance of their connection?

Apparently done sniffing, Della rested her ear over his heart. "How long does... *it* last?"

"Depends." Cal rubbed his tired eyes and fought back a yawn. "Not so scary after all, is it?"

"The knot? No, it doesn't hurt." As if to prove her point, her hips wiggled, jostling his dick and forcing him to release a half-tortured, half-grateful groan. At this rate, his knot would last all damn night. When they'd resettled their sticky bodies, she propped her chin on his chest, a thoughtful crease in that noble brow. "How old are you?"

"Not exactly sure," he said through another yawn. "Close to fifty, I reckon." Cal stretched one arm behind his head, chuckling softly. "Are we resuming the inquisition? Thought maybe I'd earned a bit of a break from all that."

With a half-hearted scowl, she laid her cheek back on his chest and muttered, "I'm old enough to be your great-grandmother."

Absently, his fingertips explored the silken skin of her back, enjoying and luxuriating in the impossible softness of her skin as he pondered the implications of her age. Old enough to be his great-grandmother, yet never claimed by an Alpha. Odd. In his life, Cal had traveled from the Gulf of Mexico all around the former western USA and now up to this stretch of northwest wilderness. Nowhere had Omegas outnumbered or even numbered close to the population of Betas or Alphas. As a result, plenty of Alphas took Beta mates, deciding they'd rather have something than nothing. Even if the Alphas Della lived among failed to recognize her Omega nature, why hadn't she been claimed as a Beta? Hell, as a *woman*?

"I know you're one of the Old Ones," he said, "don't bother me none."

Raising her head, she pinned him with a wary look that melted his heart all over again. "The Old Ones?"

"Folks like you, who survived through TheEnd and keep on living. Some became Alphas, some Omegas. Some stayed unchanged Betas, though I don't suspect many of them are around anymore."

Her head assumed a quizzical tilt. "Hunter calls them *transformed* Alphas. I haven't met any *transformed* Omegas. If that's even what I am."

Cal raked his gaze over her face, a primitive warning sounding in his brain. Their sex had shifted something in her. Even without a bond, he felt it. The barrier between them crumbled as she'd joined with him, in body *and* spirit. No woman could fake something like that, and no reasonable woman could deny it. Yet that's what she appeared to be doing.

"I've known transformed Omegas," he said carefully. Uninvited memories pushed forward in his mind. Faces of family members he hadn't allowed himself to recall in decades: his father, his half sister, his cousin. Still more faces crowded to the surface behind those: his desolate mother, his furious brother-in-law, the rest of his formerly tight-knit Pack, all angry and mourning and accusatory, all aligned against him for tearing the Pack apart.

"Like me, you mean?" she asked, jarring him from his dark reverie.

"No one's like you." Emotion added a gruffness to his tone. Shoving the invasive memories away, he returned to the puzzle of his stubborn mate. Sleep called to him, but apprehension held him back. With his knot tight in her body, the time to clear things up was now.

Della refused to believe she was Omega, and as far as he could reckon, he needed to find a way to bridge the gap between what she believed and what he knew to be true. That meant finding out who she *did* believe herself to be. Cal brushed a curtain of hair off her forehead. "So, who were you, Della, Who Takes Care Of Herself?" he asked softly.

Her sharp eyes, usually so focused and steady, went hazy with pain or memory or some combination of the two. "Adeline," she replied, her voice flat. "State Senator Adeline Catherine Maria Cabrese-Rao representing senate district thirty-nine in the great state of California." He stared wordlessly, absorbing every monotone word of her recitation. "Daughter of four-term US Senator Michael Anthony Cabrese and wife to Rakesh Rao, billionaire inventor, sister to Captain Anthony Joseph Cabrese."

"Holy shit." Astonishment rolled through him. Born well into the AfterEnd, Cal still understood the power behind such an illustrious family. Beyond her pedigree, his Della had been someone of note in her own right, with her own accomplishments and ambitions.

"Before the bombs fell, I was getting ready to announce my candidacy for US Senate, to run for my father's seat since he was retiring." She added bitterly, "Don't look impressed. None of that shit means anything now. I'm not sure it ever did."

As his knot began to ebb, Cal cupped her cheeks to prevent her from detaching and rolling away. He didn't know what she needed right at this moment, but he wasn't about to let her retreat inside of her nightmares and regrets. He had a feeling she'd spent far too much time there already.

No stranger to regrets, Cal recognized the signs. He could read the blame underneath her controlled countenance, but a few very key differences set them apart. He alone bore responsibility for the deaths of his father, sister, and so many others. They died as a direct result of his poor leadership and decision-making. Yet Della blamed herself for... what, exactly?

Pressed against him, her body went lifeless and cold. Skin to skin, having made explosive love, they were closer than they'd ever been, and yet her spirit dissolved beneath his fingertips. The fiery Omega who'd held a knife to his throat had disappeared and been replaced by this withdrawn shell. She was hiding from him again. Withdrawing deep within herself, retreating behind an unseen wall she erected between them. What the sex had torn down, she rebuilt in an instant.

He hated it. He hated every single invisible, offensive brick of it.

Goosebumps broke out over his skin, a tactile sign of unease. "Tell me." he said, utilizing the slightest degree of Alpha command. "Tell me what happened."

She met him with a challenging stare. "How much do you know about the events of TheEnd?"

He drew in a long breath. "My Pa was one of the Old Ones. He made sure we had a grasp on American history, both leading up to and through TheEnd. He'd already been living for many years 'off the grid,' as he liked to call it, before TheEnd. Had a ranch, did some farming, so when things fell apart, he took a bunch of his neighbors in, became the start of our Pack."

Della's chin jerked in curt understanding. "If he was off the grid, I was forged by it. You might know the coasts were hit first?" Cal nodded, relieved she at least kept talking, even if her words sounded robotic to his ears. "When the first bombs fell, I was in Sacramento with a handful of other legislators and the governor, of course. We organized as much as we could, mobilized emergency services and such, but what do states do in the face of such catastrophe? They reach out to the federal government for backup, but within the week, DC had been leveled, too."

Contempt sharpened her words. "Even if anyone remained to direct help, who exactly was coming to help? *People* are help, but by then, the entire population had been affected—if not directly then via fear and panic. We evacuated Sacramento. Partly from civil unrest and partly because no one knew where the next bombs would fall. Satellite systems were sabotaged, communication down everywhere... it was chaos." She slid her eyes back to his, a cut-glass hardness in their blue depths. "I couldn't do anything, couldn't help anyone. Couldn't make a fucking phone call. Nothing about my position or who I was mattered in the end. Nothing did." She paused and wet her lips. "I didn't drop the bombs. I didn't cause TheEnd, but the things I believed—about people and government and the essential goodness in the world... I was wrong about *everything*." She hissed the final word, the betrayal as fresh as the day it happened.

That, he could understand. After the accident, the things Pa espoused about the meaning of Pack evaporated in the snap of a finger. Packs supported and protected each other, no matter what. Except, when Cal's failure cost the Pack lives, he'd been drummed out and exiled without any consideration for protecting him, as a member of the Pack, from their grief and rage. Those cuts hurt, but they weren't the deepest ones.

Then, Cal saw it. As clear as the stream that flowed outside the cave, he saw to the bottom of Della's empty eyes. Despite her claims, she suffered not from the loss of ideals but the loss of something much more profound. The long-buried desperation, abandonment, and pure undiluted grief rang out to him because he'd witnessed it before.

He'd *caused* it before.

The muscles in his throat tensed and tightened to the point of discomfort. "Your husband. What happened to him?"

As she parted her lips in genuine surprise, her vacant veneer shattered like ice falling on rocks, replaced by alarm. "Wh—what?"

It all made sense. Her aloofness, her reticence, her steadfast commitment to not taking a mate in the hundred years since the end of the modern world. As pragmatic as she was, Della would comprehend the strategic benefit of being someone's mate, and he refused to believe no one had ever offered for her. While he hadn't met all the Alphas at Morris Hill, there were more than a few, with the exception of Silas, who would've treated her with kindness and respect, at the very least.

His gut told him Della had undoubtedly rebuked any offers that had come her way. No matter what she said, losing something as abstract and esoteric as her ideals would make one question oneself, but only losing *someone* caused this sort of desolation.

Deep, forever-seeping wounds she concealed with isolation and irritability. Wounds as flimsily papered over as his own. Wounds he couldn't protect her from, no matter how ardently he tried, and, horrifically, he recognized that particular impotence of being a bystander as a loved one suffered, knowing there was absolutely nothing he could do.

Unable to have this conversation on his back, Cal sat up, rearranging the soft length of the female till she sat cradled in his lap. His cock slipped free from her silken envelope, but he couldn't even relish the gush of their co-mingled fluids that spilled over the tops of her thighs. Agitated by this conversational turn, he angled his head, putting his face in her whole field of vision so she couldn't run away. His pulse battered his ears, telling him how close he edged to something absolutely critical to understanding this woman who'd be his mate.

"Your husband, Della. What happened to him?"

CHAPTER SEVENTEEN

Della

A thunderous press of emotions loomed, rumbling like a distant avalanche and filling her with just as much terror.

It was the sex. The sex ruined her. His seduction so skilled and covert, Cal had sliced her open with surgical precision, the cut so quick and sure she hadn't realized till it was too late. Emotions she'd sought in the pages of her photo album hemorrhaged out of her in gush after spurting gush. For decades they'd stayed dormant only to return at her most vulnerable moment. Not at home in her cozy cabin surrounded by safety and security when she might be able to process them, but bared before this Alpha, unprotected as he snooped around the walled-off corridors of her heart.

Pain flooded those hidden cloisters and dimly-lit coves, collecting anguish she'd sequestered for the people she'd lost. Family, close and extended, friends, colleagues, acquaintances, young and old, men and women alike, but Cal hadn't asked about them. He'd stuck his finger in the wound and asked about Rakesh.

Rakesh, her loving husband whom she'd not thought of *once* as she'd fucked this Alpha on a dirty cave floor in the middle of nowhere. Guilt crested like a crimson wave. How could she? How could she talk about Rakesh with combined slick and semen still slippery on her skin? How could she even whisper his name when Cal had driven his knot so deep he'd pushed out the memory of any other cock she'd ever known?

Even worse, how could she force the damning words past her lips? Rakesh hadn't failed to protect her; *she'd* failed to protect *him*. Like she'd failed her father and brother and staff and every single other constituent who'd voted for her and every single one who didn't.

Pressing her fingertips to her eyelids to avoid Cal's compelling gaze, Della labored to stanch the bleeding. It was the past. It would always be the past. Only the here and now mattered.

Solve the problem, solve the problem.

Things had gotten out of hand. Her sense of smell, this transformed Omega business, her own lust, all of it diverted her attention from her goal. She needed to rewind this unspooled mess to get back to safety. She needed to go *home*. Whatever connection they'd forged in the course of the lovemaking—no, the *sex*, just sex—had to be severed.

As if fleeing a predator, Della scrambled off Cal's lap and reached for her discarded shirt. "I'm tired," she said, stuffing her head into the garment. Eyes averted, she pushed arm after arm through, yanking it as far down as she could to cover her lower half. It didn't go nearly far enough.

"Della." Displeasure crept into his voice. "Della, look at me."

She folded her arms over her chest and refused his command by turning her head to stare out the cave opening. "This isn't what you think it is, Cal." Determined to fix this, she spoke with as much confidence as she could muster. "You seem like a nice enough man,"—she paused to purse her lips—"for a kidnapper, I suppose, and maybe bedding an old woman is interesting to you as a novelty. But, beyond that, there's no happiness to be found with me." Della clenched her jaw. "I don't have anything to give you."

"No." He barked the rebuke. "That's not true."

No? Not true? She wanted to laugh. He didn't care for her inquisition? Didn't appreciate her attempt to get to know him and devise a solution to this mess that would serve both of them? He *thought* he wanted her, but only because he didn't know any better, didn't know what a gnarled, dried-up wreck of a person she was.

Well, then, the gloves were off. Squaring her shoulders, Della charged headfirst into a reckless new strategy: blatant, painful, unhinged honesty. "You said you wouldn't lie to me, so I'm giving you the same respect." She cut him a side-eyed glare, not backing down at the hardened set of his mouth. "Sex is all I can offer. There's simply nothing else."

After a single taut second, he sprang into action. Groping for his pants, Cal heaved himself to his feet, glowering as he fastened his fly, his patience seemingly exhausted. Hazel eyes flashed with accusation and... hurt. The look chilled her, and a tense quaking started in the muscles between her shoulder blades, a biting discomfort at his obvious irritation.

Alpha is unhappy.

A sweet, feminine voice crooned inside her head, and Della smacked her palm against her brow. Was she *hearing* shit now? More concussion symptoms or a sign of impending insanity? No shit, he was unhappy. This was the AfterEnd; who in the fuck got to be happy?

He won't hurt you. Take care of Alpha, and he'll take care of you.

She stifled a snort. Ignoring the irritating voice and its smug declarations, Della snatched at a blanket that unfortunately reeked of their union and covered her lower body. Cal seethed, his hostility like the pounding surf against her weary spirits.

"Listen." Heaving a great sigh as if fighting for serenity, Cal squatted before her. The heat of him seeped into her as if the thin layers of clothing ceased to exist. Della shuddered, remembering the touch of his skin crushed against her own, his weight on her body, his knot sealing them together. Coffee-cinnamon scent braided a web of deliciousness around her, his aroma somehow more complex and wonderful after their joining.

More, that cloying voice said. *You want more.*

No. No, she *didn't*.

Cal interlaced his fingers so tight the knuckles cracked, thankfully distracting her from those base physical musings. No more of that shit tonight. He cleared his throat. "Whatever happened, exactly none of it was your fault. No one would expect you to do anything more'n survive. You did that, and I'm grateful for it because it brought you to me." His chin lowered, and his voice took on a warning tone. "But that don't mean you get to dictate what you are or aren't doing for me. Not now, not ever."

Heat shot to her head like a volcano blast. The fucking gall of this guy. Even for an Alpha, it strained believability. He had no difficulty telling her all the things he wanted from her: be an Omega, be his mate, take his knot, blah blah blah. But she didn't get a say in any of it?

Fuck that. Fuck it all the way to hell.

"I'll tell you what *you're* doing for me," she sniped, diving into the conflict like a pilot on a suicide mission.

"Tomorrow, you're taking me back home to Morris Hill."

"Like hell I am." Cal spat the words out.

His constructed calm shattered, and the pungent scent of Alpha anger spiked the air. Della wrinkled her nose against the stench as two things became apparent. One, he did *not* like her telling him what to do. Two, although his ire peaked to a new level, it failed to rouse any kind of fear response in her body. Just like that first night, she felt safe with him, even if it made no sense.

"You can fuck me again if you feel the need," she tossed off, as if he hadn't spoken, "before we leave in the morning."

Fists clenched, he bore down on her with his vibrating outrage, the nerve she struck zapping and popping like an exposed wire. "Let's get one thing straight, Omega." Cal stabbed at the rock between his thighs with his index finger. "Just because I held off the claiming bite, don't think for one goddamn *second* you're in charge of what's happening here. You are not in *any* position to be dictating demands."

Sliding her gaze up from his emphatic finger, Della raised an imperious brow. "Oh, I see. I was wondering when your big bad Alpha was going to show himself. What a surprise he's as tedious as all the others."

A growl burst out of him and ricocheted around the cave. Not a sexy growl, either. This one approximated the warning snarl one animal might give another. "You think I'm like all the others?" Several snorted breaths through flared nostrils later, he sneered, "I don't think you want to know how differently this could've gone."

"Oh, I know," she snapped, unable to hide the wobble in her voice. She knew all about what Alphas were capable of. After a slow blink, understanding showed in his eyes, and his features softened. Della's body felt simultaneously empty and laden with lead, and her head started throbbing again.

Cal rose to his feet, stomped one foot, and then the other into his boots. He stalked to the edge of the bedding and retrieved the jackknife, tucking it deep in his pocket. Turning his back, he stormed to the cave entrance like a black cloud, hovering on the threshold to dart one last glare in her direction. He coasted a cold look over her before saying gruffly, "Get some rest, but this isn't over," before disappearing into the night.

All the righteousness left her in a dismaying puff of smoke, but a heaviness centered in Della's chest, growing with every crunching stride Cal took away from the cave. Her throat ached with bitter defeat. She'd lost sight of herself, lost track of her objective, and fumbled the entire evening. As if moving through a fog, Della laid down, arranging a blanket on her body and feeling more alone than she had in her entire life.

CHAPTER EIGHTEEN

Della

Where in the fresh hell was he taking her now?

The thought rolled through Della's still-sleepy brain, bringing a cross purse to her lips. Cal had roused her at not-quite dawn with a firm hand on her shoulder, hauling her out of bed and handing her a clean-smelling, Alpha-sized shirt to change into. Groggy, she'd put it on without arguing but tied a thin blanket around her waist for good measure as there was still no sign of her pants. With a jerk of his chin, he silently announced they were heading out of the cave tout de suite. Della stuffed her feet in her shoes and followed, neither of them speaking as they tromped a precarious path from the ridge down to the water.

They walked as the sun trudged out of its own bed, the forest still mostly suffused with quiet early morning peace. The bubbling creek grew as they followed its lead. Water streamed over the jutting rocks with more and more vigor, taking up the space where conversation would've naturally gone. Neither of them said a word.

It had been a weird night.

Alone in the cave after their blow-up, worries danced a jig on her unquiet mind. Where had he gone? Would he return? He wouldn't leave her there, would he? How had things gotten so off track? What was she going to do? Hours spent tossing and turning and being taunted by the mingled sex scents that perfumed the cave. The fire dwindled to coals with their dull orangey glow and then faded to ash, leaving her in velvet darkness while her circling thoughts refused to quiet.

Eventually, Cal returned and threw himself onto his bedroll, mere inches from hers. Close but not touching, Della's body honed all her attention on the hulking black lump of his form, instantly preoccupied with maintaining the scant space between them on principle. Unbothered, he fell into a deep sleep, snoozing gently as his familiar scent bathed her reassuring comfort. Warmth toasted her cheeks as she remembered how, shame-filled yet desperate for unconsciousness, she'd finally given up, traversed the darkness and the careful distance, to bury her nose in the fragrant groove of his spine. Exhausted by conflicted feelings and confused thoughts, she allowed herself that one concession. For her reward, Della inhaled one luxurious breath and then promptly passed out.

For whatever reason, Cal deferred any mention of her middle-of-the-night snugglefest thus far this morning. Yet with every step and shift of the satchel he carried, the long groove of his spine peeked in and out of visibility, teasing her for what she'd done the night before. Even worse, her fingers itched, dying to launch herself at him, to reclaim everything she'd missed during those quiet hours of slumber and complete a thorough exploration of every inch of his rich, russet skin.

These sorts of thoughts were foreign. In fact, Della's own body felt foreign. Somewhere in their frenzied joining yesterday, something critical freed itself inside her. Some long-buried, suppressed part now wailed for attention with every breath she drew, demanding restitution for the years of ignoring her skin's hunger for another. Their argument, as brutal as it had been, did not weaken the hunger. It grew more intense and insistent, and most concerning of all, it all centered on *him*.

You want your Alpha, the need inside of her crooned, its voice so loud it bounced around her head like an echoing shout over a canyon. *You need him to claim you.*

Nope. She neither wanted nor needed to be claimed. With effort, Della tore her thoughts from that path and grounded herself in the now: her feet crunching over the damp, pebbly ground, the sweet early summer air lifting the hair on her forehead, the faint scent of sulfur on the breeze, and the strong, wide expanse of Cal's back as he forged the path ahead.

She sighed. Demanding he return her to Morris Hill had been a misstep. She knew, better than anyone, Alphas's tenacious stubbornness. Of course, he wouldn't take kindly to a direct order. But, thrown by the sex and his question about Rakesh, she'd panicked.

That itself was incomprehensible and vexing, as Della, under normal circumstances, was far from that rash and volatile version of herself. Yet the feelings crashed through her too fast to wrangle, the impotence and the bitterness so thick she could choke. She'd laid all her cards on the table and lost.

They arrived at some destination understood only by Cal. Signaled not by any explanation or verbal acknowledgment but by the unceremonious drop of his pack on the ground. With a cool glance up at her, he bent to rummage through it.

Now fully awake and not focused on walking, their argument from the night before seasoned the air like the ozone before a storm. One thing about Cal she'd observed in their short time together: he rarely shut up. Whatever he was doing, the man chattered on, the syrupy lilt of his accent smoothing everything with his easy affability. This new silence? She didn't like it.

Della cleared her throat. "Is there a reason we're out here?"

Without looking up, Cal grunted and produced a tangled net out of one of the many pockets. "Fishing."

"You want me to go fishing?" Incredulity spilled from her lips. "I'm not even wearing pants."

He tossed her a look, his expression exquisitely neutral. No teasing tilt to his lips, no crinkle at the edges of his eye, no sign of the dimples whatsoever.

It... *stung.*

In their relatively brief acquaintance, he'd never treated her with anything other than amused consideration, with a healthy dollop of charm on top. Even angry, he'd noticed her fatigue and ordered her to bed, never losing sight of his concern for her. This blandness and silence—sapped of all his warmth—repulsed her. She *hated* it.

"Don't see what pants have to do with it," he continued, his fingers working through knots in the netting. "The way I figure, if I don't keep an eye on you, there's no telling what you'll get up to. Might find something else to hold against my throat."

Hackles up, Della steeled her spine and raised a haughty chin. "You're expecting an apology, I suppose?"

"Naw." Setting the net aside, Cal turned his attention to untying his boots, tugging them off, and rolling his pant legs up to his knees before stripping off his shirt. His shoulders, a yard wide and coppery brown, made her mouth water. Backing away, Della perched herself on a rock, letting her gaze unabashedly cascade over him, unable to ignore how his brown nipples pebbled in the crisp air or the way the corrugated muscles on his sides rippled as he moved. The strong line of his clavicle stood out like a raised barrier between the thick angle of his trapezius and the muscled expanse of his pecs. What would it feel like to sleep with her head pillowed on those?

"Ain't gonna fault you for trying to protect yourself. In fact..." His hand disappeared into his pants pocket and reemerged with something metallic in his palm. He tossed it up in a casual flip before lobbing it at her. It sailed through the air, and Della caught it on reflex, the hard metal ferrying his body heat directly into hers. "I went ahead and sharpened that up. You can have it."

Puzzled, she hefted her hand, the knife cupped in her palm. "You'd give me a weapon?"

His shoulders gave a small flick, like a shrug he couldn't be bothered to commit to. "Sharpened or dull, that piddly knife in your shaking hand is no real threat." The coolness in his manner thawed and a new vehemence stirred beneath his hazel gaze when he lifted it to hers. "I said I wouldn't claim you, and I didn't, but I only agreed because I want you to trust me, not because of that." His head angled toward her outstretched palm.

Emotions swooped in her belly. Part embarrassment at her hasty, ill-conceived actions the night prior and part begrudging appreciation of his strategy. Without her realizing it, he'd slipped trustworthiness right past her defenses and embedded it in her heart. *Damn it,* she *did* trust him. Not to claim her, not to hurt her, and not to do anything other than what he said he'd do.

Della ran her thumb along the spine of the folded blade, amazed she was holding it again. Quickly, she flipped it open, so discombobulated she flinched as it clicked into place. Sunlight lit the edge, bright and shiny from its sharpening, a beautiful, deadly thing. When had he...?

Last night. He must've spent the hours away from her honing the blade to this lethal edge. The image ran forcefully through her mind. Cal, shirtless, aggravated, scowling, painstakingly bringing the blade back to life in the light of the moon. For her.

"I understand," she murmured, afraid that if she opened her mouth to say anything more, she'd disclose the emotional maelstrom threatening to pull her under.

"Not sure you do," Cal declared before bending again to his work. "You've been on your own for so long now, you don't get what's happening here. Everyone should have a good knife. Me giving you one, that's me taking care of you because that's my job now, my privilege, and my pleasure." He spoke with a curtness that burned, but the words and the sentiment behind them dispelled any of her leftover anger. "That's also why I didn't leave you this morning, thought you might be scared if you woke up alone."

He got to his feet and spread the detangled net between his outstretched arms to give it a little shake. He folded his brow and pinned her with a critical squint. "I hope you weren't too frightened last night.

You should know—" Cutting his words, he huffed in exasperation. "You should know I didn't go far. You were never in any danger."

Carefully, Della refolded the knife, rubbing her thumb along the spine of the closed blade. She hadn't been afraid. Even in the pitch-black cave, dark after the fire died, she'd worried about him and the implications of their fight, but she'd never felt fear.

"Honesty. Integrity. Openness. Dependability." Her own words paraded through her mind. The condescending recitation of things she valued in a person, hurled in Cal's face like a mockery of things he would never, ever be. Only, *god dammit,* had he snuck those qualities inside her defenses, too?

"I know." She attempted a weak smile, her head spinning tumultuously. "I wasn't scared."

A breath whooshed out of him, a trace of relief in the gust. After another half-hearted shake, he dropped the net to his feet. Standing tall, hands on hips, he stared out at the rushing water, a muscle in his jaw ticking.

"Don't want to fight with you," he said finally, his words barely audible above the rushing water.

Harvesting her conviction from the night before, Della braced herself to open the can of worms he'd apparently decided to push to the dusty, forgotten corner of the pantry. She wasn't angry, but the issue remained unsettled. "If you want to protect me, and you don't want to fight," she said evenly, "then you need to take me back to Morris Hill."

The line of his jaw hardened to stone. "Not gonna rehash that." He tracked her eyes with his, and Della shivered with the harnessed command in his voice. "We're not going back there, and that's final."

Della bit down hard on her lip, bottling the rising tide of worry. "So, what's your plan here? We live in that musty cave now? Indefinitely?"

He drew his brows together. "Working on a plan," he hedged, releasing her from the intense eye contact. Della tutted at his unsatisfactory response, and he continued, flashing her a resentful glance. "Thought we'd stay here a few days, rest up, make sure your head is okay, and then head east. I've heard about a few places where they have electricity up and running where you might be more comfortable." He rifled a hand through his hair. "Or we could find a new Pack."

Della's stomach caved in like she'd been punched. Head east? Out into the world? Away from Morris Hill?

Morris Hill was more than her home; it was her *refuge*. A peaceful, safe community where she let her guard down for the first time since TheEnd, if only a little. Before arriving there, she'd run from violence, fought off attackers, scrounged for food, and seen people die from stupid accidents and simple infections. There was no safety out in the world.

Pulse pounding against the backs of her eyes, Della spiraled into her waking nightmares. So fucking assured of his own ability to protect her, he thought nothing of venturing somewhere else, somewhere unknown. And then what? Encounter whatever depraved monsters controlled the resources and electricity wherever they went? If not that, then… join an Alpha Pack? Cold terror clawed her spine. Della knew Alpha Packs. Cal would have to fight his way in. That was how they operated, even Hunter's. But while Hunt only required a good showing—kick ass or take an ass kicking—other Packs demanded more. Kill or be killed.

If Cal died during their journey in some stupid Alpha conflict or even while trying to fight his way into a Pack, she'd be on her own. Again. It wouldn't even have to come from a Pack. Who's to say they wouldn't encounter some traveling band of miscreants tomorrow, the next day, or next week? Cal could fight off one or two, maybe three, but more than that? No. They'd kill him for the simple pleasure of it. Or they'd beat him to the brink of death and make him watch as they violated her, and he wouldn't be able to do a fucking thing a bout it. She'd be taken, killed, enslaved, or some other god-awful, unimaginable scenario. It wasn't an idle speculation of her overactive imagination. She'd *seen* shit like this go down... until she came to Morris Hill.

Protests sped up her throat, all stuck together in the race to get out. The jackknife tumbled from her shaking hand, landing on the rocks with a soft scrape. "Cal..." she whispered, unable to form the words to explain, to make him understand. He paced a step closer, attention rapt. "I... I need to go back. I can't be..." She circled her head to their surroundings. "Here."

She lifted her chin and put all her fear and apprehension out in the open. Let it shine through her expression, hiding nothing. He saw her? He wanted to see her? He could see this. Here. Now.

Cal held the look, his attention never wavering or recoiling from whatever he saw on her face. Then, a low, vibrating note wiggled into her chest, elbowing aside the cacophony of emotions cramped together. Desperate, she latched onto it, welcoming the reprieve from all the memories and anxieties drawn far too near to the surface. The sound flowed through her, and she embraced it, let it bump over all her tense muscles and jostle the knots free. Her shoulders, drawn up to her ears, slumped under the seductive throb.

"I know you're scared," Cal said, low and soothingly, the purr turning his voice to melted butter, "but you gotta trust me on this. We *can't* go back there."

Trust Alpha. He'll protect you, that soft, feminine voice coaxed in time with the undulating rhythm. And, *oh hell,* she wanted to believe it.

"There..." Della clutched at her focus, feeling the vibration reorient itself, changing from a distraction toward something else entirely, waking up the hunger that lived in the marrow of her bones. She ought to resist it, she ought to hold tight to herself and her needs, but after the surge of fear and the uncertainty of the last two days, she'd simply ran out of resolve. "That's where my life is," she said weakly.

He inclined his dark head, his eyes glimmering but resolute. "We'll make a life somewhere else. You and me."

"But..." Fight dripped out of her drop by drop, squeezed out by the low rumble, until only a vague outline of her arguments remained. "But... you can't drag me away from my home in the middle of the night and expect me to say, '*Oh yes, please, Alpha, that's a great idea, Alpha, thank you, Alpha.*'"

Yes, that's right, that irritating inner voice rejoiced. *He's your Alpha*, it said, as if to mock her for inadvertently giving voice to her deepest, darkest secret. Sarcasm or not, it didn't matter because now the words had left her lips, and there was no taking them back.

Pupils blown to black, Cal's muscled chest bunched and heaved with each raggedy breath, and things got even worse. That inner voice, summoned from its shameful depths, took possession and ran through Della's fracturing self-control. *Look at him. Alpha's big and strong and beautiful. You don't need to worry.* Unable to stop herself, Della listened. Knees weakening, she indulged in a long, visual drink of the Alpha, standing tall and assured, a wild creature at home in the wild surroundings.

He curled his full lips. "Say that again."

Heat billowed low in her belly. "I need to go back."

"Not that part." He looked her over seductively, and Della's stomach tightened to a near cramp, locked in his unwavering hazel spotlight. "Call me Alpha again."

CHAPTER NINETEEN

Della

Della's pulse ticked upward to what surely must be a dangerous level. "I was being sarcastic," she managed to croak.

Long legs ate up the distance between the water and her seat on the rock, all the while making that deep *hmm*ing noise that wove through the air and tickled her in places it had no business tickling. She tilted her chin up, his body filling her gaze as he stalked closer.

Hmm. He made the noise again, roughed up and veering uncomfortably closer to that infernal growl. With a final lurch, he invaded her space, immediately burying his nose in the crook of Della's neck. A surprised squeal left her lips, and she made to jerk away, the movement stopped by Cal snaking his all-too-quick arms around her waist.

Sharp teeth slid along the thin skin of her neck. "But it rolled right off those luscious lips, didn't it?" His rumbling voice sent her eyelids into a spasming flutter. "Say, 'please Alpha' again, and I'll give you what you want."

Flashes of the night prior played in her mind like a film. Every sordid minute writhing on the cave floor grabbed her like a giant hook, as if to drag her out of this moment and back into the memory.

She was losing it, absolutely losing it.

A fresh burst of his scent exploded through her senses and hauled her to the present. Coffee and cinnamon and masculine musk blended together. It fused and synthesized to become something altogether new, something uniquely, exquisitely *Cal* that activated some hidden switch she'd never known she had.

"Please, Alpha," she mouthed the words, barely loud enough to cross the spare inches between her lips and his ear. "I want to go home."

Cal's hands flexed around her middle, holding her in place as his nose slid up the sensitive skin behind her ear. He inhaled loudly, breathing her in as she did him. What did he scent when he filled his nose with her?

She didn't have time to ask, as the next second, he freed that unrestrained growl. Della's lower belly throbbed hard, the blood flowing to her swelling sex like a mini climax of its own. A trickle of slick wet the blanket she'd fastened into a skirt, highlighting the vacant space demanding its own attention.

"You've said that." Quickly and purposefully, he untucked the blanket from her waist and spread it out beneath her bottom. Immediately his hands were on her skin, rough and assured and *perfect*. Thumbs rubbing circles on her inner thighs, his magical hazel eyes skipped up to hers, and the lustful yearning in them stole her breath. Was she looking at his desire or a reflection of her own? "Is that the only thing my little queen wants?"

The circling thumbs inched closer to her core, the swelling, achy part of her body centering all her attention. Della's reason shuffled closer to a cliff edge, scrabbling for a foothold of sense to withstand this spiraling insanity. She knew her task, they'd been talking about going back to Morris Hill, and now a few simple caresses and a near-growl had her ready to spread her legs and beg for all the pleasure he'd surely give her if she asked.

Last night she retained a distant hope of resistance, but today she knew how this went, how this *felt*, how *he* could make her feel, and there was no more denying it. Later, later they would need to figure it out. The return to Morris Hill and the question of the claiming and all that. But, right now? She was here, in this moment, and those worries couldn't touch her.

In answer, Della shifted her weight, spreading her knees and propping her feet up on the rock. Making her decision, she exposed herself without a single ounce of reserve. If she were going to allow herself this incredible thing, she would reach out and take it with her whole self. His heated gaze turned molten, and a strange, singular power tangled alongside her mounting desire. Since he'd stolen her away, she'd been at his mercy, but in this, he was very much at hers.

"If I'm the queen," she whispered, "you should be on your knees."

Throat bobbing with a low groan, his eyelids stuttered closed and then opened again. Slowly, he dropped to one knee and then the other, his gaze never faltering from hers as he dipped his head to hungrily mouth along the length of her inner thigh. Della's muscles shook at the stimulation on her energized flesh, lost in the way he looked at her like she was his doom and salvation all at once. Her heart pounded in a visceral salute, an acknowledgment of the same.

"Goddamn, Della," he breathed, gently sinking his teeth into the flesh of her thigh and then licking the unbroken skin. "You show me your puffy, wet pussy anytime you want, and I'll be on my fucking knees in a second. Makes my mouth water just looking at you."

With another low moan, Cal brought his mouth to her heated sex. The reaction to his touch was swift and strong, and her back arched so hard the muscle cramped. His lips and tongue moved not with tentative, testing, or teasing strokes but with a full-bodied commitment to devour everything she'd offered up to him with appreciation and ravish. Staking a path through her sex, he glided over and alongside her clit, winding her coil of pleasure tighter and tighter. Head fallen back between her shoulder blades, Della's closed lids shimmered with rosy warmth as the sun climbed higher. It was heady and luxurious and indulgent and perfect.

"Oh shit," she breathed, the sensation spiraling too soon, too fast, too hard to control. Fingernails scraped against the rough surface of the rock. She wanted this to last but didn't, but *did,* but didn't, but *couldn't.*

A large Alpha hand spanned the soft flesh of her belly, his fingers spread wide, holding her in place. Della groped for that hand, needing more of his skin on hers to moor her to earth as her connections frayed and snapped with every wrenching, building second. Images flew through her mind: hazel eyes glimmering with a grudging approval as she fumbled a knife against his throat, his face contorted and beautiful as he'd taken her body, his shadow cast large on the wall like a hulking, mythical, feral beast as he surged into her and delivered the final peak of his exquisite knot. No longer afraid of it, her body shuddered as her release neared, thinking of nothing but that final moment of all-consuming fullness.

Waves of pleasure crashed. Her thighs closed around his cheeks, holding him against her. Time seemed to stop as her body evolved within itself, her cells and very essence rearranging to accommodate this new reality, this new way of being, of surrender and acceptance and electric connection. Her lungs became a vacuum, her breaths suspended between inhale and exhale, and shards of sunlight splintered into constellations of stars. She couldn't breathe, couldn't think, couldn't cry, argue, rage, or do anything other than combust and reform anew.

Omega.

The word purred into her consciousness. That inner voice, soft and humble, tucked it into her brain like a lover's goodnight kiss, and Della let it be. Maybe not forever, but for now.

The pulsations were hardly a faint echo before Cal was on his feet, gathering her up and lifting her off the rock as if she weighed nothing. She snapped her eyes open, arms flailing to his neck for stability. "Cal," his name grated past her panting, parched lips.

"Hold on." With her legs wrapped around his waist, he braced her back against a large tree. Well off the ground, her thighs stretched wide over his broad abdomen, and she looked down, loving the raw, unashamed vision of her glossy curls tickling the ridged contours of his belly.

Cal cupped one hand on her ass as he fumbled with his pants, freeing his cock from its prison. It sprang up, nudging against her, hard and hot and insistent. Della circled her hips, caressing the tip with her core, smearing it with slick. Moaning, Cal slumped forward, resting his forehead against Della's as if having trouble staying upright.

"You want it?" He breathed against her mouth, dick nudging gently between her lower lips. "You want my cock, Omega?"

Needing more of him, she ran her hands over his cheeks, treasuring the gentle abrasion against her palms. She grazed her lips across his, mingling their shared air. "Not before you kiss me."

After one deep, shuddering breath, Cal flexed his hips upward, thrusting into her body as his mouth crashed against hers. His lips were hard and searching, crashing into her like a breaking storm, and she met him with the same wild vigor. He tasted like coffee and sun and Mexican hot chocolate mixed with leftover morsels of her own flavor hidden in the recesses of his mouth. The taste sang in her veins, vibrant and colorful and so fucking *alive*. Alive in a way she'd never thought she'd feel again.

She drank him up as his rigid length drove forward in long, careful, steady thrusts. Pulling almost all the way out before sliding deep again and again, luring her body back on another journey, another path up toward the peak. All the while, he fervently kissed her, never letting up in his intensity.

"Your lips, Della, oh my *god*." His voice cracked, a sign of how affected he was by this, and Della dissolved completely. Everything around them ceased to exist—the scratch of the bark against her back, the rustle of the wind in the trees, the bird calls greeting the morning, even the cramps in her legs and the strain from being pinned between an enormous tree and an enormous man. All of it faded away, leaving her aware of only his taste in her mouth, the feel of his tongue as it delved between her lips, his hand's groping clasp as it snaked under her shirt and found a breast, his hips rocking between her thighs, and the escalating joy of fullness and impending release.

Yes, that inner voice sang, *give it to him. Give Alpha* everything.

Della wedged a hand between them, combing through her curls to add pressure to the spot she needed it. With every hard thrust, his abdomen brushed against the back of her hand, turning her on and intoxicating her with the simple, exquisite feel of skin on skin.

The ecstasy soared. "More," she said, her free hand dropping to his waist, urging him tighter in an unsubtle demand. "I need more."

His lips pulled free of hers, their shared breaths slamming together in the narrow space. "You got no fucking idea what you're doing to me, do you?" he said. With a massive heave, he jostled her higher, changing the angle of his strokes, coming into her faster and somehow even harder, his cock touching a different spot that cranked everything up another level. "No idea how fucking perfect this hot pussy feels on my dick."

Della's head bounced against the tree trunk, his words tumbling over her like a filthy waterfall, hauling her under and deeper into their union. Sounds left her lips, a deranged mix of *oh god* and *fuck me*. Della whimpered, her climax skating on the edge where anything could tip her over. One stroke, two, maybe three? One small word or some extra caress, and she would fly into a thousand million pieces, spinning off into infinity.

As if he knew, Cal licked up her throat and then nibbled his way down, his teeth finding their way to the claiming spot high on her shoulder at the base of her neck. "You wanna be mine?" he said, a taunt buried in his tone. He nipped the spot in a gentle tease, biting down but not enough to break the skin. "You already are, you know."

You want it. Tell him you need it. Let him claim you.

The voice commanded, but Della slammed her teeth together, feeling like her soul was being ripped in two. God, she wanted it, yet at the same time, she didn't. She wanted to fall over but also hang onto this delicious, terrible edge for the rest of her life. She wanted none of it, all of it, and so much of it that she couldn't contain any of it.

Cal's voice brought her back, vibrating against her skin. "I want *you*, all of you. Let go, Della, I've got you, and I'm not letting go."

The sun burst from behind a cloud, blinding everything as her insides went incandescent. Cal closed his mouth over hers, swallowing her scream as he kissed her through the final strokes he needed—one, two, *three*—to come tumbling into free fall along with her. They clutched at each other, all grasping hands and clenched muscles, erasing space between their bodies. His lips, soft but firm, hovered away from hers, parted as he breathed through his stuttering, post-orgasmic exhalations.

Time passed. Maybe a minute, maybe ten. A cloud edged in front of the sun, and their small corner of the forest dimmed once again. Della's head lolled against the trunk, her movements sluggish like her body was encased in honey. A glossy, golden sheen colored her vision, Cal's sweat-glazed skin burnished and gilded and so beautiful she needed to squint. He thought she was beautiful? He was a work of art.

Below, the swell of his knot pressurized, not kicking off another climax as it had the night before but spurring something even more dangerous to expand inside her: emotion. It roiled inside her chest, dark, and potent and impossible to ignore.

She'd come so close. So close to asking him (demanding him!) to finish it. To sink his teeth in and be done with it once and for all. The words had teetered on her lips, *"Take me. Claim me. I'm your Omega. Make me yours."* Yet some morsel of self-preservation held them in check.

She wanted him, maybe even needed him, but she also needed to go home. Morris Hill needed her, and once she surrendered to his claim, there'd be no going back.

CHAPTER TWENTY

Cal

Arms filled with a fresh load of firewood, Cal climbed the narrow ridge back to the cave. The knowledge that Della waited inside filled his chest to bursting with warmth. He knew she'd stayed where he left her because, for one reason, he could pick out her scent anywhere, and for another, he'd kept the cave within eye and earshot as he'd gathered the wood.

Cal lowered his neck to pass through the cave entrance. "I'm going to head back and check the fishing net. Do you want to—"

The scene before him ate the rest of his sentence. Della stood in the middle of the cave, face concealed in a heavy blanket, while every other piece of clothing and bedding was strewn about in a chaotic rummage pile. He stood, arrested in dismay, as Della snuffled a long, highly audible inhale of the blanket surrounding her face.

"Better," came the muted voice, "but still a little off."

He shifted from foot to foot, working to make sense of it all. After fucking her against a tree in the early morning (which he highly recommended and needed to do again sometime very soon), he'd somehow finagled the blanket and laid them down, all the while laughing together about the silly awkwardness of trying to move around while attached at the crotch. Not an easy task, but worth it to spend the next quarter hour stroking Della's long hair and chatting about what bird calls they recognized in the aviary chatter. She'd been quiet, then. Quiet, but present with him in a new way, like something righted itself inside her. He didn't know what to make of it but lapped up those serene moments like a kitten with milk.

Nothing at all like this current outburst of industriousness.

"Della?" he asked gently.

The blanket fell from her face, revealing his Omega, her eyes shining and cheeks flushed. She frowned and held up a palm. "Don't move!"

"What?"

Tossing the blanket to the floor, she scurried over and made a grab for the firewood load. "Here, let me take that."

"Hell no." He swiveled his shoulders, keeping it out of her grasping hands. "I'm going to set it down over there." He jerked his chin to where he'd tossed the small pile of branches and logs he'd collected over the past day. Except, an empty space existed where the pile had once sat. His head swung around the cave. "Where's the rest of it?"

"Oh!" Della smiled brightly. "I relocated it over behind that pile of rocks, see? You can stack it over there, and it won't be so messy spilling out everywhere." She folded her arms over her chest and, tapping her pointed chin with an index finger, surveyed the cave with critical regard. "Now, I think the best place for the bedding is actually over there." Moving her finger away from her chin, she dropped it to point toward the far side of the fire ring and, with a decisive nod, hustled around, bending to scoop up the bedding she'd scattered. "Some of this needs to be aired out, but I'm going to get it all set up for now and see if I like it. Are you sure this is everything you brought?" She glanced over her shoulder with a suspicious gleam. "You don't have any other blankets or anything packed away, do you?"

Cal eyed the flaccid assortment of his emptied-out bags. "Uh... no. Looks like you got it all." He crossed the space, stacking the firewood as directed in the newly relocated spot. A spot which, to be clear, he didn't judge as any more convenient or preferable to the old one, but Della's thinking about this had far surpassed his.

Task finished, he turned around to find Della sitting on her haunches, folding and stacking the bedding, patting it down and arranging it in some highly specific yet completely impenetrable pattern.

Nesting, his brain supplied.

Oh, shit.

He had an Omega nesting in the makeshift home he'd brought her to. An Omega who'd spent the better part of the last three days denying her Omega nature. An Omega who was about to go into Heat. Go into Heat in a cold, echoey cave, he clarified with a wince, not a soft, cozy nest like she deserved. Twin strikes of guilt and desire shot through him, desire winning out as he fixed on the way her rounded bottom wiggled as she worked. Tension built in his groin, the thrumming of his pulse loud and heading due south.

"Della..." His voice grated like gravel. They'd only returned from setting up the fishing net a few hours earlier, but already his body activated and declared it was ready to go. Making love to his adorable, nesting Omega in her Omega nest? *Hell yes.* And if it distracted her from any more discussion about returning to Morris Hill? Even better.

They'd danced around the sore subject all morning, but if he studied her face, the trouble oozed out from behind her calm exterior. He had no answer to give her, though. Because, no matter what, claiming mark or not, giving her up was no longer an option.

"This one." She rose to her feet, pinching a thin blanket between her forefinger and thumb. "This one needs to be hung outside. It reeks of another Alpha." Screwing her mouth up in a disgusted grimace, she strode toward the opening.

"Here." In two steps, Cal caught her up, wrapping his arm around her waist and plucking the offensive blanket from her fingertips. Beads of sweat pearled on her hairline, her cheeks ruddy. She'd complained of feeling warm and crampy on the walk back to the cave, but he'd chalked it up to resolving symptoms of the concussion and encouraged her to take a nap.

She hadn't, choosing instead to rearrange his hastily set-up campsite. With an affectionate squeeze to her bare bottom (he decided right then he'd burn those pants), he tossed the blanket toward the entrance, freeing his other hand to provide similar attention to the other half of her ass. The juicy curves overflowed his palms in a deeply satisfying way, even more so when she wiggled into his hold. No, he had not spent enough time with this particular feature.

A slow grin slid onto his face. "Can't argue about being an Omega now, can you?"

Della glanced up from where she'd been rubbing her nose into his shirtfront, scenting him as naturally as any Omega he'd ever met. "Huh?"

Cal tipped his chin lower, dusting her nose with his. "You're going into Heat, darlin'."

"Is that why I'm so warm?" She rubbed at her sweat-glossed forehead. "I know it's chilly in here, but I feel… hot and… weird."

Slowly and seductively, her gaze raked down the front of his body. Black currant and juniper, laced with a sweet hint of slick, filled his nose. He cupped his palm along the silken swell of her hip and tucked into her waist, drawing her close. A smirk brewed on his lips. "Any other feelings you'd like to share?"

Her focus drifted to the newly-assembled single sleeping pallet, and her cheeks flushed a deeper shade. Wild energy stormed in his veins, and Cal shuffled forward, directing Della's backward steps toward the makeshift bed. "You gonna invite me into your nest, Omega?"

She glanced over her shoulder at the destination. "Is that the standard protocol?"

The laugh spilled out of him, charmed beyond words at her formalized phrasing. He loved this loosened up, lusty version of Della but adored the way she retained her unique formality even in a rapidly escalating moment. He'd never known an Omega like her. There'd never *been* an Omega like her, of that he was absolutely sure.

"Typically." He added a little rumble to the word and was rewarded when her eyelashes fluttered prettily on the high arches of her cheekbones.

"And then what happens?" she breathed, her fingers restlessly clenching and tugging his shirt fabric like she wanted to rip it off and eliminate that small barrier between them.

He wouldn't be upset if she did.

Once her heels touched the edge of the bedding, he paused their forward momentum. A nest boundary demanded respect, and hesitancy from deep inside halted his steps. They teetered on the threshold of not only the nest but also something profound and singular. While he'd never personally serviced an Omega in a Heat, he'd been a bystander to enough to know people and relationships were changed no matter the participants' initial intent. Omega Heats were varied in length but almost always boundless and overwhelming for everyone involved. Alphas and Omegas alike lost their heads and made decisions they'd later reconsider or even regret.

He didn't want that for himself or for Della, yet the persistent beat of desire throbbed in his pelvis like a fist wrapped around his spine, dragging him away from his more sober considerations. Cock swelling, his stomach drew taut, and his teeth gnashed with harnessed desire to bite and claim. But Della didn't want that. That final brink she refused to traverse when she was in her right mind, and he'd be damned if he crossed it when she wasn't. He might be Alpha, and Alphas claimed, but in his soul, he knew if he proceeded without her consent, without laying down her willing tribute to their bond, she'd never forgive him.

Hauling himself back from the metaphorical ledge, he brushed his lips over her forehead, trailing a line of kisses along her proud brow and up to the dampened hairline. The moisture cooled his lips and ardor enough to refocus on the beautiful woman quivering in his arms and everything he needed to do to fill her Heat with mind-bending pleasure.

Lowering his mouth to her ear, he whispered, "You invite me in, then I come into your nice, clean nest and do some very dirty things." Her resulting shiver rippled under his fingers. "The only question is"—snagging the hem of his borrowed shirt, he lifted it up and over her head, baring her skin to his impatient hands—"are you gonna beg for my cock like a good little Omega, or are you gonna pretend you don't want me to use this tight little cunt any fucking way I want?"

A breath hissed through her clenched teeth, her shoulders quaking in response to his coarse words. Would she even be able to respond, or had she already descended too far into Heat delirium?

Working a hand between them, he tangled his fingertips in her curls and lingered at the top of her slit, stroking and teasing the mix of soft and wiry textures. He could get plenty addicted to that sensitive little spot. Sighing, Della sagged against his supporting arm as more of her honeyed perfume released into the air. Slowly, her hips began to squirm and twist, seeking stimulation deeper into her sex. She liked it, too.

Stifling a groan at the wantonness on display, Cal chuckled darkly and flicked a tongue along her dewy hairline, savoring the salt-enhanced burst of her flavor. "Yeah, I know what you want, little queen. You're too stubborn to say it, but here's the thing." Abruptly, he stilled his fingers, and a woeful whine broke through her daze as she wiggled in protest. "You have to invite me into your nest, so I'm gonna need to hear you say it."

Fisting handfuls of his shirt, she raised her eyes, defiance slithering behind the arousal sheen. "An Omega would know what to say, but I can't say I do."

And goddamn if that resistance didn't make his dick approach dangerous levels of hardness. With a thumb on her petulant chin, he tilted her face toward his. "You say, 'Come in my nest and fuck me, Alpha.'"

She slipped her soft, pink tongue out to wet her lips, and he had to stifle another groan. "Come in my nest and fuck me."

He held back, waiting for her to complete the phrase. She didn't, responding with silence and another flare of sapphire-blue opposition, offset by a sensuous curl of her lip. Was she fucking with him? "Come in my nest and fuck me, *Alpha*," he corrected, accessorizing the phrase with a warning tone. He slid his hand from her chin to her neck, circling his thumb over her galloping pulse.

Not to be outdone, Della reached for his aching cock and gave it a good firm squeeze through his straining pants. Caught off guard, Cal grunted, and smugness twisted her pink mouth. "Are you going to knot me with this big Alpha cock?"

An unrestrained growl erupted from his chest. "Yeah, I am." Cal firmed his grip around her throat. "And you're gonna come so hard they'll hear you screaming for miles."

A thick swallow rolled down her neck, and her husky voice vibrated against his palm. "Then come in my nest and fuck me, *Alpha*."

CHAPTER TWENTY-ONE

Della

For the second time, Della followed the slope of Cal's perfectly formed back as he tromped through the woods at a brisk pace. After two days spent alternately fucking and sleeping, with occasional breaks for eating, being upright brought a much-needed change.

Strange, this Heat business. A bizarre mash-up of puberty and menopause all rolled into one horny, never-ending hormonal blur. The Heat dulled her wits. Her sluggish, distractible brain clambered to hold on to *any* thought more substantial than *I'm ready to fuck again now*, which left her little time to process this whole Omega business.

The fresh air helped clear some cobwebs from her logy, sex-addled brain, and her thoughts strayed back to her last notable "female" milestone: menopause, when menses finally ceased. She never knew if it was brought about by natural causes versus a side effect of inadequate and inconsistent availability of food and then multiplied by the unfathomable stress of navigating the time after TheEnd. By that time, fertility ranked so far down on her list of concerns that her only feeling was relief that she wouldn't have to improvise menstrual supplies any longer. One less need to take care of.

Common knowledge presumed that Heat cycles marked a time of enhanced Omega fertility, but for a newly transformed Omega at a very advanced age, the chance of a pregnancy struck her as remote. How could her dusty ovaries have any viable eggs kicking around after all this time? A pregnancy now would be nothing short of a miracle of saint-like proportion. Despite her dubious fertility, with the onset of this Heat, she could no longer deny the reality of this Omega transformation. Certainly, she'd never experienced anything like that before. What that meant for the rest of her life, she had no idea.

So, she dutifully marched behind, ignoring the battered soreness between her legs and the fact that she'd not put up a single word of protest when Cal ordered her to put her shoes on. Had she sunk so far into her Omega nature—still weird to admit that, even to herself—that she acquiesced to his casual dominance without a second thought? Where were they going again?

Oh, right, to check on the net. What was it with men wanting company on fishing trips?

The parallel to her former life struck her fast and hard. When Rakesh developed a fly-fishing obsession, he'd also cajoled her to come along as he trudged through Montana or Wyoming or wherever-the-hell-else to find some epically mythical spot.

"Can't you enjoy your rich-guy hobbies and leave me out of it?" she would grouse every time he proposed another trip.

And, every time, Rakesh would take her in his arms, flashing his wide, brilliant smile, so white and beautiful against the deep bronze of his skin. *"Not very patriotic of you to turn your nose up at experiencing the vast natural beauty of this fine country, Congresswoman,"* he would tease.

"I fail to comprehend how standing waist-deep in water for hours qualifies as experiencing beauty," she would say, and then poke his nose, a playful *boop* that never failed to stretch his grin even more.

But she'd done it. Hating every soggy, boring minute, she'd done it for him.

Uneasiness leached into her reminiscence. Rakesh would never begrudge her taking a lover, but as her eyes roved over the contours of Cal's body, the feelings stirred up were far more tangled than simple lust.

And that was a problem. A big one.

After Rakesh died, she vowed to survive. For him, for the memory of him and the short time they shared on this earth. It was the least she could do to honor him as, God knew, there were no funerals and memorials and gravestones and twenty-one-gun salutes in the years following TheEnd. They hadn't even buried the dead most of the time, choosing instead to burn them in great, heaping, stinking piles.

At the time, she'd been grateful for the loss of her smell.

So, for Rakesh, she survived. Even when she'd been so terrorized by depravity and violence she thought she'd never sleep again, she'd survived. Even when she'd watched women get dragged off to be raped or killed by bands of feral men, she'd hidden and survived. Even when she'd scavenged for moldy food because her body neared collapse, she'd survived. Even when her womb expelled the early pregnancy and she'd said goodbye to the last piece of Rakesh left in the entire world, she'd survived. For him.

But, for herself, she made a different vow.

If she had to survive, then she'd do so without ever opening her heart to anyone ever again. Because Della knew, deep in her soul, that another catastrophic heartbreak was the one thing her ravaged heart couldn't endure.

"Here it is." Cal's rumbly voice broke through her thoughts, and he flashed her a lazy grin, dimples winking in full force. "You wanna have a seat and take a load off?"

He jerked his chin at the oversized rock she'd perched on two days ago, the same one he'd laid her out on before delving between her legs like a starved animal. With a small hum of acknowledgment, Della glanced away, embarrassed at the memory as well as all the others that transpired since this accursed Heat began. Cal got plenty out of the arrangement, but now that she had the available brain cells to pay attention, shadows graced his under eyes, and lines of strain bracketed his lips. He looked unmistakably worse for the wear, yet this peculiar concern for her kidnapper unlocked another host of anxieties, highlighting her rapidly evolving feelings for him.

Hard to complain about some thorough fucking after a century of near-abstinence, but Cal's care far exceeded her carnal needs. Without complaint, he saw to all the other daily necessities: making food, gathering firewood, getting water, washing dishes, clearing ash from the firepit, and a thousand other tasks he completed while she snoozed between bouts of sexual frenzy. Hell, he fluffed the improvised pillow and *tucked her in* at night. Not to mention the way he gently untangled snarls in her hair and cleansed between her legs with warm water and soft cloths. True, he basically "signed up" for these duties when he stole her from Morris Hill, but the niggling thought persisted: any other abducting Alpha would be far less considerate.

Tenderness welled in her chest, and her thoughts converged on a simple but horrifying truth: the more time they spent together, the worse this inconvenient affection would become.

She had to get away from him.

Mindful of her footing, she kneeled on the slippery stones at the water's edge to scoop a few splashes of water on her face. The glacier-fed stream cooled her overheated cheeks, and she scrubbed briskly, as if she could cleanse away the conflicting mess surging through her. Sitting back on her heels, she plucked a small pebble from the ground and tossed it into the water, where it landed with a merry *ploop.*

The stream swished along, too brisk to reflect her countenance, but she didn't need to see it. She knew her face, knew the lines that, unlike Cal's, never softened no matter how much rest she got. He said he didn't care about her age. But... what if he hadn't taken the implications all the way to their logical conclusions? With Alpha aging being what it was, even in his fifties, Cal remained a young man in his prime. Why saddle himself to someone like her? She'd outlived a normal human lifespan, but who knew how much longer that would last? What about a family? Children? What about adventure? He already had two Pack brothers loyal to him. Did he aspire to break off and lead his own Pack someday? He was more than capable, but how would he do that with Della in tow?

The reasons and arguments piled up like a cairn commemorating this impulsive and foolhardy courtship. Being with her made no sense.

"I can hear you thinking clear over here." His teasing drawl poked through her brooding. She flicked him a look, noting that under the canopied trees, his hazel eyes turned a luminous, mossy green. They shone on her with a saucy wink, and her heart clenched in inconvenient adoration. Boots removed and pant legs rolled to his knees, Cal waded into the shallow water, grimacing at the frigid stream. "Come on, let's hear it," he added when she didn't respond.

Della tucked a strand of hair behind her ear. "It's nothing."

"Uh-huh." He took a few more steps, sloshing toward where he'd set up the net like a sieve. "Well, if you're not gonna tell me, I suppose sitting there looking pretty is good enough."

Della snorted and got to her feet, muttering, "You say that, but it's not necessary, you know. Maybe I was passably pretty once, but that was a long, *long* time ago."

Cal paused, hands on his hips. "So I can't say you're pretty now? What's your point?"

Feigning nonchalance, Della brushed some dirt from her sleeve. "I suppose if you've been living with Alphas for too long, you'll be taken by the first woman you see. That's simply—"

Cal tossed his head back with a hearty, rich laughter that had him clutching his belly, derailing her thoughts and melting her defenses completely. As long as she'd lived, had a man ever been more beautiful when he laughed? "I ain't been living under a rock,

Del," he finally wheezed. "I've seen and scented plenty of women, Beta *and* Omega. Hell, I scented those two unmated Omegas back at Morris Hill, and they did absolutely nothing for me, all right? So if you're finished making specious arguments, maybe you can take my word for it and let me rustle up our lunch."

At that, her own surprised giggle bubbled out of her. "Specious?"

His chin lifted in a non-subtle challenge. "Yeah, specious."

"Okay, well..." She lowered her blanket-wrapped bottom to the rock—*still no sign of her goddamn pants*—composing her expression into one of neutral curiosity. "Here's a completely reasonable argument. What about children? You're a young Alpha, so surely you'd like some pups of your own someday."

Cal's shoulder jumped in the smallest of shrugs. "Never really thought about it."

The pathetic attempt at indifference irked her. "Well, maybe you *should*."

Ironically, a picture emerged in *her* mind: Cal, by a creek just like this one, teaching a few adorable, hazel-eyed, school-aged children how to fish while a couple of smaller ones turned over rocks looking for crawdads. Granted, she'd only know him a few days, but possessing his particular brand of quiet, laid-back patience and strength, he'd make an excellent father.

Fully engaged, her imagination went wild. Maybe the whole brood would be on a campout, sleeping rough for a few days with bedding littered around a firepit with a fire going. Would their Omega mother be close by foraging for nuts and berries? Or would she be enjoying some quiet rest at home? A ball of discomfort lodged directly in her throat. Whoever that woman was, she most definitely was not Della.

Impatiently, she cleared the obstruction. "Heat notwithstanding," she brusquely continued, ignoring the cross look on his face, "I can't have children. You should think about that since you're so intent on"—she flapped a testy hand between them—"*this*."

Face tilted to the sky, Cal heaved one giant sigh before splashing out of the stream with such vigor he seemed to be trying to kick all the water from the creek onto the land. The crunch of sand and pebbles signaled his approach, which she stubbornly refused to acknowledge until two large palms gripped her upper arms. "Della, look at me." Shifting only her eyes, she gave him her wary attention. "What the hell is going on? I thought we were past all this."

Her eyes shot open. "Past all this? What's all this?"

His brows speared together. "Whatever it is you're trying to do here. This weak and transparent attempt to convince me that you're not my mate."

Della shuddered. That word again. *Mate.*

"Cal, I am *old*," she said with forced patience. "My face is lined, my hair is faded and half-gray, and my boobs are deflated. Whatever it is you think is between us, it must be the Omega pheromones and scent or whatever. It's obviously potent stuff."

He tipped his face forward, bringing them eye-to-eye as heat simmered in his hazel depths. "You're right. That *is* what I'm responding to, little *Omega*." He emphasized the word with the smallest of growls, and her sex perked up as if it had its own set of ears.

Stupid pussy. Della ground her back teeth. "That's my point. Whatever you're doing, you're not thinking about this logically. What I said that first night is still true: I can't give you what you want. Or need."

He wet his lips and quietly challenged, "How do you know what I need? I don't recall you ever asking me." Big, warm, Alpha-sized hands slid up her arms to her neck and into her hair. With a gentle fist, he angled her chin up to capture her full attention. The lines of his face softened and shone with a sincerity that plucked a deep chord in Della's chest. "Della," he began, voice gritty and raw, "you're a gift I'd never dared to hope for and a blessing I don't deserve."

Against all her inclinations and arguments, Della's heart cracked open like an egg, oozing a mess of affection all over her knotted-up insides. He couldn't possibly mean any of that, a part of her protested, yet the earnest devotion on his face argued the point more than words ever could. No question, he believed the words he said, and—her stomach somersaulted into a free fall—she believed he meant them, too. Sound rushed in her ears like she'd plunged to the bottom of a deep pool. Love. He was talking about *love*.

"And," he continued, oblivious to her emotional chaos, "since you didn't ask, I'll tell you. There's nothing I want or need that you can't give me." Inclining his head, he pressed a kiss to her brow.

Dizzy with feeling, Della groped for a line of logic to follow through this madness. "What about what I need?"

"You need to be safe, cared for, and protected," he explained, "and that's what I intend to do. That's what I *am* doing."

Della's mouth turned to sand. "You can't protect me from everything."

Case in point: he couldn't protect her from all these inconvenient feelings rampaging through her chest. He couldn't protect her affections from blooming in the lazy Sunday warmth of his appeal. He couldn't save her from the heartbreak she risked by surrendering to this relationship, not as a biological need but as an emotional one. He couldn't stop her from falling in love with him.

"*Yes,* I can." Sudden vehemence ignited behind his eyes. "Maybe I messed it up once, but I'm not making that mistake again. Not with you." As if proving a point, he smashed his lips to hers, sealing the declaration with a kiss that weakened her knees. Reeling, she gave herself over to it, running her hands up his strong back, mashing her breasts to his bare chest, moaning into his mouth.

How easy it would be to totally succumb. To disappear inside this insane romance and ride it till the end, wherever that took her. She felt like a helium balloon, weightless and bouncing in the breeze, striving to detach and ascend and touch the blue, blue sky. Only a thin but tenacious ribbon of anxiety tethered her to the earth, and for the love of everything, she couldn't cut the string.

CHAPTER TWENTY-TWO

Cal

Heart still thundering in his chest, Cal set Della back on her rock perch and took a few slow, gliding steps backward, curving his lips in a smile. "As much as I enjoy refuting these points you're trying to make, I gotta get our lunch figured out before you start trying to climb me like a tree again."

She pulled her knees up to her chest and hugged them tight to her body, curling into an adorable little ball. Worry creased her face, despite her best effort to wipe her expression clean. "So, are you going to tell me where you learned a word like specious?"

He waded into the water up to his knees, biting back a curse at the chill. "Pa had some very particular ideas about his children and their education. Very big on vocabulary."

"Yeah?" The worry disappeared from Della's face, replaced by intrigue.

Cal nodded, relieved she showed interest in a topic other than Why I'm Not Your Mate. She'd abandoned the I'm-not-an-Omega argument—the onset of her Heat put *that* issue to rest—but seamlessly pivoted to this equally exasperating one. Although, compared with talking about Pa and what happened in his Pack, maybe it wasn't so bad after all.

"He was a lawyer but left it to become a rancher, even before TheEnd. He schooled us through most of his university and law textbooks." He shot her a bitter glance. "He liked a lively debate."

"You didn't care for it?" Della gnawed on her bottom lip, now totally engrossed in his reminiscences about Pa. *Shit*, he really didn't want to talk about this.

"Pa was a stubborn man," he said evenly. "Had a great deal of... expectations."

"Of you?"

"Uh-huh." Cal grunted and bent to wrangle a fish caught in the net, coming up with a flopping trout. He tossed it on the shore. Two or three more and they could get back to the cave. He didn't like being out here longer than necessary.

"My dad had a lot of expectations for my brother," Della mused, sliding off the rock to pick up a stone. "Wanted him to follow his footsteps into politics. But Anthony enlisted in the navy, instead."

Cal snatched another small trout from the net, debating whether to set it free or eat it and decided on freedom for the little guy. "Put his hopes in the wrong kid, did he?"

Della laughed. "He got over it." She whipped a flat rock and snorted when it dropped into the water instead of hopping along the top. With a stern look, she tried another and managed a few paltry skips. "Unlike Ant, Dad was happy with everything I did. Maybe he didn't expect anything, so everything was a delight. Maybe it was because I was a girl. I don't really know, but when I showed interest in politics, he supported me any way he could." She dusted the dirt off her palms and faced him. "Do you miss your Pa?"

All the old, haunting guilt flamed up his throat like acid indigestion. He swallowed and swallowed again, the sour taste coating his mouth. "If I do," he said quietly, "I got no one to blame but myself."

Della took a step toward him, riveted. "How do you mean?"

His eyes pinged from landmark to landmark: rock, stump, moss, fern, anywhere but meeting Della's earnest gaze. Why had he mentioned it? Why tell her his darkest secret? Why were these memories crying out for attention now when she teetered on the verge of actually accepting him, accepting *them*? He carried the burden of shame and learned to live with it, but in this moment, he knew Della's condemnation was the one thing he couldn't handle.

Thickness gathered in his throat. "I killed my Pa... and some others." Cal couldn't feel his feet. The numbness burned and throbbed like an open wound, but compared to the pain and fear gouged in his chest, it barely registered. "Got banished from the Pack I was born into, from the Pack I was meant to inherit, to lead. I can never return or I'll be put to death."

Movement flickered at the corner of his vision, Della's hand flying up to brace against her chest. "What happened?"

Restless, he wiped his hands on his pants, rubbing and rubbing at the thick denim as if he could wash the blood from his hands. Too late. It was too late to save his family, too late to salvage his Pack, too late to hide this shameful secret from her. "There was a bridge." Voice choking, he paused to clear his throat. "The Pack was going on a trading trip, like the Morris Hill Alphas, and Pa put me in charge of scouting the route to make sure it was safe. I did. I checked it out and double-checked… but there was a bridge."

Everything around him ceased to exist. Della, the creek, the fish fighting against the net, the woods, the breeze, the sky. Nothing touched him. Nothing warmed that desolate place inside him, where all he could do was stare at that fucking bridge. Rusted metal and chipped concrete, like everything else in the AfterEnd, it told the story of the decay of a civilization. All those impressive monuments to engineering were laid to waste, left to taunt the people who pecked out a life among the ruins like chickens scratching a dirt yard for worms.

"It crossed a river that flooded occasionally." He heard himself talking, his voice faraway and sad. His chest hurt like he'd never take a full breath again. "I don't know how many times over the years the bridge had been submerged. There's no way to know, but I scoped it out. I rode over it with my horse several times. It wasn't pretty, but I thought it was safe enough." Chin tucked against his chest, and his shoulders heaved in a shame-filled sigh. "And it was safe, for one Alpha and a horse. Not safe for an entire caravan with loaded wagons and livestock."

A petite, feminine gasp lanced through his turmoil, and he glanced up. She stood motionless, compassion shining in her eyes that only twisted the knife. He'd meant what he'd said earlier that Della was a blessing he did not deserve. Because of this, because of what he'd done to his family, his blood, his Pack.

"There was no warning." Cal's voice barely rose above the bubbling water, but he pressed on, unable to stop the story now that he'd begun. "One snap of a beam, and then everything dropped. Those that weren't crushed outright drowned before we could get to them. Everyone on that bridge died. My Pa, my sister… Ten adults,"—he paused to choke back another mouthful of bile—"two children."

It was an accident. A simple, stupid accident that could've happened to anyone, but it didn't matter. The pain ate at his soul like the myth of Prometheus and the vulture. An inexhaustible supply of guilt for his conscience to gnaw on for the rest of his life.

"They blamed you? Your Pack?" Della asked, her voice soft with concern.

He jerked a nod, his body stiff but moving again. "My sister's mate, my brother-in-law, he was angry, furious, and desperate. They had pups... my nieces and nephew... and I killed their mama. And my ma, she wasn't much better with Pa being dead. Everyone lost someone; it destroyed the Pack." This part of the story came easier. The part where they banded together against him and decided on a punishment that would change his life as neatly as he'd changed so many others'. "No one knew what to do. *I* didn't know what to do, how to bring everyone together. Pa had intended for me to take over as Alpha when he passed, but my brother-in-law challenged me an... well... I couldn't even muster up a real fight." He lifted a shoulder. "He took all his anger and hurt out on me, and I was happy to let him. When it was over, he was Alpha of Alphas, and I was banished."

He'd lost everything he'd held dear: his home, his family, his future, and in their place, guilt and regret took up a perverse vigil to keep him company at night. Unable to look at her, unable to risk the reflection of his shame on her face, Cal turned to his task. With a few rough tugs, he unfastened the net and chucked it out of the water in a sodden tangle, like this was any other fishing trip and he hadn't laid his most traumatic history at her feet.

Eyes downcast, Cal splashed through the water on unfeeling feet, dread pummeling his insides. He needed to look at her, to face the consequences, and get it over with. Hiding in his head was a chickenshit Beta thing to do. At the edge, he stepped onto the pebbled shore when the force of a small body almost knocked him back on his ass. Della hurled herself into his arms and, high on her tiptoes, hugged his wooden body as if she could make up for all his years of solitude in one single embrace. He encircled his arms around her narrow back, knowing he didn't deserve this comfort but needed it all the same.

"Della," he whispered, an anguished plea to withhold her proffered comfort, which only made her cinch tighter. Her soft curves molded to his body, as tight as any sexual embrace they'd yet accomplished, but all the sweeter for it having absolutely nothing to do with her Heat. His heart swelled in his chest, not with guilt but with the sneaking realization that, for the first time, she was willingly and enthusiastically comforting *him*.

"It was an accident," she hissed in his ear. "You *have* to know that. It wasn't your fault."

Overcome, Cal buried his face in the crook of her neck, breathing in her sweet black currant scent. If he didn't ground himself in something tangible, he feared he would fly apart completely. The whispered words trickled into his blood, pumping to every inch of his body with every galloping *da-dum* of his heart.

It's not. Your fault. It's not. Your fault.

He wasn't sure he believed it. Wasn't sure he ever could believe it, but for Della to believe it, to say it out loud in solace for his aching soul, it was enough. More than enough.

She pulled back, every line of her face set in seriousness. "What they did to you was hurtful and *wrong*. But you punished yourself more, wandering for decades, never settling down with a new Pack. Haven't you?" A shaky sigh rattled out of him, all the confirmation he could manage to this final unmasking. "Until you met Hunt and came to Morris Hill. What changed? Why join a Pack now?"

She rasped her knuckles over his beard scruff, and he captured her little fist, bringing it to his lips with a rueful flick of his tongue. "I got tired."

She paused, her mouth pulled to one side, an unconvinced twitch of her cheek. "So why fight with Silas? Why steal me so you can never go back? I don't understand."

A sudden lightness washed over him, like the bucketload of badness he carried inside him got dumped out on the ground. He sighed in resignation, not even feeling any resurgence of anger at the mention of that asshole Silas. "Silas, being a lazy fucker, refused to do the full patrol route we were assigned that day. He and I had words about it, which resulted in my kicking his ass to persuade him to finish it. Once we got back, he tried to make it look like I attacked him to cover up his laziness."

"But..." Della's face contorted into the look she got when she geared up to pursue something bothering her, a look he now knew very well. What he also recognized, however, were the faint drops of perspiration collecting at her hairline and the growing pink cast to her pale cheeks. Another burst of sexual hunger hovered on the threshold, and he needed to get her home. "But you could've stayed and talked to Hunt... Why steal me and make things worse?"

Cal scanned every inch of her pensive, flushed face, drinking it up like parched earth absorbed a gentle rain, filled with the same desperate, grateful wonderment. He raised his rough hands and cupped her delicate, soft cheeks. "That Pack didn't mean a goddamn thing to me except that it led me to you."

She locked her hands around his wrists. "Cal..."

Leaning forward, he pressed a kiss to her feverish forehead. "I could lead a long, lonely, unnatural life— a lone Alpha without a Pack—and somehow make the best of it." Thumbs stroking her cheekbones, he looked deep into his Omega's eyes, a deep and powerful feeling strumming in his veins, "But I knew I couldn't bear to live a single fucking day without you, Della."

Reclaiming her lips, he hugged her to him, letting all his angst and passion flow freely, letting it season the taste of their kiss in all its messy complexity. Yeah, he'd left his friends behind and abandoned his Pack for a second time. Sure, he'd claimed an irascible Omega who'd fight him every step of the way. And, yes, he'd brought her to this place with only the clothes on her back and the solemn promise that he'd care for and protect her with every fiber of his being. It wasn't perfect nor even ideal, but it was everything he wanted and exactly where he needed to be.

CHAPTER TWENTY-THREE

Cal

Della stretched her arms above her head like a lazy cat in a patch of sunshine. The soft smile she aimed at him morphed into a massive yawn, making him chuckle as he arranged kindling to start a fire. She'd snoozed in bed till almost noon, and he'd done his best to be quiet and let her sleep.

After another late night working off a surge of Heat lust, she needed her rest. And while he couldn't believe this would ever be the case, he needed some too. Not that he didn't enjoy fucking Della into a noddle-limbed puddle several times a day, but he didn't know how much more he could take before claiming her once and for all.

Each time they came together got better and hotter and more explosive, and the urge to sink his teeth into her flesh grew stronger and stronger. The compulsion roared in his blood, and he labored under the competing demands to keep himself in check while also attending to Della's needs. Honestly, he skirted the edge of his control every single time. Last night, he'd gnashed his teeth and torn through the blanket tucked under her shoulder, shredding the fabric like a teething puppy.

Five days had passed since she'd held the dull knife to his throat, and they hadn't spoken about a claiming bite since. Selfishly, he wanted to hear it from her lips (preferably begging for it between breathless moans as he sunk his knot deep and tight in her cunt). He'd coaxed plenty of desperate pleas from his Omega over the course of her Heat. With the proper inducement, the little queen would beg like the lowliest guttersnipe.

"Fuck me hard, Alpha."
"I need your knot, Alpha. Please give it to me, please."
"Fill my mouth with your Alpha cock, I want to taste you deep in my throat."

Aware of a tightening in his pants, he glanced at his yawning and sex-messy mate. Hell, maybe he wasn't ready for her Heat to end after all.

But nagging survival concerns intruded on his amorous musings. Once he got this fire started, he'd cook up the last portion of porridge. The bread was long gone, and his dried stores depleted. Sure, he could hunt and fish to feed them, but even salt, which made a basic diet palatable, dwindled. Plus, Della needed things like fresh vegetables and fruit to reset her system after a Heat.

No question. They'd have to move on. And soon. He scrutinized her a bit closer: her coloring normalized back to pale pink, and no beads of sweat dotted her hairline. If her Heat had passed, they could make preparations to vacate the cave and plot a course east. Rubbing crust from her eyes, she reached for the hastily discarded pile of clothes on the floor. Shaking them out, she took a quick sniff and wrinkled her nose. "Ugh. Maybe I wish my smell *hadn't* come back. These clothes need a bath." Face adorably screwed up, she delicately sniffed herself. "And I do, too."

Cal grinned. "We could take care of that today if you're up for it."

The hot springs weren't far, but they had yet to pay a visit. He'd held off mentioning it to her, but between her Heat episodes, he'd patrolled the area aggressively and regularly. A few times, he'd sensed Alphas on the periphery of his detection, but no one had come as far as the hot springs or beyond.

Despite his worries, the woods remained eerily quiet, which was both a relief and a disappointment. Honestly, he expected a better effort from the Morris Hill Alphas. If not for concern for Della, he'd figured they would at least pursue him to save face since he'd stolen something of "theirs." Perhaps Simon concocted some story that drew their attention elsewhere. In the chaos of that night, Cal could've ridden in any direction, and it would be impossible for them to search all possible routes away from the settlement. They would've had to make hard choices about where to search and easily could've made the wrong ones.

Raking fingers through her long hair, Della separated sections for plaiting. "Does it smell like rain?

All I can scent is myself and, well"—she blushed—"you."

Warmth billowed in his chest. "I'm not complaining, but I'll go check. If it's all clear, we can go." He pointed a finger at her nose. "*After* you eat something. You need to get your strength back up."

Quirking her lips, she gave him a jaunty salute. "Yes, sir."

With a quick, playful tug of her hair, he jumped to his feet and strode to the cave entrance. Midday sunshine poured in, prompting all sorts of images to form in his mind of Della, *naked*, luxuriating in the hot springs.

Today could be a very good day indeed.

Ducking outside, he looked up into a cloudless blue sky and sucked the clean forest air into his lungs. Immediately a whiff of something out of place throttled his good mood. Sweet and delicate, Omega scent drifted to his nose on the breeze. Apprehension coursed through him, and all the blood flow diverted to prime his frozen muscles. He leaned further out the opening, and another gust shot up his nose. Not one scent, but there were two. Straining his ears, he picked up the tinny notes of two chattering voices drifting through the forest. His stomach solidified to a stony brick. What in the fresh hell? Why *the fuck* were Omegas wandering through this area?

He breathed deeply again, sifting through the forest smells for any accompanying Alpha odor. Nostrils flaring, he tried again, picking up a weak Alpha tang, not strong in any one direction, but definitely here somewhere.

Alphas! Near his Della! Omegas forgotten, black fright ripped through him, and he slipped back into the cave.

"What is it?" Della asked at full volume.

"Hush," he hissed, with enough alarm that she was on her feet and at his elbow within a second. If there were other Omegas here, might Della call out and betray their position, perhaps in an attempt to save herself? Surely not now, after everything they'd been through? Yet she still didn't wear his mark. That fact poked uncomfortably between his ribs.

Refusing to risk it, Cal moved before she could sense the intruders, securing her shoulders with one arm and covering her mouth with the other. Her body stiffened, and he brushed a reassuring kiss along her temple. "Someone's out there," he whispered directly in her ear. "I don't know friend or foe, so I need you to stay quiet. Can you do that for me?"

She nodded as much as she could move within the tight confines of his arms. Her back braced to his front, he edged them closer to the entrance, craning his neck to look down without sticking his full head out in the open.

"... this is too far." An Omega's voice floated into the cave, directly below the cave entrance. "Riddick said anywhere past the hot springs is off our territory."

"And you think he's keeping her captive on our territory? How much sense would that make?" the second Omega retorted before opening her mouth to bellow. "Della! Della, are you out here?"

All his worst fears confirmed, Cal's grip seized tight around his Omega, and she whimpered, trying to crane her neck outside to look at the search party. "Hush," he hissed, more aggressive this time.

The entire situation revealed itself to him in a rush of confusing and contradictory facts. Two unmated Omegas were wandering through the woods on the edge of the Morris Hill Pack's territory, looking for Della. Heart thudding, he sniffed the air again, tasting their pure Omega scents as well as another hint of Alpha musk. Was someone with these Omegas? A guard or chaperone? They ought to have one this far from home. What the hell was going on? He pivoted his nose this way and that, trying to locate the Alpha, but the scent registered too faint to be accompanying the Omegas.

"Della! Della! Where are you?" the first Omega joined in, half-heartedly calling out before addressing her companion with an exasperated sigh. "Rue, this is stupid. It's been a week already, they're long gone. We need to go back."

"Hang on a minute. Don't you scent Alpha on the breeze? Someone's here or has been here." The defiant Omega, a slight young woman with a stubbled head, cupped her hands around her mouth and tried again. "Della! Della!"

One thing was clear to him and probably Della as well: no Alpha accompanied these two on their excursion. Given the second Omega's discomfort, Cal concluded they had set out on this highly dubious venture without telling any Morris Hill Alpha what they were doing. Which meant the Alpha tang he'd detected had nothing to do with these two and likely originated from some other foreign presence in the area; one that posed a threat to both the Omegas and to Della.

Stupid, naïve, irresponsible Omegas!

Della's nails sliced into his arm, her body trembling. Brows pinched together, skin pulled taut with strain, the tears welling on her lower lids made him feel like a total piece of shit. Here were two Omegas worried enough to endanger themselves to come look for her, and he stood in the way of their reunion.

Once he let Della go, she would kill him. "*Shh*," he murmured in her ear, barely audible. "You can scream at me once they're gone."

After a few more feeble calls, the Omegas tromped back toward the hot springs, their voices dejected as their chatter and scents began to fade. Cal listened intently, all of his Alpha senses tuned to the outside world to survey the threat to those young Omegas and, most importantly, *his* Omega.

"I'm gonna let you go"—he kept his volume lower than the aggressive call of a bluejay in a nearby tree—"but you need to be silent. Someone else is out there."

Della nodded once, and he dropped his hold on her. Immediately, she spun to face him, a tear roaming down her cheek. On tiptoes, she grabbed his scruff and jerked his ear to her mouth. "There's Alpha scent in the woods!" she whisper-screamed. "They're in *danger*."

"I *know*." His head pounded. Impatience rolled off her in waves. She clearly wanted to go after the Omegas herself. Or, at the very least, send him to chaperone their return to wherever they left their horses. But leaving the cave risked tainting the air with his scent, which would be obvious to any nefarious Alphas prowling around, not to mention risk having their safe haven discovered and leaving Della vulnerable without protection while he tracked the Omegas.

Fuck. Fuck!

Della's fists pounded on his chest as she continued to berate him in a harsh whisper. "You have to go help them!" He snagged her fists in one of his own, fixing her with a silencing stare while his brain spun itself in circles.

He had no way of knowing how many Alphas might be sneaking around the dense wood. His instincts told him only one, but he couldn't verify that for certain. If he left the cave, he could very well be walking into a trap or a fucking ambush. Sure, he could hold his own against one Alpha, maybe two, possibly three... but beyond that? What if he scented a scout and an entire Pack encroached behind him? He'd be held captive or killed, and then who would protect Della?

A tense minute passed. Then the thrashing sound of large bodies moving through brush rustled on the wind. Della froze, her nostrils flaring as Cal sniffed again, getting a choking nose-full of dirty Alpha stink. Color drained from Della's face.

The sound grew closer. Releasing her fists and holding up a finger, Cal shifted them farther back into the shadow of the cave's entrance and reached for his knife belt. If he'd had his way, he'd drag Della to the pitch-black back of the cave and leave her there while he investigated. But, knowing the stubborn woman, she'd not only protest, but she'd come out of hiding as soon as he stepped one foot out the door.

His fist clenched around the leather handle of his buck knife in impotent aggravation. *God dammit.* He hadn't faced an attack totally alone and unprepared for years, and now he looked down the barrel of one with his Omega at risk.

"Why don't we grab them now?" an Alpha voice rose up from outside the cave, entirely too close for comfort. Instinctively, Cal pushed Della behind him.

A second voice chimed in, angry and agitated and loud. "That prick has been holding out on us! He said they only had *mated* Omegas in that fucking settlement. Motherfucker lying through his fucking teeth! If they let those two stroll away unnoticed, who knows how many they have?"

"What're you thinking?"

The coarse susurrus of big feet crunching tender plants ceased as the pissed-off Alpha stopped to think. *If he worked any harder at it, he'd hurt himself,* Cal thought bitterly.

"Change of plans," the Alpha said. "We don't wait to meet up with that prick. We wait till it's dark, surprise them and take the Omegas and horses for ourselves."

"And the Alphas? He said they have a dozen or so. We can't hold off that many."

An evil chuckle wafted through the air. "They can't fight us if they're fighting a fire. We'll burn the whole fucking place down."

Della sucked in a gasp, her hand flying over her mouth at the noise she'd made. Cal reached behind and gave her hip a soothing pat. Those two asswipes made so much noise with their mouths and their feet that he sincerely doubted they'd hear anything louder than their own farts.

"And the Omegas back at camp, what'll we do with them?"

His nerves tensed. These fuckers had *Omegas*, too? But they wanted more; they wanted to steal the Morris Hill women and intended to burn the place down to do it. Oh, holy shit, this situation was bad. Really, *really* bad.

The plotting bastard grunted. "We'll have to take them, tie 'em up and stash them in the woods while we work. They'll keep their mouths shut if they think they'll be getting fed."

The Omegas were hungry, too... Starved? Abused? Imprisoned? He felt sick, all his protective instincts instantly at war with each other. Protect Della, protect the Morris Hill Omegas, protect these nameless, faceless Omegas unfortunate enough to be in a Pack with these two repugnant Alphas.

"Hey." An ominous pause descended, and Cal held himself stiff, fighting the urge to poke his head out and get a good look at the bastards. "Are you picking up any other Alpha scent? I'm getting something, maybe another Omega, too..."

A long, brittle minute passed while Cal held his breath as if he could keep his own smell locked away by not breathing. If he could track those Alphas, they could likewise track him right to the cave. Once Della's Heat arrived, he hadn't been especially careful to hide his tracks as he'd gone to and fro. Silently, he cursed himself. *Sloppy.*

"Eh," the leader grunted in response. Feet crashing through the underbrush again, his voice started to fade. "We're close to those hot springs, so it's probably leftover from whoever boiled their balls in there today. Come on. Those Omegas are long gone. Let's head back to camp."

The Alphas continued on their way, heading north away from the cave, but instead of relief, a tight throb pulsed at the base of Cal's skull. The information avalanche of the last few minutes promised an almighty headache: Omegas ambling unprotected, searching for Della and coming uncomfortably close to finding her; rogue Alphas planning a merciless attack; someone—Cal suspected he knew who—in league with the rogues and feeding them information about Morris Hill.

All of it enough to make his stomach cramp with worry.

Della, his not-yet-claimed Omega, shook behind him. *She* was the priority, he reminded himself, and that clarified things. He needed to think of a way through this mess. None of it would touch his mate, not while he lived.

CHAPTER TWENTY-FOUR

Della

Della's thoughts swirled so fast and furious she wondered if her concussion had resurfaced again.

Rue and Zorah had come looking for her. *Her*. The poignancy socked her right in the guts. Days had passed with no sign of the Morris Hill Alphas, but these two small Omegas braved the risk, putting themselves in more danger than they even knew, for *her*. How had they gotten away from the settlement without anyone noticing? How had they spirited horses out from under Sloan's nose? Cal said they were a half day's ride from Morris Hill. Surely the girls hadn't walked the whole way here. And, for all that was holy, how had they avoided being nabbed by those two disgusting deplorables skulking around the forest?

Their pungent Alpha stink seared her ever-more-sensitive nose with every breath. They reeked of filth, evil, and lust—a bad, *bad* combination. Shaking with fury, Della tipped forward and rested her nose in Cal's back, sucking in deep inhales of his soothing scent to displace their rankness from her nostrils.

Slowly, the tense line of Cal's shoulders softened, and Della ventured a small tug on his shirt.

"Who were they?" she whispered. "Where did they come from?"

Cal spun around, and before she could speak again, he'd gathered her up and carried her into the black recesses of the cave. His eyes blazed out from dusky sockets, bearing down on her with a fierceness that sent her pulse into palpitations.

"I think they're gone," he said, voice still pitched low, "but we should be careful. There may be more."

She fisted his shirtfront with both hands, yanking him toward her. His stubborn chin, with the impossibly handsome cleft, harshened in the shadows, taking on a maniacal contour. "We *have* to warn the settlement. If we leave now—"

"No."

The word slammed into her like she'd run face-first into an invisible door. "But—"

He gave one tight head shake. "I said no, Della. We're staying here tonight, and then in the morning, we're going east. We'll start over, you and me."

A shriek leaped up her throat, but she gulped it down, struggling to keep her voice under control. "What? No! We have to warn them—"

"No, we don't." His tone was hard and unyielding, unlike any she'd yet heard from him. Her mouth fell open, confusion and disbelief dancing a tango in her head. "Going back there is walking headfirst into a trap. I won't put you in danger, so don't ask me to."

Heat flamed up her neck, losing her battle to keep her voice down. "So, you're going to let Morris Hill burn? Let those girls be taken captive? They came looking for me." She slapped a palm against her chest. "And now you're asking me to abandon them to those monsters without a fight? What about the other Omegas? And all the children?" Fury propelled her forward, and she pushed at his immoveable chest.

"Keep your voice *down*." Cal crowded her against the wall, flashing his hand up to circle her neck as he bore down on her like a man possessed. "I am *not* risking you," he snarled a low promise. "Not for them, not for *anything*."

"But... but..." Della worked to still her flailing chest, hysteria looming a few scant breaths away. "If we warned them..."

"They will take you." His beautiful lips curled around the harshly whispered words like they were an insult to him. "If we go back to 'warn' them, they will *take you from me*!" The force of his hushed vitriol hit her like a slap to the face, and Della recoiled, stunned by the unexpected forcefulness from laid-back Cal.

The stone wall dug into her back, and the Alpha's stony intransigence imprisoned her front. His broad torso heaved tortured breaths, and Della's chest hurt as all the nightmare images crashed through her mind in a chilling sequence. Morris Hill on fire, the Alphas dead, the Omegas captured, the children... slaughtered? Abandoned? Her home and everyone she cared about gone.

No... not again.

She couldn't go through that again.

Desperation. Pure, undiluted desperation made the decision. It placed her hand on top of his and squeezed his fingers tighter around her throat. "Then claim me." Her words were hoarse, but their meaning plain. "Do it," she commanded, louder and with more resolve. "They can't separate us if we're bonded." Her voice cracked on the last word as the reality exploded in full focus. Claimed. Bonded. Irrevocably tied to him.

"You'd do that?" His expression turned wary, thumb caressing the base of her neck. "You'd submit to me? Now?"

White noise crashed in her ears. Della had known a great many Alphas in the AfterEnd. Some she'd run from, hid from, and protected others from. Others she'd bargained with, worked beside, argued with, and lived among. Yet none had ever made her feel a fraction of the things she'd felt for Cal in the last few short days. Not even Hunter, her onetime best friend, ever came close to inspiring her to make an offer such as the one she willingly, impulsively threw in front of him.

Yes, he'd stolen her away from her home, but he'd been patient, caring, and attentive. He was clever, humble, and honest. The night prior, drunk on sex hormones, she'd come perilously close to begging him to claim her without anything near as serious at stake. So, no, she wasn't scared of being claimed by Cal.

She was afraid she was falling in love with him.

Her stomach wrung itself to the point of pain. Could she do this? Could she really, truly break the vow she'd made to herself a century before?

The faces of the Morris Hill residents—the Omegas and the pups and, yes, even the aggravating Alphas—paraded through her mind. Not as they were now, living and whole, but as ghosts in her memories, gathered with the ranks of all the others who'd died while Adeline Cabrese improbably lived on.

She couldn't stop the events of TheEnd, couldn't mitigate the aftermath, but this time she *had* something that she could do to prevent a catastrophe from befalling her community of twenty years. If the horror those reprobates discussed came to pass, how would she ever forgive herself?

Tilting her chin up, she linked eyes with Cal. "If you promise we'll go and warn the settlement, then yes. Do this thing, and I'll be yours forever. If that's what you want."

He stepped into her, the hard ridge in his pants a clear reaction to this proposal. "There's no going back on this," he said, voice rasping. "You'll wear my mark, your scent will change, you'll be bonded to me and only me. Everyone will know." He leaned into her space, his lips a hairsbreadth from her own. "Wherever you go, you'll never run from me. Wherever you go, you'll be mine."

Della's entire body trembled: from fear, from longing, from pure, unbridled exhilaration. *Yes! Alpha wants you! Let him take it!* Her inner voice rejoiced. She steeled herself against it, held herself back from pressing her neck into his hand and escalating his grip on her throat, stopped herself from touching his lips with hers, reeled herself back from the edge of insanity, if only in her mind. It seemed important, critical even, that she held something back.

He can claim me, she argued with that inner voice, *but I can't love him. I won't. I refuse.*

The silent reiteration of the vow soothed her frazzled nerves the smallest of degrees. "Promise me," she forced out, "we'll warn the settlement. No lies. *Promise.*"

His grip closed around her throat, the pressure as much a vow as when he spoke the words, "I promise."

Feeling Cal's uneven breath on her damped skin, Della licked her lips and surrendered. "Then do it."

He came at her then with mouth and tongue and hands and teeth. His calm so shattered he tore the clothes from his body, leaving them in piles and tatters as he lifted her up and carried her to the bed that, somehow, had become *theirs*. Unable to hold on to any amount of reserve, spurred on by the depth of his need, she failed to stem the tide of rising lust. She might stop her heart from loving him, but her body was wholly his.

Dropped to her feet near the sleeping pallet, the messy pile of makeshift bedding beckoned as if everything that had happened since she left Morris Hill had led her to this exact moment. Behind her, Cal's naked body pressed to her own, his urgency singing like a struck tuning fork. Holding her in place, he kissed her shoulders and neck with sloppy, open-mouthed hunger. He cradled her breasts, hefting and squeezing, rubbing his thumbs over her nipples with proprietary aplomb, and she arched into his touch, wanting more and more, and never enough.

"Are you going to beg?" he goaded, adding that delirium-inducing growl accenting his words. Slick rushed from her body, and Cal wasted no time snaking a hand in to catch the first drops on his waiting fingers. Growling, he stroked through her hot sex, spreading the wet in large, sloppy swipes. His palm clamped over her pussy, a delicious shudder radiating from the tight hold. "Beg for my cock, little Omega queen."

Della gasped. Did he even know what his words did to her? Overwhelmed, she could barely see straight through her lust-clouded vision, could barely make sense of all the sensations zinging over her skin, barely aware he wanted something more from her. He wanted *words*. A damp palm smacked her pussy, and she yelped, both from surprise and the answering spasm in her core. "Do it," he snarled in her ear.

Her body a vibrating string, she spoke in a broken whisper, "Please fuck me."

"Not good enough." He delivered another smack. "More."

Della's knees wobbled and threatened to buckle. She inhaled through her nose and out her mouth, feeling a future she wasn't sure she could handle hurtle through time and space and into her reality. But the time for doubt and equivocation had long since passed. The threshold of the bed, the *nest*, waited, as did her Alpha.

Her Alpha, her Alpha, her Alpha.

The chant resounded through her head like a drumbeat, that wicked inner voice ecstatically dictating the next words that flowed from her tongue. "Fuck me, Alpha. Fill me with your big cock. Do it now. *Please.*"

Hands on her hips, he urged her forward and whispered in her ear, "On your knees."

The words crackled through her nervous system, and her body obeyed, falling to all fours, cushioned by soft bedding that already bore the evidence of their mating. After days of her Heat, their intimate scents mingled, adding a certain sordidness to complete the erotic tableau. In all her years, Della never once thought she'd crave that kind of coarseness. But once Cal uttered those shocking words, they wove into her psyche, hooked deep, and supercharged her arousal. On her hands and knees, she lifted her ass in supplication to the fevered mess of their lust.

Cal's huge body hit the bed behind hers. His thighs, firm and so perfectly *solid*, kicked her knees apart. The strain registered in her hips, a delicious stretch, opening her to the moment as well as the man. "Cal," she groaned, restless with impatience as every second stretched thinner and thinner. This joining differed from the others. Gone was the slow, sensual climb. This was hot and fast and *huge*. *"Alpha."*

"That's right. I'm your Alpha." Huge hands stilled her hips, and with one quick motion, he entered her, rocking her forward with the force. Della fisted the cloth, the filling sensation so deeply satisfying she let out a thankful groan. "Say it again," he ordered, the sound of his voice as erotic as anything else touching her, as erotic as anything she'd experienced in her whole, long life.

"Fuck me." She said on a moan that echoed around the cave as she thrust herself back, grinding her ass against his thighs and belly and, most importantly, stuffing herself with his hardness. He slid out and punched back in, ready and willing to grant her request. "Fuck me, Alpha. Make me yours."

"Oh my god." His voice skated over her skin, deep and gritty, yet full of wonder.

Faced away from him, she felt everything more. His hands soothed up and down her spine, skimmed over her hips, and separated handfuls of her bottom so he could fuck into her deeper. Every stroke thudded from her core to the top of her head. Grappling, she braced on one elbow and reached back, anchoring her hand around his thigh to cling tight and urge him on. He liked this. In response, he snapped his hips against hers faster, hands groping wildly for whatever handful of her he could find, moving from place to place, restless and greedy, her thigh, her belly, her breast. He took what he wanted as if driven by his desire rather than catering to hers.

And that made her *crazy*. Seizing one of his wandering hands, she brought it between her legs, situating his fingers where every stroke of his cock would rub exactly *right* on the strong, capable hand.

Another growl rushed out of Cal, reverberating along her back and forcing more slick to gush from her body. "Come here," he said, fisting a handful of her hair and hauling her upright till her back hit his chest. Wrapping a hand around her throat, he made a sound more animal than human, embodying the worst Alpha stereotype she'd ever allowed herself to imagine. "Are you mine, Della? Are you mine to do with what I want, whenever I want?"

Questions she'd asked herself many times over the years, listening to Omegas wax rapturous about their Alpha mates, reared their heads. What was the appeal of sex with an Alpha? How could a knot ever feel good? Who'd ever want to be the focus of that sort of unhinged attention? To be locked together with a snarling beast of a man who could move you and hold you and fuck you any way they pleased without a single thing you could do about it? Who'd want to feel so helpless and vulnerable and deprived of control?

Turns out, she'd been wrong about a lot of things.

Cal could do any and all those things without causing fear or disgust because she—the realization bowled her over—*trusted* him and wanted him as fiercely as he wanted her. She drew her arms back to circle his head, desperate to get her hands as full of him as his were of her. The softness of his hair tickled between her fingers, and the side of his neck glossed her palm with his sweat. All she could imagine was spinning around and licking it up, savoring his salty musk on her tongue.

The touch of sharp teeth on her skin brought her back to the moment. As he'd done many times before, he nipped at the spot, bearing down on the verge of breaking through. Excitement roared through her, and her body thrummed on the edge, waiting for the pain and the rapture at the same time. With his hand buried between her legs and his cock thrusting from this new angle, every inch of her skin opened and pressed against his. No secrets remained to be discovered.

Fistfuls of his hair in her palms, she pulled his head harder against her neck and angled her head away, offering the spot as her final act of submission. "Do it. Do it now."

The first puncture caught her by surprise and spurred a raw, whimpering cry. But as his teeth tore through skin and vessels, the pain flowed into pleasure, the excruciating merged with the erotic, and everything came together in a blinding flash. She trapped a scream behind her teeth as her climax crested on the heels of the mark. Blood trickled over her skin, running between her breasts, spilling down her shoulder blades and smearing against his sweat-slicked chest. All of it so fucking primal and dirty and insane and *sublime*.

Pulsations started deep in her core and exploded outwards from there, dissolving into a million points of sensation, blowing her completely open as something brand new unfurled deep in her chest. A glowing dot nestled behind her sternum and declared itself to be home. As Cal's orgasm flamed into life and he pulsed inside her, the remnants of her pleasure blended with his so that every last bit of tension in her muscles spun out into the universe and exploded into everything and nothing at all.

Nothing but this new version of Adeline Cabrese, this reborn Della, and the tiny particle of light nuzzled against her heart, whose name was Cal.

CHAPTER TWENTY-FIVE

Cal

If Cal thought his middle-of-the-night flight from Morris Hill was harrowing, it had nothing on the return journey. They left the bulk of their supplies behind in the cave, bringing only weapons, water, and what little food could be eaten on the road. Despite this, keeping up a solid pace required constant struggle.

First off, they had to walk the entire way. What had been a half-day trip on horseback turned into an arduous most-of-the-day journey on foot. Second, the impending attack threatened like a gun to the back of the head. Cal nearly gave himself whiplash the entire trip, his head in constant rotation, all of his senses on alert. How far behind were the rogue Alphas? Did they have horses? Would he and Della be overtaken or run down? Nightmare scenarios, each one of them worsened by the fact that he now had Della in his care.

His sweet Della, in no condition for the strenuousness of the journey, marched on without a complaint. Despite her age, he'd never questioned her strength and vitality, but less than a week prior, she'd suffered a concussion, followed by an unexpected Heat that culminated in an aggressive mating and claiming. Even worse, the fresh mark on her shoulder pained her the entire way. Anxious to reach their destination, she never voiced discomfort, but her anguished winces grated like a broken rib inside his torso. He checked the wound at every single break they took (which weren't many), his feelings a maddening mix of sympathy, guilt, and shameful satisfaction.

Painfully aware her body needed food and rest, several days' worth of both, instinct screamed at him to abandon this foolish quest and tend to his mate. He could make a rudimentary shelter with pine boughs anywhere along the route. Build her a fire, rub her feet, and purr her into a deep sleep. In the morning, they could reverse course and return to their cave, giving Della a chance to rest. Then, in a few days, set out for somewhere new, hopefully somewhere *safe*. Forget about Morris Hill and the ingrates who cared not a whit about her there.

Except, that wasn't quite true, and he knew it. Those two young Omegas had come looking for her, against all sense and reason and any basic awareness of danger. If he were their father, he'd be sorely tempted to tan both of their hides for such flagrant disregard for their own safety. They had no idea the depth of their foolishness, how lucky they were to ride off unmolested with those feral Alphas stalking them through the woods.

Those same feral Alphas who could, at this very moment, be stalking them.

Danger on their heels, danger waiting for them in Morris Hill. Danger loomed on all sides. Nausea crawled up his throat, bolstered by resurfacing memories of another journey, one that started out benign and ended in disaster. His father, dead. His mother, bereft. His village, broken. Him, banished. He'd lost every single thing he'd loved. One false step, and it all crumbled beneath his feet.

He glanced again at Della, the fear parked like an overloaded wagon on his chest. She belonged to him now. Defiance surged in his veins. She wore his mark, there was no changing it, and he would die before he let the Alphas of Morris Hill come between them. Della *wanted* to be claimed. She'd asked for it herself, and with the tie that bound them together now, that faint thread linking his heart to hers, no remorse or regret emanated from his determined mate. Fatigue, hunger, anxiety, pain? Yes. Regret? None at all. If anything, he caught the edges of her defiance, rearing up in response to his, as if to bolster each other from the coming storm.

As night arrived, the peaks of the Morris Hill structures finally came into view.

Della stumbled at the sight, her hands hitting the ground with a dull thud as her body gave way to the fatigue and strain. His guts roiled in a bout of fresh anxiety and guilt. He'd thought her on the verge of collapse, but maybe she'd finally run clear off the end. Throwing off his pack, he dropped to her side, wrapping an arm to support her torso as she sluggishly righted herself. She dusted her hands against each other, her palms scuffed and bleeding in a few places. The muscles across his shoulders cramped with worry, and he fought down the urge to take Della's stumble as a poor omen of what they were about to walk into.

"Come on." He helped her to her feet, his heart clenching when she shot him a grateful look. The faint lines around her lips stood out in a face creased with worry, a reminder of her age and everything she'd survived to get to this moment. Trauma and loss and none of it her fault; she'd outlasted chaos and destruction and kept herself alive and whole only to give herself to him.

The significance of her gift hit him again. He knew she'd done it to save her village, to convince him to return, but he couldn't help but believe there'd been more to it. The ease with which she'd offered it up to him, as if it hadn't been far from her mind to start, made him want to believe she understood what he could give her beyond this current crisis: comfort, love, and safety.

Although, so far, he'd given her exactly zero of it. He rubbed his palm up and down her back, a brisk reassurance to himself as well as her. They'd deal with this, they'd manage the attack, and then they could have some fucking peace. He had to believe that. "We're here, okay? We'll go warn them like you wanted, all right?"

She clamped her hand on his forearm, the tight squeeze a sudden surprise. "Let me talk to them, okay? They'll listen to me."

"Della—"

Reaching up, she trailed her fingers alongside the swollen, inflamed mess of a claiming bite. "I have to get out in front of this and make them understand it isn't what it looks like. They need to hear it from me. You have to trust me on this."

He swept his gaze over her face, everything inside him revolting at Della leading the charge back into the settlement. In his soul, he understood there was no way through this but to battle the Alphas of Morris Hill for the right to keep his mate. He was the Alpha, he ought to be in front. They would come for him in an attempt to protect her. It's why he didn't want to come back, why he would've preferred to stay far, far away from here.

But, if he'd done that, Della would've never forgiven him. Of that, he was certain, and the knowledge he'd have hurt her in this way made the choice for him. She'd submitted to his claim, she wore his mark, but it wasn't enough. Their newly-forged bond tingled in his chest, her side a mess of hesitation and doubt about her feelings for him, and he could sense the way she held herself back from letting the connection blossom fully. She hadn't made a mark on him, and to demand it at the time would have been greedy and brutish. It would have to come from her when she was ready. And, to be honest, he didn't deserve it. Not right now, not like this. He'd held her hand and walked her back into the lion's den. What kind of a protector did that?

Unable to resist, he bent forward, resting his forehead against hers and breathing in her wholesome scent, all sweet and floral and sweaty. "I trust you. I don't trust *them*."

"Come on," she whispered, patting his cheek. "Let's get this over with."

She moved to go, but he shot his hand out, circling her arm, hauling her back against his chest. "One more kiss, darlin'." His lip pulled up at the corner. "For luck."

He took her mouth then, savoring her plush lips and gentle tongue, and his chest risked caving in under the weight of all his feelings rushing to the surface. Clenching her clothes with his hands, he pulled their bodies flush, not wanting to relinquish an ounce of control as the moment rushed past him.

"Cal," Della said against his lips, bracing herself on his chest and pushing him away, "we have to go." She slid her palm along his tight jawline, and his heart broke all over again with the subtle affection in the gesture. "It'll be okay."

He did it then, his body nearly cramping with resistance, but he let her drift from his hold, his eyes glued to her back as she charged toward the village, wearing the pants he'd washed and returned to her before they evacuated their cave. After several days without them, he much preferred to watch her putter around with a bare lower half, but no way in hell would he permit any of these fuckers to see her that way. The pants sagged in the butt, evidence of the weight she'd lost in the course of the Heat and the consequence of living rough. Another thing he'd need to remedy once this night was over.

"It's dinnertime," she explained over her shoulder, legs pumping faster with a renewed burst of energy. He hoped there would be enough left over for Della to eat. "Everyone will be in the mess hall, which will make things easier. We can talk to them all at once."

Cal grunted, not wanting to reveal his foreboding about the impending confrontation. In no time at all, they crossed the distance unimpeded. No posted guards, no watch, no security whatsoever. No wonder this rogue Pack planned an attack; Morris Hill had become complacent and took their safety for granted, and they were about to pay the price.

Della pushed open the mess hall door as sudden panic flared in Cal's chest. What if the village was silent because everyone was already gone and some trap awaited inside?

"Della wait—" he said, stepping in behind her as hundreds of eyes—Alpha, Omega, and pups alike— turned toward him, all of them spitting with surprise, suspicion, or outright hatred. Whispers hummed from one side of the room to another as a hush fell over the rows of benches and tables.

Everything paused for a taut, pregnant moment, a collective breath holding. Cal surveyed the room, zeroing in on Simon and Matteo, his two loyal friends in this pack of wolves. Matteo flashed a glance at Della, his face lit with surprised delight, and Simon gave an imperceptible chin dip, the unspoken message plain: his friends were with him. He returned the gesture, beyond grateful to have the assurance, although doubtful they'd be able to turn the tide if things went south.

As if some secret signal had been given, the room exploded. Chairs and benches were thrown back and crashed on the floor. Pups were wrangled and drawn away by worried-looking Omegas. Alpha footsteps thundered on the wooden floors to surround them in the time it took for the door behind him to slam shut. The smell hit him first: musty, Alpha musk from far too many, ripe with the tang of impending violence. After days of breathing in fresh air and Della's pure scent, he wanted to gag as the smell rammed into his mouth so intense he could taste it.

He reached for Della, wanting her against him, but it was too late. His hand closed on a sickening grasp of air. An Alpha he didn't know pulled her away, protectively tucking her into their midst like reshelving a book. Enraged at someone handling what was his, Cal lunged, his movement checked by hands locked on his arms and shoulders, trapping him in place. A wicked snarl ripped from his chest. "Don't touch her!"

"Wait! No! Stop! It's okay, it's okay!" Della screeched, her eyes wide and scared as she fought to get free from the Alpha who strapped an arm around her chest. "We need to talk! Colt!"

"For fuck's sake, let her go!" Cal thrashed with all his strength, hurling himself against the—*three? four?*—Alphas that held him back.

A face appeared in front of him, a vision of lethal disdain blocking his view of Della. Fucking Colt. "Pretty stupid to come back here," the Second said quietly, his eyes spitting daggers. "What did you think? You could waltz back in and everything would be forgiven?" He shook his head with disgust.

Cal harnessed his urge to fight and forced himself to mimic Colt's overly controlled tone. "It isn't like that." He jerked against the Alphas holding him, feeling his right shoulder strain to stay in the socket.

"Colt," Della demanded, "stop this *now*. We need to talk."

The desperation in her voice tore at his insides, and he flexed his neck this way and that, trying to make eye contact, to reassure her that he'd fix this, he'd get them out of this and back together. But Colt drew his fist up, catching him on the jaw instead.

Cal's head snapped back, his vision fizzing out into white for a moment, coming into focus as the second fist hit him from the other side. The skin on his cheekbone popped under the impact, opening a cut that immediately began to ooze. Alphas snickered and jeered, Della screamed, and the sound of her pain stabbed at his heart more than the blow ever could. Too frightened to guard her emotions, her fear lashed at his insides, the bond snapping and angry and scared.

"What's going on?" A deep voice cut through the din, and Cal blinked and blinked again, trying to rearrange his brain cells to see who was speaking. Two blows wouldn't normally affect him, but taken by surprise, pinned in place, and unable to dodge even in the slightest, the punches landed harder than any Colt had delivered in their prior fight. And maybe they'd been thrown with more *oomph* as well. Jealousy flared deep inside him. Did Colt have designs on Della? Is that why he hated him?

"Hunter, listen to me," Della pleaded, and Cal looked up to the formidable Alpha striding into the middle of the group. Hunter wasn't the tallest, or even the broadest, of the Morris Hill Pack, but what he lacked in physical parameters he made up in sheer arrogant presence. The room stilled around him. "There's a group of rogue Alphas on the edge of the territory to the north, and they're planning to raid Morris Hill." The words flew from Della's lips, rushed in her desperation to relay the message. "Tonight. Please, you have to listen."

Hunter's shrewd eyes scanned the room and collided with Cal's. Without breaking his gaze, Hunter stepped to where Della was restrained a mere yard away. Nudging her shirt collar to the side, he displayed the fresh claiming bite, swollen and nasty and stained with blood as they hadn't had time to properly clean it. A fresh wave of hisses and discontent rumbled through the Pack. As plain as an admission from his own lips, right there out in the open, evidence he'd broken the hallowed Morris Hill rules about only claiming willing Omegas. Della had been willing, but fat chance of proving that to them in this particular moment.

"You did this?" Hunter asked, deceptively calm. "You took her from her home and did this?"

"That's not important right now," Della stammered, desperately clutching Hunter's sleeve and tugging for his attention. "There's a threat to the settlement."

"Yeah, right," a voice sneered to Cal's left. *Silas.* "They're making up a story to distract from what he's done. Don't fall for it, Alpha."

"That's not true," Della shot back. "We overheard them. They were stalking Rue and Zorah in the woods earlier today. The girls are lucky they got away."

"Listen to this," Silas scoffed. "Boogeymen hiding out in the woods. It's a fucking tall tale."

Several voices joined in at that point. Della still pleading her case. Colt snarling something and curling his fist like he was lining up his next punch. Silas, shooting his lazy mouth off and a few other Alphas telling him to shut the fuck up.

Hunter held up a palm and faced Cal, his expression stony. "You wanted to join my Pack, and you helped me find Kess, so I welcomed you in." He thrust an index finger toward Della, his face twisting with anger. "And this is how you repay that trust? You steal a woman away from the Pack and claim her against her will?"

"It wasn't. He didn't." Della's voice broke. "I'm *fine*."

Hunter scoffed and threw a glance over his shoulder. "You don't look fine. You're dirty, exhausted, covered with blood, I can hear your belly rumbling from over here, and every Alpha in here can smell him all over you."

Pink shot into her cheeks, and she opened her mouth, yet no response jumped out.

Cal wet his lips, tasting his blood. "No disrespect to you, Alpha, but if all that's true, why would I bring her back? Why not take her, claim her, and keep on moving, get far the fuck away from here?"

"To insult our Pack," Colt spat. "You were pissed about what happened with Silas and the patrol, so you snuck off in the night like a fucking dog, taking her along for spite, and now you've come back to rub it in our faces. That's all this is."

Cal's lips twisted in a cruel, mocking grin. "When I want to insult you, *pup*, I'll do it to your face."

Expression contorted with rage, Colt pulled back a fist for another punch, only to be stopped by Hunter sliding between them and laying his hand on the younger Alpha's chest. "That won't help."

In the brief reprieve, Cal circled his gaze around the gathered Alphas, making careful eye contact with a few familiar faces as he made his argument. "What's between Della and me is between us, and she'll tell you the same if you'd listen to her. We came back here, you *stupid fucks*, to warn you." He glared at Colt and Hunter in turn, willing his reason and good sense to prevail. "I didn't want to, but it's important to her, and that makes it important to me. So you can spend all night yelling or sucker punching me when I can't fight back," he sneered at Colt, "but you're wasting time and leaving your people vulnerable."

A thoughtful pause overtook the group, and Cal found Della in the crowd. Her face had fallen, a hollow sadness taking the place where the impassioned argument had vacated. Those precious lines of her face stood out stark and forlorn in the fading light, incongruously paired with an expression of such open bafflement and disillusion. She looked simultaneously young and old and so hopelessly *lost.*

In his chest, their bond twanged like an out-of-tune guitar, the notes sour and grating, and he cursed himself again for bringing her here. Should've gone their own way and left all this behind when he had the chance. That future wavered, fading like a desert mirage, and panic clawed at his guts. He needed to get to her, to take her in his arms, to give her his purr, and remind her of everything they'd shared.

"I know she's a part of your Pack," Cal continued, forcing himself to stay calm, stay reasonable despite his surging turmoil, "and I know this looks bad, but right now, you need to listen to what we're trying to tell you. There're rogue Alphas north of here, maybe making their way here as we speak. They want your food, your horses, and they want your Ome—"

"Fuck this guy and fuck this bullshit story," Silas interrupted. "Unmated Omegas wandering around by themselves. What a crock of shit. Sloan, wasn't Rue helping you all day in the stable?"

"She was..." Sloan scraped a hand over his jaw.

"But you got called down to the fields, so how would you know?" another Alpha pointed out.

"Are you saying Rue and Zorah took two horses and went for a joyride alone, and you didn't stop them?" Riddick hurled the accusation at Sloan.

"Hey, fuck you." Sloan's face turned red. "I was pulled in three different directions today. What the fuck were *you* doing?"

Riddick snorted and folded his arms over his chest. "Not misplacing Omegas, that's for sure."

A few others joined in, shouting harassment at either Sloan or Riddick or telling one or both of them to shut up.

Cal cleared his throat, raising his voice for this last reveal. "The ones coming here know all about you. Someone in this Pack is in league with them and feeding them information." He shifted his glare to Silas. "I'd sure be interested in knowing how often Silas here has been doing the patrol route alone. Della and I have no reason to lie, but he's awfully invested in discounting what we're saying."

Hunter zeroed in on Silas, and Cal saw the cogs start to turn. Colt straightened his shoulders, looking less like he was going to punch Cal again and more like he was actually reconsidering the situation.

"It's the truth, Hunter. Please listen," Della whispered into the contemplative quiet. "Cal didn't do anything I didn't ask him to. Let him go. *Please.*"

If her pleas affected him, Hunter did not show it.

"We need to sort this out," Hunter said finally. "Until we do, Colt, you take him." Hunter jerked his chin at Cal. "Silas, you're with me. Logan, get Della home and get her something to eat." He pointed an index finger at Cal's mate. "Stay in your cabin. Don't make me have to come track you down."

"No!" Della jolted back to life, clawing at the Alpha who restrained her, his face set in a grim line as he adjusted his grip on her to subdue her flying fists. "Where are you taking Cal? What are you doing with him?"

Her anguish screeched through the bond and the stunned air of the mess hall. Several nearby Alphas took involuntary steps away from the snarling hellcat, their eyes wide with disbelief as to what they were seeing. This was not the Della they were used to. But, the Della they were used to was not Cal's fierce little Omega.

Knowing it was just as pointless but unable to sit idly by as his Omega suffered, Cal renewed his struggle, shouting into the chaos. "Don't touch her! You're going to hurt her!"

"Hunt! He didn't do anything wrong! Colt! Stop this!" With the energy of pure Omega fury, Della thrashed and fought while screaming at anyone and everyone in earshot. "Let go of me! I need to be with *him*!" She stomped on the Alpha's foot hard enough to make him swear, and a second Alpha stepped forward, stooping to restrain her kicking legs.

"Get her out of here," Hunt commanded, hiking a thumb toward the door.

"No! Don't do this! Don't! Please! Let me go! Cal!" Two Alphas carried her toward the door, pinned on her side like a rolled-up carpet. Her eyes, hysterical, roved to find his, abject terror in their depths.

Cal strained hard against his captors, saying soothing words she had no chance of hearing over her own bellows. "Della, just wait. I'll take care of it. Just sit tight, okay?" He forced the reassurance down the bond, but it, too, got drowned out.

"Cal!" Outside the mess hall, her screams faded into the night, but the turmoil surged through the bond unabated. "Cal!"

The anguished note in her voice pierced his precarious control. His Omega was hurting, and she needed him. With a final gust of strength, he yanked away, desperate to get to her and ease this torment. Pain erupted in his right shoulder as the joint jumped the socket, nearly buckling his knees as his arm hung limp. He cursed, his vision snowy as the physical pain cut through all the other sensations slashing and hacking at his body.

"You should let me go to her," he panted, sweat prickling at his temples. "She needs me."

Hunter's expression went hard, and ice slithered down Cal's spine. "We got it from here. Della's no longer your concern."

CHAPTER TWENTY-SIX

Della

The same Alpha stood in the doorway as the last time she checked. With an aggravated huff, she squinted at his unfamiliar face in the darkness. He had the look of an aging movie star who'd spent too much time in the sun: handsome, but weathered. Staring back at her, his arms folded like a bouncer guarding the entrance to a chic nightclub, complete with the air of stone-faced boredom.

"Like I told you before, Alpha says you have to stay here." His gaze turned pitying, which only riled her harried nerves even more. "You should just go back inside and try to rest. I'm sorry, ma'am."

"Ma'am?" With a guttural *argh*, Della slammed her creaky old door in his stupid, serious face. She'd been in her room for hours, long enough that her first set of guards had been replaced by this idiot, whom she didn't recognize but who clearly was a leftover from before TheEnd. No one said ma'am in the AfterEnd. She whirled to face Rue and pointed at the door. "Who the fuck is that?"

Sitting calmly on her bed, Rue scratched at her stubbled head. "Jake. He's new."

"Yeah, no shit, he's new." Della marched across the floor, resuming her pacing circuit around the small cabin. Periodically, she threw open the door to see if whoever was charged with keeping her inside might be persuaded to let her go. Thus far, every Alpha responded with the same aggravating answer as *Jake*. Minus the ma'am.

She'd been at it a long time, maybe hours, but what was time when her entire life was blowing apart at the seams—again? The golden orb inside her crackled and arced like a shorting-out circuit. Emotions skittered through the bond—deep, lancing pain and clenching frustration, fragments of anxiety and strife. The only consolation Della could take from it was that it meant Cal was still alive and at least somewhat awake. Somewhere. But where was he? What would they do with him? What had they done with him? No one would tell her shit.

She'd fought with Logan and Mick like a feral animal as they'd bundled her into the cabin. Eventually, Logan took her face in his hands and commanded her to calm the fuck down. His exact words, *"Your Alpha won't be happy if you hurt yourself,"* cut through her rampaging hysteria. No, Cal wouldn't be happy if she hurt herself, and disregarding her own safety felt too much like a betrayal of his concern. Sequestered in her cabin, guarded like an inmate, she felt more imprisoned than she ever did back in the dank cave. Longing for the cave—for the simplicity of the two of them, sleeping, eating, living, and screwing—took on a life of its own. Yeah, it was unsophisticated and dirty and raw. But, after several lifetimes of inescapable numbness, it was also everything she needed. She'd woken up in that cave to both her Omega nature and her isolation. Having been put slightly back together, her chinks filled in and her wounds tended, she remembered how good it felt to be whole.

The tears came then, gushing and ugly, smearing the dirt and grit that coated her face. Logan hugged her shoulders and fetched her food and hot water sufficient for a rudimentary bath. Moving in a terrified daze, she sluiced the sweat, dirt, and sex fluids from her body, awkwardly rinsed her dingy locks, donned some clean clothes, forced down some dinner, and then was left with nothing to do but wait and strain her ears for any sounds of disturbance from the camp.

Yet only silence answered.

The dinner congealed in her stomach like a mud pie. Her head was stuffed with cotton, her eyes encased in sandpaper, and her chest—*good lord, her chest—* throbbed a proclamation of disaster. She'd calmed enough to attend to the bond, seeking that connection to him with almost obsessive regularity, desperate for any kind of reassurance. But that brilliant dot of light, the one birthed inside her with Cal's searing bite, only vibrated with despair.

Even worse, she couldn't tell: was it her despair, or was it his?

Her own pummeled her mind like crashing surf; every swell a reminder of her naivete at believing the Morris Hill Alphas would listen and do the right thing. Why had she believed that? Her, of all people? Had it been the passage of time? Had all these decades blunted the hard lesson of TheEnd: that people and structures in power always, always fail in a crisis? Or had she been so wrapped up in the ecstasy of the last few days with Cal she forgot how stubborn and prideful Alphas could be?

Della wrung her hands, cracking her knuckles even though she'd cracked them three times already. She knew better than to trust them to do the right thing. She knew it, but she'd done it anyway. Hell, she'd *begged* Cal to *claim her* to ensure they wouldn't be parted. And look what it got her? Trapped in her cabin, shut out of any preparation or decision-making, and tied to an Alpha with an uncertain future. So much for the sanctity of Alpha-Omega bonds.

"You're going to wear a hole in the floorboards if you keep that up." Rue's wry voice cut across the cabin. "Come sit." Rue patted her bed. "I'll braid your hair."

Shaken from her ruminations, Della faced the young Omega, who lounged on her bed, doodling idly with a stubby pencil and a notebook that looked worse for the wear. Since the Omega had come to live with her, Della'd kept a polite but careful distance, telling herself it was as much for Rue's benefit as her own.

But that was before. Before Della's skin remembered the touch of another's, before her body awakened a craving to be touched and caressed and held, before her soul remembered to ache for comfort when she was hurting inside.

Rue wanted to brush out and braid her hair? Della almost cried at the offer.

"I never said thank you," Della said hesitantly, lowering herself to Rue's mattress, "for coming to look for me. It was very brave."

Rue's shoulder lifted, so thin it looked like a knife cutting through her T-shirt. "The Alphas searched for a few days, but they thought you were long gone. But then, two days ago, Livvy wandered into camp, and I knew they'd missed something."

Della snorted. "It took that horse a week to make it back?"

A smile played on Rue's lips. "She took her sweet ass time, that's for sure. Here"—Rue nudged Della's leg—"face that way."

Della did as she was told, turning toward the fire as Rue produced a brush and began working through the half-dried tangles. They sat in peaceful silence for a long time. The only sounds were the crack of the fire and the gentle scuff of the brush. A long, shuddering breath whisked out of Della, her mind slowing for the first time all day.

Rue began tugging the lengths into strands for braiding. "I can't wait till my hair grows back. Grandmére would brush and then braid it like this," Rue murmured, her throat hinting at the swallowed *r* of a French pronunciation. "She liked things to be neat and tidy, *une Madame Blancheville.*"

"Was that her name?"

Rue giggled. "No, it's just a saying. It means a... woman who likes things spic and span."

Della's mind flashed back to Amma and her spotless kitchen and the salt-and-peppered braids coiled around her head. "My husband's grandmother was the same." A small smile stole onto her face. "I miss her."

"I miss Grandmére, too." Hesitation rolled off the young Omega. "You... you had a husband?"

Della half turned to look over her shoulder, noting Rue's open and curious face, and then turned back to the fire. "A long time ago."

Rue's hands made short work of the task, efficiently organizing Della's hair and then tying it off on the end. "What was he like?"

"He was..." Thankful for the distraction from her worries, Della let the old memories infiltrate the present. "He was a good man. Handsome. Brilliant. We met when he was lobbying my father for something or other and invited us to a party on his yacht."

"What's a yacht?"

Della shifted on the bed, bracing her back against the wall so she could look Rue in the face. They'd never spoken this much in all the weeks they'd been living together. Regret filled her at how much Rue longed to connect and guilt for how little she knew about her. "A very, very large boat. So big there are rooms on it for sleeping, eating, cooking…"

Rue pulled her legs up, folding them under and tucking herself into a little, avidly-listening ball. "And he lived on it? Your husband?"

"Oh no, no." A bitter laugh scraped past Della's throat. "The yacht was for fun." She sighed. "The world before TheEnd drowned in excesses. There were many who lived like kings."

Rue's dark lashes flew up. "So that made you a queen."

"No, not exactly." Egalitarian to their core, she and Rakesh had been copilots, co-CEOs of their complicated lives, but she'd never been Rakesh's queen.

Only one man had seen her that way: a queen without a country, hiding in the shadows, living half a life so nothing could be taken from her again. Tears scalded the back of her throat, and she caressed the bond, searching for some trace of Cal. It glimmered weakly in her chest, rife with misery and discomfort, faltering like he hovered on the verge of unconsciousness. She strained harder, like extending a hand to someone hanging off the edge of a cliff, desperate to feel a firm push from his side of the connection. Nothing came, and the tears pushed their way up her throat.

"But you loved him?"

"Who?" Della's froggy voice cracked, and she refocused on the Omega in front of her. Rue rested her chin on her fist, fully entranced at the story of Della's life in the before times. "Rakesh? Yes, I loved him." Rue's lifted brow silently asked the next question. "He died in a fire," Della said in a resigned tone, letting the memories unfurl one by one like a slow flip through her photo book.

Memories of her palatial home ticked by: her favorite chair by the pool, the pile of books next to her desk waiting to be read, the outline of her bed, unmade and untidy, her last thought that she ought to make it because how nice it would be to come home to a properly made bed. Refusing to face the inevitability of the coming inferno. A wave of affection for her former self poured from her heart. If only she'd known what was to come.

But, then again, what difference would that have made? What would she have done differently?

"There were fires everywhere then, in all directions. Rakesh had wanted to leave sooner, but I refused. Instead, I went door to door and tried to round up my neighbors. You see, some were elderly or had young children, and I was trying to get everyone together, to take what we could and go." The old sadness crept in around the corners, yet it lingered in the realm of memory, not encroaching into the present. Della could see it there, could acknowledge it, but the old aches had lost their hold on her. "He went back for something, a dog, maybe? He always loved dogs. Anyway, we got separated."

Della cut a glance to Rue, who listened like she'd never heard a more riveting story. "A tree fell and cut off the exit. The last time I saw him was through flames shooting ten feet high in the air. I screamed at him to go around, to try to make it, but he wasn't moving. He smiled at me and waved, waving goodbye. He looked oddly… peaceful? Like he'd accepted it, like he was ready to die." A distant pain squeezed her heart. "My neighbor, Mai, dragged me away. Like, literally dragged. I left bloody scratches up and down her arms, the poor thing. I had nightmares about it for a long time: the flames, the heat, the smell… dreaming that he'd tried harder to find a way, or I fought more to get to him."

Years she'd had those dreams, and every time she woke up, she took that pain and stared it in the face, promising herself she'd never feel pain like that again because she'd never love someone like that again.

Whether it was possible to immunize herself against future hurt didn't matter, she'd sworn to try.

Only to fail at it again.

"You were lucky though." Rue's voice pulled her from her thoughts.

Della's head snapped to her. "What?"

"He didn't want your last image of him screaming in terror. He loved you so much, he protected you from that. It was his final act of love." A sad smile wavered on her face. "I can't even imagine what it feels like to be loved like that."

Della stared, tongue-tied, at the young Omega. If she hadn't been sitting down, she might've crumpled to the ground.

A sacrifice. Rakesh hadn't failed to fight for her. In those final moments, he hadn't given up and left her alone in the AfterEnd. He'd spared her the only way he could. He'd stared into the face of death and saved her from one last devastation.

It was an act of love.

Rue reached out and grabbed her hand, clenching it emphatically between her own. "I'm so glad you're back so they can protect you from *him*."

Della blinked, struggling to understand the conversational turn as Rue's face twisted in disgust. "Who?"

"The one that took you. The bad Alpha."

"He's *not* bad." The words shot from Della's mouth.

Rue pointed an accusatory finger at Della's claiming bite. "Look at what he did to you! They should put him to death. Everyone's been saying so."

Terror seized her heart in an iron grasp. Put him to *death*? Della's fingers tightened so fast Rue flinched and extracted herself from Della's grip. "Is that what they're saying?" Della demanded, pushing the words past her breathless lungs. No, that couldn't be right. They didn't *put people to death* in this Pack. That was barbaric and insane! Surely Hunter wouldn't take such drastic measures. Bands fastened around her ribs, cinching like a vice. She'd thought he wouldn't separate a bonded couple either, and look how that turned out.

Rue nodded her fervent agreement with this form of justice.

"He's *not* bad." Della jumped to her feet and took a few jerky steps toward the door, her hands wrapped around her head. "He saw something that made him suspicious of this place, and he was right to be suspicious. They won't hurt him... they *can't.*"

Cal's face those last few minutes came back to her, his kind eyes reassuring, convincing her everything would be fine, even as they'd yanked his body this way and that, wrenching his shoulders and arms in unnatural angles. *Oh god.* If they killed him, would that be her last image of him? Subdued and struggling to comfort her?

Chest burning, she stumbled to her bed and pressed her palm to her sternum, gasping shallow breaths. Closing her eyes, Della grappled for their connection, opening herself to it in a way she'd never before allowed. The effort settled her tortured respirations, and she breathed into it further, seeking the man on the other side of the link. The orb responded with a soft ripple, like the smallest pebble thrown in the smoothest lake, and its warmth saturated her insides, surrounding her with the comfort of losing herself in his arms.

The memories of their time in the cave knit together like a tapestry. Salacious and mundane moments displayed in a picture for her examination. A picture of patience, humor, and tenderness so exquisite she wanted to cry. A picture very much like love.

A wave rolled through the bond, an answering push to the emotion she'd released. Love reaffirmed and reflected back.

Della's eyes flashed open to discover Rue asleep in her bed, the fire almost out, and silence on all sides around her cabin. She stared up at the ceiling, sending a determined push through the bond. A promise. This wasn't the end, not for him and not for them.

CHAPTER TWENTY-SEVEN

Cal

The shackle closed around his ankle with a sickening *clink*, and resignation pinned him like pressure at the bottom of the ocean. Satisfied, the Alphas who'd hauled him into the room slowly backed away, edging toward the doorway of the underground room. Sacks of food and other supplies piled in the space and perfumed the air with spices and the faint vegetal sting of onions. He'd never been down here, but it appeared to be a storeroom of sorts, beneath the mess hall, a single, dusty window the only source of fading daylight.

Storeroom plus improvised prison cell.

Cal swiped the sweat from his brow with his working shoulder; the other hung limply and grotesquely from his side. "I'd like to ask why y'all have a spare shackle and chain just lying around down here, but I'm afraid I don't really want to know."

Colt twisted the key in the lock and then stood, the key in his white-knuckled fist. "We figured it never hurt to be prepared."

"Well,"—Cal bent his knee, and the heavy chain scraped against the concrete—"you're wasting time with this when you should be preparing for what's about to happen tonight."

The Alphas at Colt's back shuffled restlessly, and Cal shifted his gaze to them. "Y'all shouldn't be standing here. You should be setting up patrols for every quadrant. Send Heck or Alek up in a tree to be lookout. Get the Omegas and pups hidden and secured somewhere safe."

"You said they were coming from the north?" An Alpha with rich brown skin stepped forward, his eyes serious but wary.

Cal nodded. "I saw them in the area near the hot springs, but they could be clever and come from any direc—"

"Shut up," Colt snapped, flashing a glare between Cal and the question-asker. "We got it under control."

"Do you?" Cal lifted a challenging brow. "'Cuz it seems to me you got four guys down here going to a lot of trouble to restrain a wounded Alpha when you should be making arrangements to keep the Pack safe."

A muscle ticked in Colt's cheek. "The Pack's safety is not your business."

"Della's my mate," Cal seethed. "And if something happens to her because of y'all's negligence, I swear to you, there will be no safe place for you to hide on this entire green earth."

Colt scoffed and shook his head. "Yeah, wouldn't want to see anything happen to Della, right? Like her getting abducted from her Pack, you mean? Stolen away and dragged over hell's half acre, returned half-starved with a claiming bite and reeking of Alpha seed? Something like that, you mean? Wouldn't want to see anything like that happen."

Cold shame poured into his veins like oil, and anger lit the match behind it. No denying he did those things, but fuck this asshole for throwing it in his face like he was in the wrong when he didn't know the first thing about it. What he had with Della was the furthest thing from wrong.

Cal took a fortifying breath, striving for patience. "We can rehash all that once this threat is dealt with. Della ain't no wilting flower. She'll tell you herself what happened between us."

A look of pure contempt darkened Colt's face. "Della is a hysterical mess. She's not in any condition to talk to anyone. Another thing she can thank you for, I suppose." With a disgusted shake of his head, Colt turned to leave. "He can't do any more damage down here. Let's go."

The Alpha who'd spoken earlier flicked a worried glance between Colt and Cal. "Someone should stay with him, don't you think? A guard? Just in case?"

Colt threw of smirk over his shoulder and stuffed the key deep in his pants pocket. Cal's stomach bottomed out, a nightmare he hadn't even considered playing out. *Colt* was keeping the key to his restraint? Dread engulfed him like a bag thrown over his head.

He was never leaving this room.

"You heard him," the Second sneered, "he says we gotta prepare. So, let's go prepare."

He strode toward the door, his big feet tromping up the short set of stairs to the outside, taking the key to Cal's freedom with him. Ignoring the spiraling panic of being left alone in the dark basement with the key walking off in Colt's pocket, Cal shouted one last warning to the Alphas queued up to follow, his voice thin and strained. "They got Omegas with them. Don't know how many, but don't let them get away without rescuing those girls."

"You sure about that?" The Alpha who spoke up turned and met his eyes, looking less wary and more alarmed.

Cal dipped his chin, his gaze never wavering. "Swear on my Omega's life. They were talking about having Omegas but wanting more. I got no idea what they're doing with 'em, but it didn't sound good."

The Alpha tensed his jaw, determination squaring his shoulders. "All right, man. You sit tight. I'll remind Hunt to come take a look at your shoulder."

"Don't worry about me." Cal tried for an unconcerned grin and jiggled the chain. "I'm not going nowhere."

He held it together until the last Alpha filed out and the door slammed shut. But when the metallic sounds of a second lock snapping closed jangled through the hazy dark, his stomach began to heave. Rolling to his good side and then awkwardly up on three limbs, Cal's exhausted body labored to expel every drop from his roiling guts. The day's meager food long digested, so only a revolting thread of bile and stomach acid drooled out of his mouth. A sour taste poisoned his mouth, and he heaved again, so hard his stomach clenched to the point of pain and his throat screamed in abused agony. Spots swam in his vision, the combined sick and weakness finally catching up with him.

Cold sweat prickling on his neck, he sat back on his heels, tilting his head up and pulling in deep, desperate breaths. He had to stay awake, stay alert. No matter how much he hurt or how much he wanted to lie down and pass out. He couldn't disappear into unconsciousness, not while the bond flailed in his chest. A never-ending symphony of distress howled from Della's side, so loud and deafening he couldn't get through to her. If only she'd settle enough to let him through, he could soothe her through the bond. But, at the moment, her anguish blared at top volume and drowned everything else out.

"Della is a hysterical mess." Well, Colt got that right. Her weak, flailing limbs fighting off Alphas twice her size without a single thought for her safety burned in his mind. A shameful, selfish part of him adored her possessive Omega instincts on full blast, but underneath that dwelled a dark sense of failure. Separated from his suffering Omega, he could do none of the things Alphas were meant to do: comfort, care, protect, defend. Desperate to claim her, to secure that final attachment, to have her for his own, he'd made a choice he might regret forever. If something did happen to her in the coming conflict, he'd never forgive himself.

Slowly, Cal situated himself, sitting upright with his back braced against the ancient water heater and his good arm cradling the bad. It wasn't like he could go far. The cuff around his ankle linked to a thick chain, which had been welded to the water heater bolted to the concrete floor. With his working arm, he tugged at the attachment without daring to hope it would break. But all he accomplished was making a racket of the clanking, grinding links.

What. A. Fucking. Mess.

The bond clanged a bleak note in his chest, out of sync and miserable. When had things gone so wrong? Had the decision to return to Morris Hill been the final mistake? Or had the last week been one long exercise in poor judgment? Fighting Silas? Stealing Della? Claiming her? Not bringing Simon and Matteo along with him them? An endless supply of second-guessing and self-condemnation was all he had left to keep him company. Where had he gone wrong?

Eyes closed, he sensed Della on the other end, also swimming through misery, wading through darkness to find her way back to him. His tired thoughts strayed to better memories, recalling the sweetness of her scent and the way it concentrated in his favorite spot. Snuggled into the crook of her neck, rich with silken, unblemished skin, warm and fragrant beneath his lips, she'd shiver and sigh when he kissed and nibbled. He recalled the fierce set of her lips when she held that knife to his throat, battling not just with him but with herself and her body's escalating awakening. Her Omega, just under the surface, fought to come out. So delicate but so strong. Beautiful and precious and *his*.

*

Cal's eyes shot open, senses on high alert and straining for any hint of what yanked him from sleep. His head throbbed; a tension headache so severe he swore his eyeballs were about to pop out of his head. Had he been asleep? When had he drifted off?

It was fully night now, and without a lamp, murky darkness enveloped him. Frantic, he tugged on the bond, seeking Della through the haze of pain and black night. She was there, and the bond hummed a slow, steady cadence, like the shushed beating of a heart.

Peaceful. At rest. Cal breathed a small sigh of relief. Like him, she slept, and for now, she was safe. As safe as she could be, given the circumstances.

Reassured, he rubbed at his aching eyes as all the anxieties returned in full force. He'd done everything he could to warn the Morris Hill Pack. At least a few of them appeared to take his warning seriously. Hunter was cautious, not an idiot. He wouldn't be so foolish as to fall for Silas's bullshit. Whether or not they'd take the precautions Cal would if this were his Pack, he couldn't predict.

A shudder racked his body at the thought of what might've happened had those rogue Alphas discovered him and Della during one of their trips out of the cave. They'd been close—far closer than he knew—and could've easily come upon them unawares. Cal had no doubt he'd fight tooth and fist to defend his Omega, but he wasn't arrogant enough to think he could best a whole group of Alphas. He could tally the mistakes he made, both obvious and less so, but he'd done one thing right. The Morris Hill Alpha would protect Della and the other Omegas better than he could've as a lone Alpha in the middle of nowhere. No matter what happened to him tonight or even in the morning, banished from the Pack or once again exiled, he hadn't stranded his lovely mate alone in the wilderness.

A scratching sound tickled his eardrums. He held his breath and listened. A mouse or rat? No, much too loud of a noise for a rodent to make. A minute of silence passed, and he began to question his own perceptions. Was he hearing things now?

Boards creaked above his head, and he got his answer. Heavy footsteps, a single pair of boots, moved fast and with purpose. Alarm raced up his spine, but he held himself rigid, not wanting to risk any chain noise to disclose his presence. Something was happening, and he didn't like it. More scuffling and then quiet again. The minutes stretched into tortuous lengths as he waited.

His next careful breath brought the answer: smoke. A thin, acrid trail slithered into his nose, and an ominous warning echoed through his mind.

"They can't fight us if they're fighting a fire. We'll burn the whole fucking place down."

Outside, the night waited in silent, bated breath. Nothing stirred, no shouts, no calls, no alarms. A string of curses rolled through his mind. Where the fuck were the Morris Hill Alphas? How had this wannabe arsonist snuck past them?

The footsteps clomped over the floor, more confident now, no doubt making his hasty escape. Omnipresent smoke contaminated Cal's every breath, and a storm of undiluted fear rained down.

He was chained to the floor, and the building was on fire.

CHAPTER TWENTY-EIGHT

Della

The pounding started deep in her brain. It hammered through her unconscious, jerking her from a slumber born of utter exhaustion.

"Della! Get up!" She opened her eyes to discover Kess was the owner of the unfamiliar voice. To her right, Rue grasped Della's arm, hoisting her upright. "You have to come now. We're under attack."

"Where's Cal?" Fully awake, Della reached for her shoes, ramming her feet inside and following Kess's confident strides toward the door. Passing her bookshelf, she swiped the knife Cal had sharpened for her and tucked it into a pocket. "Where did they take him?"

"The storeroom," Kess said grimly as she swung open the door. "The women and children are in my cabin. We have to go *now*."

"What—" Della's words turned to ash when she stepped into the terrifying night. Flames, originating in the center of the settlement, shot up, licking against the night sky like a hungry dragon's tongue. Her hand flew to her mouth as the sickening smell of fire invaded her nose.

Oh god. No. Not again.

Her knees threatened to buckle as the muscle memory took over. Fire. You had to run from fire, but terror rooted her to the spot. Everything went in slow motion for a never-ending second as her brain pieced together what she was seeing, her thoughts a deranged cacophony of worry. The storeroom. Kess said Cal was in the storeroom, the cellar under the mess hall. The mess hall currently going up in flames. The bond flared up a sputtering, desperate warning, one livid with terror and agitation.

Kess roughly tugged her arm, imploring her with wide, white-ringed eyes. "We have to go!"

Della knew what she had to do. Adrenaline flooding her blood, Della shook off Kess's grip and took off, heading straight for the fire.

"Della! No!" someone behind her screamed. She raced across the grass and gravel, moving as fast as she could while sticking to the shadows as her head swiveled to take in the scene.

On the far side of the mess hall, a heated battle waged between a tangled mess of hulking bodies. Illuminated by the firelight, smoke obscured her view, and Della couldn't make out how many were Morris Hill Alphas and how many were the invaders, nor could she tell who, if anyone, was winning. Shouts and screams and the dull roar of fire polluted the peaceful night.

Della swore under her breath but didn't slow, running top speed toward the inferno. *The mess hall.* Of course, how had she not anticipated that? Blood surging with adrenaline, her legs pumped a brutal rhythm on the hard-packed ground. Heat blasted against her face every step closer, and the smoke and fumes singed her airways. Coughing, she pulled her shirt over her nose and ran toward the back of the building where a cellar door, half sunk into the earth, lived, thankfully away from the battle. Her hands closed around the handle, and she yanked, immediately feeling the wrenching strain on her shoulder when it didn't move.

What the fuck?

A lock hung on the side, newly bolted in since the last time she'd had cause to visit the door. Probably installed in response to the missing food. *Fuck!* A crack of a skylight ripped through the air as it crashed and threw up a flurry of sparks. Every minute the situation became more desperate. Della whirled around, searching for something, *anything,* to break the lock, landing on the ring from the firepit.

Ignoring the Alpha battle, she tore across the distance, grabbing the biggest rock she could. Turning back, her ears filled with her own heartbeat and ragged breaths and the hissing rush of the fire, like a river of pure destruction. Skidding, she careened down the three steps, crashing against the locked metal door with a thud. Hefting the rock over her head with both hands, she slammed it into the lock. The dull clang of rock on lock rose above the fire as the force reverberated up her arms. She gritted her teeth and swung again, missing the lock completely with the unwieldy weapon, smashing her pinky finger between the door and the rock in the process.

Pain seared so fast and hot she almost dropped her weapon. "Fuck! *Fuck*!"

"Here." A firm hand on her shoulder held her back from lining up another blow. A breathless Kess stood behind her, holding up a key on a tinkling keyring. "Here," she panted, "it's this one."

Dropping the rock, Della snatched the key, hope blooming in her chest, and jammed it into the mechanism. With a decisive twist, it fell away, and Della swung the door wide.

"Cal!" Blinded by the transition between the fire-bright night and the darkened basement, Della stumbled down the steps into the darkness while Kess pressed against her back. She blinked rapidly, her head whipping this way and that, trying to scan her surroundings. Heat radiated down from the low ceiling, alongside the muffled crack and snap of burning wood, a menace from above that could collapse at any moment.

"Della?" A deep voice rasped from the corner. "What are you doing here?"

Metal on metal clinked, along with the sound of a shifting body. She made out the outline of Cal heaving himself to his feet without any of his usual grace. Across the room in an instant, she hurled herself at him without any regard for his possible injuries. He caught her with one arm, the other cradled against his stomach as the sound of more metallic jangles spiked worry into her brain. Despite the danger, their bond glowed bright and happy in her chest, expanding like a supernova now that she was back in his arms.

His lips pressed to her forehead, and he gently pushed her away. "You have to get out of here. This place is going to collapse."

"Not without you." She straightened enough to run her hands over him. "What's going on? Are you hurt? Can you walk?"

"My shoulder's dislocated, and I'm chained," he explained, holding out his shackled ankle for proof. Her stomach plummeted at the sight. "I can't go anywhere."

"Kess!" Della said, panic flooding her gut. "The key?"

"It's not there," Cal said, his tone flat.

Kess ran back to the door to retrieve the keyring, tripping down the stairs while flipping through a half-dozen keys that all looked much older than the one that opened the door. "Let me try."

"What's this attached to?" Della dropped to her knees, grabbing the chain and following it to its anchoring point as Kess set upon the shackle, a key outstretched in her hand.

"An old water heater," Cal explained. "It's tied into the foundation, and I'm tied to it. Della." He fisted the back of her shirt and physically lifted her off the ground, his eyes wide and terrified. "*You have to go.*" The floorboards above groaned; another crash shook the structure, and debris fell from the ceiling. "*Now. Please.*"

Kess stood, panic all over her face, her frantic gaze bouncing between Della and Cal. "None of these work."

Della wrapped her hands around Kess's shoulders and pushed her toward the door. "Then you need to leave." Della's voice was cool but committed, and the Omega stared at her, looking dumbstruck. "The settlement needs you. You have to go."

"Della!" Cal roared. "You're going too!"

Ignoring him, Della shoved Kess hard. "Throw some of that food outside if you can, but then you need to leave." Della grabbed Kess's hand and gave it a hard, final squeeze, "Thank you for trying. Take care of my friend."

With that, Della spun, dashing into a neglected corner of the basement. If she remembered correctly, there was once a pegboard of old, rusted tools in here. Maybe she could find something to break the chain around Cal's ankle. If so, they might have a chance.

Smoke billowed through the room, burning her eyes and making it harder to see. She rubbed at them as she stumbled around, her feet and knees kicking and bumping into things. But the pegboard was where she'd remembered, decorated with rusted pliers and broken clamps hanging like an apocalyptic art installation.

She alighted on the thin contour of a hacksaw and snatched it off the wall. Old and rusted and liable to fall apart at any moment, but it only had to work this one last time.

Oh, please, God, please let this work.

"Here," she said, her lungs exploding in a hacking cough as she handed the tool off to Cal. "Let's try this."

"Holy shit," he muttered, already in motion. "Here, hold the chain."

Della fell to her knees and braced the chain with her hands. Cal used his good arm to line up the cut and saw a few passes along a link. Metal scraped on metal, the grating sound scraping across her eardrums. Della held her breath, praying to any god she could think of.

Please let this work, please. I can't lose him. Not like this.

Cal sat back on his heels and examined the blade before tossing it to the side with a rusty clatter. "Chain's harder than the saw, it's never gonna work." Della's mouth fell open, all of her unanswered prayers stuffing themselves down her throat. Cal reached out and dragged her close, covering her face with hard, frantic kisses. "You gotta go."

Her soul cracking open, she pushed at his chest, angry and hysterical and on the verge of screaming in his face. "No," she said, shaking her head. She cupped his stubbled cheeks, bringing his eyes level with hers. "I don't run from you, remember?"

A sudden calm slashed through the hysteria as her brain caught up to her tongue. *I don't run from you.* One day ago, she promised him while he'd fucked her in her Omega nest and laid his bloody claim on her neck, and she'd meant it. Her will hardened stronger than the shackle that imprisoned him.

She wasn't about to make herself into a liar.

More crashes from the upper level made the future imminently real. They were going to die there. In the midst of fire and flames and senseless violence. But neither of them alone.

Pain crumpled Cal's face, and he leaned his forehead against hers, his words gruff. "Della, no, that's not what—"

"Shh. I know," she whispered, tucking tendrils of sweaty hair behind his ears. "But I said I wouldn't run, so don't ask me to." His mouth opened and then closed again, helplessness and grief marring his beautiful face.

Peace enveloped her. Like the old movies where the soundtrack went silent right before someone died, only in Della's peace, everything crackled vivid and wild and entirely the way it should be. All of her previously eroded surfaces had been recast and reformed in the complicated, intricate shape of Adeline Cabrese, and she treasured every edge and angle and rough patch.

"It's okay," she said, wiping away the tears that dripped down his cheekbones and replacing them with soft kisses. All of Cal's anguish howled through their bond, and she absorbed and rejoiced in it, pumping pure love out in return. "I was ground down to nothing," she said directly into his ear. "I felt nothing and loved nothing, and I thought that made me safe." She pulled back and looked him square in the face, so he could see her truth as well as hear it. "But the only thing it made me was *alone*. But, right now, with you, I'm not alone anymore, and I refuse to go back."

She leaned in and kissed him like it was her first kiss and last kiss and every kiss in between all rolled into one. He kissed her back, his lips moving slow and sure, as if they had all the time in the world.

Seconds passed like minutes while the bond in her chest sputtered and dripped golden tears all over her insides. There was a certain poetry to it, she supposed, or destiny or some sick irony or simple, meaningless, idiotic coincidence, to lose two men she loved in fiery destruction.

Life was stupid like that.

All anyone could do was make the best of it, and Della knew, in this moment, she was making the best of every shitty circumstance she'd ever been handed. She was going to die here, and she had zero regrets.

Cal's chin jerked back. "Do you have your knife? The one I gave you?"

Confused, Della rummaged in her clothing, pulling it from a pocket. "It won't cut through the chain."

His jaw flexed with resolute intention. "No. But it can cut me."

CHAPTER TWENTY-NINE

Cal

An amputation. As a child, Cal had stumbled upon a gruesome do-it-yourself surgery book in Pa's library. A survivalist to his core, Pa had estimated the possibility of needing to do wilderness surgery sometime in his life, not as remote as some folks would assume.

Goddamn him for being right.

Cal had known, when he'd watched Colt slip the shackle key into his front pocket, that, one way or another, he'd die in this basement. What he hadn't anticipated, not for a single second, was taking Della along with him.

No amount of arguing would sway her. The twinkling star that lived in his chest told him everything he needed to know and nothing he wanted to hear. Her resolve reverberated along their bond like the final note of a symphony held for far too long. It flowed from her soul into his, showering him with undeserved affection meant to soothe them both. But her determination and poignant resignation to the situation drove the final nail in his decision's coffin. Too many lives had been lost because of his miscalculations and here was yet another. Not only did the bond not protect Della, it imprisoned her to a dying man, and he refused to surrender without a fight. It was save them both or die together, and Della's death was not one he could bear.

Tipping Della off his lap, he awkwardly hiked up his pant leg one-handed. His limp, useless arm hurt, the pain a dull throb in the back of his mind. His main worry was that it would limit his ability to help Della with what was to come.

"We need a tourniquet, and it needs to be tight. And Della,"—he captured her dazed and confused eyes with his own— "you're gonna have to do the cutting."

Horror spoiled the serenity in their bond. "What? No! You can't be serious!"

He stared her down, imparting all the gravitas and Alpha command he possessed into his next sentence. "I got you into this mess, and I'm getting you out." He reached out, grasping her chin in his hand. "I'm losing the foot either way. The only question is whether it's attached to me when I go or not."

Her eyelids dipped in a slow, pained blink. Then, as if something switched inside her, she shook off the bewilderment and adopted a wolfish focus. "Okay, okay." Shoulders heaving up and down with steadying breaths, she got to her feet, scanning the room. "Tourniquet. Okay. We need cloth, and there's gotta be some of that awful alcohol in here." She raced around, tearing into the dark recesses behind sacks and stacks of provisions, her face set in grim determination. *This was the Della who survived a century in the AfterEnd,* and thank god she'd chosen this moment to show up. "Here!" she yelled triumphantly, hoisting a glass container from behind a crate of potatoes.

She rushed to his side, handing it over. "Sterilize everything. I'll find something we can use for a bandage."

With his working arm, he adjusted the shackle, riding it up his leg until it wedged tight around the diameter of his lower leg. The metal circlet had enough give that he could push it up a few inches and give her enough room to make the cut. Nausea blasted up his esophagus at the thought, but he fought it down, determined to make this work or die trying.

"Here." Della had two empty grain sacks in her hand, laying one beneath the leg and tearing the other into a strip. She shot him a worried look, "There's no way that knife is going to cut through two bones."

"We'll break it first," he said grimly. Taking the cloth strip, he awkwardly looped it around his calf and held the ends for her to tie. Della executed a neat square knot while Cal grabbed the rusty hacksaw handle to use as a windlass. He placed it on top of the knot. "Tie this." She did, and together, they began cranking to wrench it tight.

Pain declared itself as the tourniquet stanched his blood flow. His tissues registered the loss of oxygen and thundered in protest. Cal gritted his teeth, knowing the worst was yet to come. "One more thing," he said through pursed lips, "I need something big and heavy enough to smash the bones."

Della whimpered. "I'm going to throw up."

"Della! For Christ's sake!"

Scrambling to her feet, she ran to the doorway and returned, hacking smoke from her lungs and holding a sizable rock that looked like a busted-up piece of concrete. "We have to hurry."

"No shit. Stand back." Taking the rock, he hefted it in his one working arm, grateful for the jagged edge he could aim at his bones like a wedge. He didn't have time to calm himself with deep breaths or peaceful meditation, his gaze centered on the lower part of his leg, and he slammed the rock down with all his strength. A sickening crack reverberated to his stomach and renewed his battle with the nausea. The jarring blow invaded like a worm, and white-out pain made him battle for consciousness. Not wanting to take any chances, Cal bit his cheek as hard as he could and struck again, this time letting a grunted curse spill from his lips when he felt the weight of his foot separate from the rest of his body.

Cal reached for the bottle of spirits, white spots bobbing in his vision. "Gimme your hands." Not looking at her face, he drenched Della in the spirits up to her elbows before moving down to douse his skin, speaking quickly in case he passed out. What she would do with his inert body if that happened, he couldn't even dare to imagine. "Once you start, you have to keep moving. Angle the blade to leave as much skin as you can, but no matter what, *keep going.*"

"I can do this," she muttered, flinching as another crash thundered from above them. Sweat ran down her noble forehead. "I can do this."

Cal grasped her chin, desperate to impart all the confidence he could. "You can do this." With a final squeeze, he held out the knife, and she took it, zeroing in on her target.

Not much remained in the jug of alcohol, but he tossed what little there was down his throat. It went down like water and was gone too soon. Holding the final swallow in his mouth, he pulled the shackled chain, keeping it up and out of the way of the blade, which lay poised and sharp against his flesh. Breath locked tight in his chest, the moment balanced on a literal knife's edge as a fresh wave of hopelessness socked him in the gut. Would she actually do it? Or would they die in a crush of fire and flame?

God bless her, the first cut was deep and decisive. Cal's neck snapped back, the last swallow of alcohol running down his throat. Its burn absolutely nothing compared to the agony of skin and muscle carved away from his bones. If his leg jerked away from the agony, well, he couldn't help it. He tightened his grip on the chain to try to hold himself still.

He couldn't watch. With his neck tilted to the ceiling, the pain took on a life of its own. His vision wavered white, gray, and black at the corners, and above their heads, the fire raged like hell had evicted heaven from the skies.

After an eternity that was probably only a minute, Cal forced his eyes to the scene, seeing his body filleted open like a freshly butchered pig. Sticky blood soaked everything, coating his lower leg and foot in his gruesome path. Alcohol-flavored bile rose up his gullet, and he choked it back down. He couldn't vomit and risk distracting Della from her task.

As directed, the blade never stopped moving. An extension of Della's hand, it became indistinguishable as the edge rotated around, making deep, hacking slashes to sever his body in as little time as possible.

"Almost there," Della said.

A booming, thunderous crack shattered the roar of the fire. A crashing board fell behind Della, sending up a flurry of sparks. Della screamed, and light from the inferno flooded the room through the gaping hole in the floor. Heat blasted his face and lungs. If one board had succumbed to the fire, the others would soon.

"Hurry!" Cal screamed through a snarl of agony. "This whole place is going down!"

"Solve the problem. Solve the problem," Della chanted to herself like a prayer.

Distantly, over the roaring of blood in his ears, snaps, pops, and cracks of burning wood polluted the air like a morbid countdown to destruction. Eyes squeezed shut, Cal braced himself for the final blow, whether it would come from Della's knife or the crush of a final, fiery ruin.

"It's done!" Della's scream ripped him back into the moment as she yanked the chain from his limp hand and slid the shackle off his leg. "Get up! Get up!" He opened his eyes to find Della on her feet, her bloody hand extended and her face dripping sweat. "I can't carry you! Come *on*!"

Dizzy and sick, Cal lurched to his knees and then his feet—*foot*—leaning on Della when she plastered herself against his injured side. His head and vision swam with dizziness and, in his wild roving, chanced upon the stump of his foot on the dirty concrete floor, a grisly sacrifice to whatever gods cared about this sad wreck of a planet. If only it were enough. With a stabilizing arm wrapped around his waist, Della urged him toward the door.

Hop after excruciating one-footed hop, he hurled his broken body toward the exit, every minute a battle between dread, pain, nausea, and the seductive pull of unconsciousness. At the foot of the stairs, she took his one working hand in her bloody ones and slapped his palm to the step. "Crawl!" she commanded, pushing on his torso to hasten his ascent. "Go!"

He wanted to scream at her to go first, to get ahead of him, to get herself safe and leave him, to tell her this was all his fault, that he deserved to die, far more than she did, for what he'd done to his family and his Pack and to her. To describe the instant when the first whiff of her scent touched his nose and how the tug deep inside him signaled the once and forever reordering of his entire existence. To explain how he'd loved her from the moment he'd seen her face alight with the gentle glow of the bonfire. To beg her forgiveness for stealing her away, for disrupting her life, and damaging her relationships with her Pack. And, most abhorrently, to confess that, despite all of it, despite all the destruction and ruin he'd brought in his wake, he couldn't feel anything other than pride and awestruck gratification that she was his mate. *Only his*. And he'd die with the single ray of light in his heart, the knowledge she wore his mark forevermore.

Yet no capacity remained to express any of this to her. Like an angry beehive, his brain buzzed incoherence, and thoughts refused to form into words. Numbly, his hands and knees moved up the steps while Della screamed words he couldn't understand behind him.

Then, his hand lifted off the steps, his body jostled by strong hands gripping his body. A deafening thunderclap shook the ground, and the flaming heavens opened, shooting embers like demonic fireflies carrying bits of hell on unholy errands.

The light in his chest flared with a final, searing burst of fear, and then everything went dark.

CHAPTER THIRTY

Della

The screams wouldn't stop. They tore from her smoke-scorched lungs like something attached to her but not *of* her, not in the way the bond that sputtered in her chest was *of her,* its brilliance fading like waning stars in the coming dawn.

They dragged Cal's limp body free of the mess hall, now a flaming pile of wreckage, while Della shrieked about being careful of his shoulder, his foot, and his head. It wasn't until they laid him down in the shadow of Hunter's cabin that she realized someone had been carrying her the entire way as well. She fought against the hold, watching Cal's head loll like a doll without stuffing. "Let me go!"

"Della!" A familiar, gruff voice shouted in her ear. "Stop!" Her head jerked to find Hunter was the one carrying her. He set her down, his face a mess of blood and soot, his age lines blackened by dirt and ash.

Her bloody hands fisted his shirt, shaking him in impotent fury. "You left him there to die! He didn't do anything wrong, and you left him!" At the sight of the blood, *Cal's* blood, painting her skin up to her elbows, hysteria stormed like a tsunami. "You didn't listen to me, and now he's going to die!"

Face grim, Hunter snatched at her flailing fists and pulled her close. Della fought his hold again, pushing and punching with all her strength, but couldn't match his Alpha strength. Through her continued raging, he hugged her so tight the grit on his shirt abraded her cheek and her tears soaked into the cloth.

"Go help him!" she cried, refusing to be soothed. Why was he wasting time? Why wasn't he helping Cal? Or was he already dead? A fresh sob blasted up her throat.

With one last, firm squeeze, Hunter eased her back and ran his hands over her hair and face, his gaze focused and scanning. "Are you all right? Are you hurt?"

Was she hurt? She didn't even know. She couldn't feel her own body, not when she couldn't tear her attention from where Cal rested inert on the grass. A bloody stump lay mangled and sickening where his foot should have been, shards of bone sticking out. Della cursed herself for the crudeness of her work. Maybe if she'd worked faster or had more skill, strength, knowledge, or *something*...

The sight broke through the last of her fortitude. "Why aren't you helping him? *Why*?" she whisper-screamed with the last of her strength.

"Paul." Kess stepped into Hunter's side, laying a palm against his arm. His face immediately softened in her presence. "No woman runs into a fire to save her abuser. If you want to help Della, go save her mate." She raised her other arm, hefting an old-fashioned doctor's bag in Hunt's direction as a more-than-suggestion. "*Go.*"

Jaw clenched, he accepted the bag from Kess, frowning again at Della's tear-streaked face. "I'll see what I can do."

He strode away, and Kess took his place, wrapping an arm around Della's shoulders. "Come sit for a minute. You're shaking all over."

Kess guided her to one of the tree stump seats by the firepit, and Della sat. Everything inside her urged her to go to her mate, to sit at his side, touch his skin, and breathe comforting words in his ear. Yet she couldn't. What if his skin felt cool to her touch? What if his breath never tickled against her face? What if her words fell on ears unable to hear? What if he was already gone? She studied him closely, convincing herself his chest rose and fell with shallow respirations, but was that only her imagination?

After Rakesh died, his face haunted her every day for years. Mirages sat atop strangers' necks, there one second and gone in a blink. Her aggrieved brain played cruel tricks. Was this the same? Was she due to repeat that experience and see Cal's hazel eyes in every Alpha face who crossed her path?

"Here." Kess shoved a cup in Della's trembling hand and prompted her to bring it to her lips. She drank deeply, swallowing past the fire-scorched tissues of her mouth and throat.

Everything around her seemed unreal and *too* real all at once. Was that Logan crouching at Hunter's side, concern creasing his face? Was Lars truly arriving with clean bandages and a steaming bowl of water? Was that Cal's friend (Simon, was it?) checking his neck for a pulse, his expression a mix of horror and grief? Was all of this happening, or was it a fever dream conjured up by her disintegrating mind as she lived the last few minutes of her life pinned under a burning building? Had she died along with him in the rubble?

"Is the attack over?" she heard herself ask.

"It's over." With the fire at her back, haloing her outline like blessed, holy light, Della considered if she truly was dead, and Kess wore the face of the Holy Mother Mary.

As if sensing her impending crack-up, Kess's hand began rubbing Della's back in a slow, soothing rhythm. The touch, genuine and kind, grounded her stroke by stroke. Yes, this was real. It was all real. She'd lopped off Cal's foot. They'd escaped the basement. He might yet die, and she'd be a twice-over widow. She'd been ready to die with him, and now she might be forced to live without him.

Inside her chest, their tenuous bond trembled like a candle fighting a strong breeze. If he lived, *if he lived*, she would fix this. They could leave, go somewhere else like he wanted, start over somewhere new. If he wanted, she would give him her bite and reinforce their connection, as barbaric and insane as the practice compared to her old-world sensibilities. She pushed the promise down the bond like a paper lantern released on the wind, hoping it floated its way to her mate, wherever he was.

"There weren't that many attackers," Kess was saying, "but somehow one or two got past the patrol to light the fire, and then that caused a lot of confusion." Kess's voice reeked of disgust and hatred. "My understanding is that most are dead, and Hunter will deal with those that lived."

Concern for her Pack elbowed its way into her awareness. "Is everyone all right? The children? The Omegas?"

Kess nodded calmly. "Our Omegas and pups are all fine."

"Is anyone hurt?"

Kess pushed a lock of curly hair from her face. "Riddick has a good slash across his face. A few others have burns, but nothing as serious as..." Her words trailed away, and Della followed her gaze to where Hunter examined Cal's wound. "Della, how on earth did you...?"

Della shrugged miserably, the only response she could give.

Kess's expression brimmed with understanding. "I knew when you tore off that you'd let that building collapse on your head before you gave up."

"Cal thought he was protecting me." Della trailed her fingers over her claiming mark. "With this. I asked him to do it, it wasn't forced..." Anger boiled up from deep in her chest. "And then they *left him there*. They left him to die."

Kess rubbed her lips together and spoke slowly. "They made a mistake."

Weighed down by too many emotions, Della sunk her face into her hands. "Cal was right. We shouldn't have come back here. We'll have to leave. If he lives, we'll go east like he wanted."

"No, Della. *No*." Kess's voice grew strong and forceful, demanding Della leave the safe avoidance of her palms. "Thanks to you and Cal, we only lost the mess hall. It could've been much, much worse. The Pack needs you and Cal."

"How can you say that?" Della rasped. "You don't even want me here."

Confusion crossed Kess's face. "What?"

The protests rushed past her lips, all her diplomacy depleted as the adrenaline leeched from her system. "Hunter told me you weren't comfortable with our friendship." Della's head swung like a resigned pendulum. "You don't even know me."

Kess's shoulders slumped. "He told me about that. He thought he'd done the right thing, but I was appalled." She shot an exasperated glance at her mate and then met Della's shocked stare again. "I'd never deprive Hunter of a friend, and I told him as much. My plan was to come talk to you and clear the air, but then you were gone, and I never got the chance." Kess rubbed at her sooty forehead. "And Hunt regretted how he left things, especially when you went missing. He was so upset. It was clear how much he valued you and how silly it was for him to push you away."

A shuddering breath quaked over Della's shoulders. "Is that why you helped me tonight?"

"I dunno." Kess tucked Della's hand into her own, squeezing it in emphasis. "Maybe I figured you'd do the same if our positions were reversed. If you stay, I hope we can get to know each other better. Now. You feel ready to go to your Alpha?"

Della let Kess help her to her feet. The first rays of sunlight stole over the horizon, raising the curtain of night beam by beam. The mess hall fire continued, polluting black smoke into the sky, but a circle of Alphas kept an anxious watch, beating back the flames and containing the spread. A new mess hall would need to be built, and the food stores would need to be replenished. It would be a hard summer and maybe a difficult winter if they couldn't recover from everything lost.

But none of that mattered.

Not as her feet stumbled to her mate's side. The Alpha voices huddled around his body, muttering in high-intensity vigil, hushed as she knelt by Cal's head. Hunter met her questioning gaze and gave her a resolute nod. Blood smudged his hands as he strung suture material for the long job of closing up the hacking mess she'd made of Cal's flesh.

Even if her mate survived, there would be infection risk, bleeding risk, and innumerable other dangers ahead. Even if it did heal, he'd be a disabled Alpha in a group that valued strength above all else. What would that mean? Maybe the wound might never heal or forever give him pain. Maybe the imprecise break would prohibit any kind of prosthesis, however primitive of one they could fashion. Her mind flashed to Cal tottering around with a pirate-y peg leg, his easy, loping gait forever ruined, and she shooed all the worries away. They would cross that bridge when they came to it.

For now, he needed only to live.

Following instinct, Della bent forward and buried her nose in the crook of Cal's neck, searching for his distinctive scent in the smoke-clogged air. She found it, coffee and cinnamon, faint and tingling warmly against her nose. Untainted by the stench of death, she identified his scent—man and musk, safety and *life*—and relished it. She drew its peace into her lungs to dispel the toxins clogging up her airways and drove away the anxiety that churned and twisted in her guts.

Satisfied, she dragged her nose up along his jaw and over his face, her hand cradling his opposite cheek. "Cal, can you hear me?" she cooed in his ear. "You can come back now. I'm safe, okay? You're going to be all right, but you need to come back. You can't leave your Omega like this. I need you."

Feeling the gratifying wisp of his breath against her face, she smoothed hair gritty with ash back from his brow and kissed him gently on the lips, on his nose, on each of his beautiful eyes, on his stubbled cheeks, and the cleft in his chin. "Come back, Alpha," she whispered against his lips. "Come back to me."

CHAPTER THIRTY-ONE

Cal

The glowing speck shimmered in the darkness. Flirting for attention, it flashed and rippled, the reddish-gold ember beckoning to him with a seductive, capering flare.

A twinkling star. A word came to him from somewhere, some knowledge base floating in the midst of so much inky emptiness. Along with it came a feeling. How he knew it was a feeling, he wasn't sure, but that's what feelings did. They birthed themselves into existence and demanded consideration.

And this one? This flickering, fluttering spark? It trilled and bounced with anticipation. It strummed and tingled, eager to lead him along some invisible path toward some unknown destination.

All he understood was that he wanted to go there. Wherever it was, it was where he was meant to be. Not lost and floundering in this bleak in-between, but charging ahead toward the thing that waited for him. Nestled against that hint of fire, he followed its path to reclaim whatever it was, already certain it was his.

*

Midnight blue.

The color greeted him like a long-lost friend. Cal clung to it like a rope thrown to a drowning man, tracing the color to its surface, where it pooled in a pair of eyes set in a face—a pretty face, worn and serious and brimming with tenderness—that gazed at him in rapturous hope.

"Cal?" Musical and breathy, the voice reached into his bleary consciousness and hauled him further to the surface. Still following the burnished ember up from the depths, he grappled for comprehension, his vision clearing enough to sweep over the room where he now found himself. Rough-hewn walls. A cozy fire. A small table and a single chair. A nice room, yet none of it held the significance of the perfect indigo in that sweetly familiar face. A single drip of moisture tumbled over and snaked a path along delicately freckled skin.

Sluggishly reaching out to thumb away the drop, his entire body ragged and grainy, slowed from disuse and dehydration. "No need for tears."

Small hands sandwiched his cheeks as she peered at him with intense focus. Which was fine with him, her touch a welcome comfort after swimming for a lifetime in darkness. "You came back. You came back to me." Her voice broke on a sob, and his leaden arms again moved, pulling her tight atop his chest, where she fit like she was made for him.

Recollection converged around the edges of his consciousness. Tucking his nose into her hair, he glutted on breath after breath, reminding himself of the berry-ripe perfection of her scent. Every inhale brought him closer to this world, the real world, one he thought he'd left behind.

How long had he been asleep?

Memories rushed back from the weird, looping purgatory. "I dreamed I died," he whispered, his hands soothing up and down her trembling back.

"No." Her reply was soggy. "Don't say that."

But the memories flowed out, and his tongue failed to stanch the onslaught. "Died and then woke up back in the cave—*our* cave—and everything happened again... with me and you... everything the same until the ceiling fell, and we died in that basement." His breath whooshed out, overcome with the remnants of that total helplessness. "And then I'd wake up again, still in the cave, like none of it had happened, and the whole thing would start from the beginning. Except I knew what was coming, and every time I'd think, 'this is the time we escape,' but it never came. And your face... oh, Della, I looked into your face and thought I'd killed you, over and over again."

Della lifted her head from his chest, and anguish fastened itself to his lungs, strangling and cutting him off from his hard-fought breath. In that wretched basement, he'd stared into those same wide, blue, terrified eyes knowing she was about to die and unable to do a single thing about it. His chest heaved, fighting the chokehold, struggling for air.

Sensing his distress, Della wiggled upward till they were nose to nose. Hearts mashed together, the radiant light connecting them pulsed with contentment and peace. "I'm not dead," she said, the tears streaming freely now. Chest glued to his, the pressure of her own respirations guided his, slowing until he could once again use his lungs. "I thought I'd killed *you*. Hunter didn't know why you were unconscious. He thought maybe the pain was too great or smoke inhalation or lack of oxygen to your brain or you'd had a stroke or—" A sob choked her words, and her face folded in on itself.

Cal wiped at her tears, desperate to make it stop, to do his duty and console her from the doubt and dread she'd been shouldering alone. It echoed through their bond, worse than the dreams of his own death, and it sickened him to know he'd been the cause of so much uncertainty and angst.

He pushed the words past his parched tongue. "I'm your Alpha. I'm meant to protect my Omega, protect *you*, from everything. But I failed. I failed so badly, Della. I dragged you into danger, and I'm so, so sorry."

He didn't know what he wanted. Not her absolution or her forgiveness—God knew, he didn't expect that, nor did he deserve it—but he kept talking, needing to drag all his shame into the open. "And the worst part?

In those last minutes, when the building was falling, I didn't even regret that I'd done it, that I'd selfishly forged this bond between us." He squeezed his eyes shut as if he could hide from his mistakes. Feeling sick, overwhelmed, and so miserable, he pried his lids open, forcing himself to face her. "How is it that every time I think I'm doing the right thing, people I love pay the price?"

Anger elbowed onto Della's features. Her lips lost their pink softness, and she narrowed her eyes into dangerous slits. "That bridge was an accident. You didn't cause that any more than you caused the fire—"

"If I hadn't put my mark on you," he interrupted, passion and guilt erupting and getting the best of him, "you could've walked away free and clear." He jabbed at his own chest. "If I hadn't bonded you to me, your life would've never been at risk."

Della lowered her brows and tilted her head to the side. "You think it was because of the claiming bite that I refused to leave?"

His chin jerked a tight nod. "A severed bond is... it's *not good*. No Omega would want to live through that."

Tears slowing, Della studied him for a long, poignant lull. He imagined the thoughts working their way through her brilliant mind as she examined them from every angle. It was one of the many things he loved about her; when she spoke, wisdom bolstered her opinions, and she always, always meant what she said. His insides shriveled, bracing and anticipating her rejection. If she severed their bond, he would miss that about her, but he would accept her truth and find a way to continue.

Her hand strayed to his face, and she traced his features with the tips of her fingers: his brows, his nose, his lips. Her touch felt like a benediction, like something holy, and his heart bulged under the weight of this gift, perhaps the last one she'd ever give him. "I told you in the fire that I tried to keep you out." Her voice was hoarse and thick with feeling. "But I couldn't. You teased, charmed, and seduced your way right into my steel-fortified heart." The full swell of her lower lip tucked between her teeth. "How could I let you go when you worked so hard to get in there?"

Pulse pounding in his throat, her heartfelt confession held him rapt in her spell. Because that's what he was, thoroughly and utterly spellbound, enthralled by the sensitive, tender creature that had burrowed into her tough outer shell for so long but who laid herself bare when she'd risked her life to save his. And, once again, her bravery exposed his deficiencies, shoving flaw after flaw in his face.

Control slipped away from him, his emotions once again spiraled into a desperate mess, and his words followed. "From the moment we met, I knew you were my Omega. *Mine*. And I vowed to protect you and keep you safe, but I didn't. *I couldn't.*"

With an exaggerated groan, Della tilted her face to the sky as her fist pounded softly against his chest. "You idiot man." She dropped her head and pinned him with a look half-incredulous, half-pitying. "Are you not hearing me? I came to save you because I *love* you. I refused to leave because I *love* you. I haven't left your side for days because I fucking. Love. You." Her ire evaporated, and she gazed down at him with all that love pouring out and spilling everywhere all at once. "Yeah, there's this connection, and I guess after all this time, it turns out I'm some weird kind of Omega. I don't understand any of it, but none of that is why I ran into that burning building. I didn't run in there because you're my Alpha or because we have this bond." She shook her head like she couldn't believe she had to actually say it out loud. "I ran in there because you're *you*."

His trembling fingers found hers, and he brought them to his lips, kissing their tapered tips because he didn't know what else to do. Every feeling he hadn't allowed hurled into him in one crushing blow. It wrapped itself around him and rocked him to his very core with astonished, heartrending gratitude.

"Cal," she whispered, those fingers scraping over his stubble, "safety is an illusion. *Nothing* is safe in this world. You can't protect me any more than I could protect myself from loving you. It's an impossible ask. The best we can do is take all the love we can find, hold it to our chests, and never, ever, give it up without a fight."

In a few elegant sentences, she'd carved a hole in his chest. Like a huge tumor had been excised, and in its place, in the wide gaping pit where all his guilt, shame, and self-doubt had lived, Della overflowed with love, affection, and devotion. Protests drained out of him. Who was he to fight her on this? Who was he to reject her precious offering? Who was he to say that she was wrong?

She was right. There was no other option. If he couldn't keep her absolutely safe, and he couldn't give her up, then, of course, she was right. She had to be. He breathed in a cleansing puff of air, discovering that rather than fear, apprehension, and despair bearing down on him as it always had, he found lightness, possibility, and grateful, reverent wonderment.

He held up his palms in surrender. "All right. You're right. Of course, you're right." Her eyes sparkled at this, and her cheeks drew up like two sweet little pillows of happiness. Lowering his hands, he snuck them around her middle, finding the edge of her shirt and slipping under to glide his fingertips over her soft, soft skin. His mouth flexed with the beginnings of a grin. "You like the sound of that, don't you?"

A wide grin spread across her face. "Maybe a little."

"A little too much." His fingers dug into her sides, tickling her enough to elicit the smallest of squirms and a tiny, girlish squeal.

"You should listen to your elders," she teased.

A rumbling growl percolated up from his chest. "Don't get your hopes up."

Smiling, he ran his hands up the length of her back, grounding himself in her strong, sturdy presence as she gazed down at him. "Do you understand what I'm saying?" The delight in her grin dimmed. "I don't need you to protect me. We're in this together, for as long as it lasts."

"I understand." He met her seriousness with his own. "And it's a good thing you do, too, because I'm not that easy to get rid of." He winked. "You had your chance. You're stuck with me now."

Craning his head upward, he kissed her nose, gratified when a smile stole onto her face. With his palms on her cheeks, he brought her lips to meet his in an electrifying kiss.

"You sure about that?" she teased between kisses. "You haven't tasted my cooking yet."

A hearty laugh rattled from deep in his chest, and he whispered against her kiss-swollen lips, "Do your worst."

CHAPTER THIRTY-TWO

Della

A loud knock at the door disrupted their amorous activities right as things were heating up.

Della scrambled upright and yanked her shirt back into place as Cal flopped his head dramatically back on the pillow, flinging an arm over his face with a groan. In hindsight, she might've been surprised a man who'd been unconscious for three days would segue directly into making out upon awakening minus one foot, and yet, she had to admit she wasn't sad about it. Sweeping a glance over Cal's bedded body, she internally cringed at the bandaged lump under the covers, dismayed they hadn't even discussed his injury.

Another knock rattled the door, and Della recognized its briskly impatient cadence. Pressing a hand to her churning belly, she swung the door open and stepped aside to let Hunter into her home.

"Hey." His sharp glance took in her tousled appearance before cutting over to where Cal was pulling himself up to sitting. Hunter quirked a brow at her, mischievousness crinkling his eyes. "Our patient's awake?"

"Obviously," she said, hiding her flaming cheeks and disheveled embarrassment by darting back to the bed and vigorously fluffing and rearranging the pillows behind Cal's back.

Truth be told, things between her and Hunter hadn't been exactly smooth since the night of the fire. He'd apologized more than once for his callous treatment of their friendship and the confusion that had left Cal chained up like an animal and left to die. In fact, a steady stream of shame-faced Alphas continuously graced her doorway since that night, each of them offering their apologies and condolences and making polite inquiries about Cal's recovery. More than one emphasized their remorse over the loss of his foot and expressed a commitment to help in any way they could with his recovery.

She'd had little emotional bandwidth for anything but worry over Cal, yet her conflicting feelings about the Pack occupied what little she had. These Alphas had been part of her life for the better part of twenty-odd years. Twenty stable, safe, productive years where she'd been able to have her own home and reconstruct some semblance of a normal life after decades of fear and chaos. Sure, they aggravated her and irritated her on the regular, but thanks in part to their efforts (along with her own, of course), she'd been able to live for the first time since TheEnd without constantly looking over her shoulder or worrying where her next meal would come from. Things she would never again take for granted.

Not that she owed the Morris Hill Alphas anything, not after the events of the past week, but her loyalty to them demanded consideration. In truth, Della wanted to believe them, forgive and move forward. But with Cal unconscious, she'd refrained from offering words of reconciliation out of respect for her mate. In her mind, Cal possessed every right to be beyond furious. For her to offer absolution on his behalf before he'd had a chance to confront them himself struck her as insensitive and disloyal, akin to adding insult to his already-significant injury. So, she'd held back, focused on caring for his inert body, and waited.

But that didn't keep her from spending many unsettled hours contemplating this eventual pending confrontation. Would Cal make nice with Hunter? What about the rest of the Pack? Or would he insist that they leave Morris Hill once he fully healed? The same worries bounced around her anxious brain as she twisted her fingers together.

In truth, she didn't really want to go anywhere else, especially now after the worst incident in the settlement's history, but she would. If Cal couldn't stomach staying a part of the Pack that almost killed him, she wouldn't argue. They would go wherever he wanted, and she would face the wide world again with him at her side.

"Cal." Hunter strode over to shake her mate's hand, and Della's gaze flashed between the two Alphas on instant high alert. "Glad to have you back with us," Hunter said evenly.

With a serious nod, Cal released the shake. "I take it the settlement is still standing."

Too anxious to sit still, Della grabbed a chair and brought it to the bedside. Hunter tipped his head to her in thanks and eased himself down, smothering a groan as he took a load off. Poor man likely hadn't slept more than four hours in the past three days.

Cal leaned back to test the pillow arrangement, tossing Della a grateful smile. With a nudge of his chin, he summoned her back to his side, where she obediently went and perched by his knees, keeping both Alphas in her sights, ready to defend her Alpha at any sign of conflict. Cal's hand came to rest on her thigh, and he gave it a friendly squeeze, pushing a pulse of reassurance down the bond.

"The mess hall is gone," Hunter said.

The corner of Cal's lip edged upward. "Kinda figured as much."

"The good news is the fire didn't spread. The bad news is that our food supply was wiped out, along with the kitchen and cooking facilities. To add to that, we gained some more Omegas in the whole mess, so more mouths to feed." He raked his fingers through his salt-and-pepper hair till it stuck out like a burly porcupine. "Priority number one is getting the kitchen and mess hall rebuilt and replenishing the food."

Della listened intently. All of this was news to her as well as to Cal. Given Cal's unconsciousness, she hadn't left his side to check on the state of things in the village. Guilt soured the churning mélange of her belly. Who was looking out for the new Omegas and getting them settled? Besides somewhere to live (all the more reason for an Omega bunkhouse now), they likely needed new clothes and everything else, and Della hadn't spared them a single thought.

"Where did you put the new Omegas?" Della asked. "How are they?"

Hunter leaned back and stretched his legs with some audible cracks. "We got 'em set up in some tents. It's not ideal, but it's dry, at least. They're a half-starved, bedraggled group, not too willing to talk to anyone. 'Course we're happy to have 'em, no one's mad about more Omegas"—his mouth formed an ironic smirk—"but it's gonna take a while for them to trust us."

"Housing would go a long way toward establishing that trust," Della said gently. "After the mess hall and the kitchen, they need somewhere more permanent."

Hunter gave a brisk nod. "Colt's on top of it. He's already got the Alphas convinced an Omega bunkhouse is a good idea."

Della smoothed a wrinkle on the bedclothes, feeling a small measure of triumph. One knot in her snarl of worries untangled. "That's good."

Cal cleared his throat. "And the attackers?"

"A few ran off when it became clear things weren't going their way. We tried to chase 'em down, but they were sneaky bastards," Hunter explained bitterly. "They distracted us by setting the fire, and I think they had some horses hidden to make a fast escape. Could've tried to go after them, but we made a decision to find the Omegas instead."

"It was so crazy that night," Della said, remembering the heat blasting off the fire as she'd frantically sawed her way through Cal's leg. She swallowed back a mouthful of saliva. "I'm surprised they all didn't escape."

"The ones who didn't weren't in any shape to make a run for it," Hunter said darkly, a renewed tension seasoning the air.

Cal's fingers cinched harder around Della's thigh, and his voice took on a menacing note. "What'd you do with them?"

Refusing to shy away from the question and its inherent test, Hunter made meaningful eye contact with Cal. "They're taken care of," he said coldly.

Cal responded with an approving grunt. "And Silas?"

At this, Hunter winced. "That's a trickier one. His story is that they ambushed him while on patrol last month. Says they were gonna kill him until he made a deal to trade his life for some food. Instead of alerting his Pack, he thought he could manage it on his own. Except they kept escalating their demands on him and then threatened to rat him out for stealing once he was in deep."

Cal's jaw worked like he chewed a tough piece of meat. "He wasn't too fucking stressed on patrol, lounging in the hot springs and napping in the shade. Quite a stretch to believe he was being strong-armed and blackmailed, if that's his story."

Cal's jaw ticked a slow pulse, and Hunter's shoulders turned to stone as they stared each other down in a silent stand-off. The confrontation she'd been dreading for days had arrived, setting her teeth on edge.

"I know," Hunter finally conceded with a heavy sigh. "Silas claims he fed them as much false information as he could, and they clearly underestimated how many of us they were going up against." Hunter rubbed an aggravated palm down his face. "I should've listened to you two that night. That was my fuck up. Tempers got triggered, and things got out of hand way too fast."

Cal's shoulder jerked in a noncommittal shrug, and the air twanged with unvoiced conflict. Della's attention zipped between the two of them, these hulking specimens who conducted entire conversations in the angle of a brow or the thinness of a lip.

Hunter's gaze slid to Della and back again to Cal. "But I do owe you an apology. Someone should've been assigned to watch you, someone who had the key. It was an oversight and, unfortunately, a very costly one, and I am very sorry."

Cal's cheeks tightened, and a muscle in his jaw ticked. "I understand y'all had reason to suspect my intentions, but you also ignored Della here. I'm new and maybe owed some suspicion, but she's one of your own. She cares about this place more'n any of you give her credit for."

Hunter winced, his brows drawn low. "You're right. She is one of our own, so when one of our own got carried out in the middle of the night only to come back with a bloody neck, well... we all went nuts."

"The mark was my decision," Della warned, not liking the two Alphas discussing her like she was a piece of furniture to be moved around, "which you would've known if you'd listened to what I had to say."

"So it was *your* decision to run off with him?" He aimed a challenging glance in her direction, and Della forced herself not to look away. "We can't have Alphas carrying women off any time they feel like it. As I recall, *you* were the loudest voice advocating for Omegas having a say in the matter."

"Of course, they have a say," she snapped, fully aware of the double bind in her argument. If she admitted Cal hadn't been in the wrong to take her, then what about the next Alpha who happened to take a liking to someone? It worked out in her case, but what if the next Omega wasn't so lucky?

"Della made her choice," Cal said, his tone low and controlled, "when she ran into a burning building." He caught her hand with his, threading their fingers together in a reassuring tug. "Which might not have been necessary if you all had given her a chance to speak when we returned."

Hunter scratched his beard thoughtfully. "I gotta say, now that I've been through finding my Omega and all that, I don't have an easy answer. We don't want Omegas to feel coerced here, but I admit the claiming urge is... uh... strong."

A pregnant pause expanded in the silence.

"I'm sure something can be worked out," Cal offered. "Maybe a trial period could be considered?" His lip quirked, and he gave Della a saucy wink. "Sometimes these Omegas take a little *convincing*."

Tingles erupted over her skin, and somehow Cal's smirk became even *smirkier*. He raised his eyebrows in a silent invitation for her to disagree, but of course, she wouldn't. Or couldn't. Or whatever.

"Here's what I don't understand," Hunter began, "I've known Della for a damn long time and never once scented her as Omega. Neither has anyone else, to my knowledge. But now, it's faint but definitely there. I've never heard of anything like it." He addressed Della. "Do you think you were some kinda latent Omega for all these years? Or do you think the mating bond *made* you Omega?"

"I honestly don't know," Della said. Having asked herself the same question and never coming up with any kind of sensible answer, she'd resolved to accept the mystery of her Omega transformation. If it gave her Cal, then how could it be anything but a blessing?

Her handsome mate shook his shaggy head. "She always scented as Omega to me. From the minute I walked into your camp, I caught her on the wind, and that was it. I had to have her." This last part he said with Della firmly in his sights, and her belly flip-flopped in response.

"So it's not faint to you," Hunter mused. "Interesting."

"And Della here got her sense of smell back, too," Cal added innocently, "which seems to be related."

The reference to her olfactory awakening in the cave had Della's lungs expanding to savor Cal's deep, rich scent, her eyelids fighting a flutter in response. Interestingly, she also picked up on Hunter's Alpha spice, but it took a backseat to that of her mate, which suited her fine.

Hunter stared off into space, his voice taking on a wistful, dreamy tone. "This Alpha -Omega shit is strange. Just when I think it's making some kinda sense... some new weirdness pops up," he ended, more to himself than anyone in particular. "At any rate,"— he snapped his head back up as he shook off those existential questions and addressed Cal—"you were right about Silas. Maybe you weren't so right about taking our Della away the way you did, but I understand why you did it. For my part, I apologize to both of you for losing my temper in the mess hall. I should've slowed down and got the whole story. That was on me. And I apologize for not making provisions to keep you safe in the cellar, brother. I understand nothing can bring your foot back, but for what it's worth, I regret it, and I hope you can find a way to stay a part of the community here."

Cal dipped his chin to accept the Alpha of Alpha's apology, and the anxiety stew trickled out of Della's belly. She didn't need Hunter's apologies (she could read the remorse all over him), but she knew Cal did. With this simple acknowledgment, her mate indicated a willingness to put the past behind them and move forward. Grateful tears welling, Della couldn't help but beam a bright grin at her mate, warmth stealing up her chest when he returned it, his green-gray-gold eyes lush with affection.

Alpha is happy. Alpha loves you, that inner voice singsonged like a smug child, and for once, she didn't feel like arguing.

CHAPTER THIRTY-THREE

Cal

"All right then." Hunter slapped his thighs, breaking up the quiet moment. "Should we talk about your injury?"

Cal forced himself to acknowledge his lower body, where a blanket hid the full evidence of his disfigurement. Maybe his injury hadn't been foremost in his mind upon returning from his extended vacation in the land of recurrent nightmares, but it definitely crouched in the corner, biding its time. All the fledgling peace he'd achieved setting his issues with Hunter aside dwindled down to nothing.

"Tell me the truth." He squeezed the words past the ball crammed in his throat. "How bad is it?"

"Well"—Hunter got up from the chair—"you can see for yourself. Della, you got any clean water to wash my hands?" To Cal's dismay, Della launched into action, vacating his side to fetch the water basin and soap for Hunter when all he wanted was to keep her close and breathe her in to distract him from the wound he was about to face for the first time.

In the heat of the moment—the literal heat of a burning building—there had been no hesitation about what needed to be done to free him from the shackle. Once Della declared she would not leave him to ensure her safety, no other option existed. Cal would never, not even for a single second, allow himself to regret that decision. At the same time, he hadn't considered what the rest of his life would be like sans one foot. Alphas, as a rule, were not known to tolerate weakness in each other. Would the injury be not only a disability but a liability?

Hunter rounded the foot of the bed, drying his hands. "How much pain are you having?"

"Some." Cal relaxed his neck against the bedframe and sucked in air through his nose. "I can still feel my foot, you know? Like if I try to move it, it's still there moving around even when I know it's not."

"It'll take your brain time to adjust," Hunter explained, squatting down and beginning to unwind the bandaged stump. "I had to file down some of the jagged edges of bone, which you were probably happy to be unconscious for, but there's nothing sharp left to come poking out of you."

Hunter's words swept past him like a gust of dried, fallen leaves, quickly forgotten. Cal's body stiffened as each wrap of the bandage loosened, knowing that at any moment, the ghastly reality of his mangled body would be exposed. Chilled air hit his skin as the last of the bandages peeled away. Overcome with a sudden rush of foreboding, Cal stared at the ceiling and braced himself in the final breath of *before*. A cool palm settled across his forehead. Della gazed down at him, her expression somber but unbothered, raining gentle encouragement on his tumultuous thoughts, and he moved his arms to circle her waist and draw her body close. He buried his head in the soft pillow of her stomach, shaking with relief and gratitude. Now that they'd hashed out their feelings, he could lay himself bare like this, knowing without a doubt she'd be there to catch him if he happened to stumble.

"Hey," she whispered, her lips pressed to his hair and her arms secured tightly around his head. "It's not so bad, handsome, I promise."

No question, he believed her and hugged her all the tighter because of it.

"In terms of healing," Hunter said, his usually gruff voice gentled, "the edges are already knitting together, no signs of infection. All told, I'm gonna guess you'll be completely healed up in about four to six weeks, Alpha immune systems being what they are. Do..." He cleared some discomfort from his throat. "Do you want to see it now or wait? I can always come back—"

"Now," Cal said, his voice firm but muffled in Della's shirt. He eased away from her, taking solace from her calm, beloved face before turning fully toward the foot of the bed.

Gone was the ghastly raw meat of his muscle and the white, exposed bone from his last memories of that night. The stump lay propped on pillows, cleaned and neat, with no trace of any of the former gore. A chaotic railroad track of sutures decorated his flesh, but Della had done as he'd directed and left enough skin to close fully over the amputation site. He rotated his leg this way and that, noting that the sutures appeared neat and uniform and not overly taut or straining.

His breath left him in a relieved hiss. It was still his body, recognizable and identifiable, except for the absence of the foot. The sight of the rest of his leg and thigh—still intact, strong, and capable—filled him with an early hope. As he'd told Della that night in desperation, he was losing the foot anyway, so the only question was whether he lost the rest of his body along with it. His hand found its way to hers, and he gave it a solid squeeze, relishing the stable, anchoring feel of her firm grip.

"Della knows how to clean it, but try not to get the sutures wet. We'll give it another few days and then get them out. Once the wound is closed, some gentle compression will help the swelling." Hunter lifted a shoulder. "I don't know anything about prosthetics or even what might be possible to make for you, but"— he met Cal's eyes with a look of solid promise—"we'll figure it out. In the meantime, I'll get someone working on a set of crutches."

"Thank you, Alpha." His voice was shakier than he might've liked, but he was well past caring. Despite the mess they'd made of their relationship, Hunter had patched him up like a true brother, and he was grateful.

Hunter tossed the soiled dressings aside and began wrapping the wound with fresh, clean strips of cloth. "It would be pretty ridiculous to let you die after everything Della did to save your life," he groused as he focused on arranging bandages with swift, practiced movements. "Besides which, we owe you much more than some stitching up. I hope you know that this Pack is gonna do everything we can to get you up and moving again."

At this statement, some final pool of unrest released from Cal's chest. Yes, Packs were supposed to take care of each other. Safety and security in numbers and commitment to each other. That's the idea Pa had drilled into him all those years ago when he was a young Alpha learning to one day take over as Alpha of Alphas. Somewhere along the line, in the fallout from the bridge collapse, that lesson had been forgotten by the people he knew and loved and whom he thought knew and loved him in return. Blind and tortured by grief, some of them sought to console themselves by scapegoating him, while others were poisoned by long years of jealousy. Either way, he'd been drummed out of the Pack that was his birthright. Betrayed not only by the people but by the principles he'd taken for granted.

But perhaps Pa hadn't been correct in putting all his faith in Cal to uphold the principles of the Pack. Maybe he ought to have worked harder to build the community and instill those values in everyone rather than putting all his focus on his one and only Alpha son. Here was Hunter, doing the exact thing Pa failed to do, working not only to protect individual Pack members but protect the idea of the Pack as deserving of protection as well.

Hence, the difficulty in dealing with Silas and Hunter's unsatisfactory answer to Cal's inquiry about that outcome. Along with the unresolved question of what Colt had been doing with the shackle key while the mess hall burned, Cal had set the question of Silas's disposition aside during their earlier conversation. But now it roared back into focus, and Cal realized he required a better answer than the one Hunter had provided, given the sacrifice he'd made as a result of Silas's actions.

"So that complicates the decision about Silas then, doesn't it?" he asked, meeting the subject in the only way he knew how: head-on.

Della started, her hand spasming where it had come to rest on the back of his neck.

Hunter frowned, giving one last squinted examination of Cal's bandaged stump before standing. "It does."

Packs had a responsibility to each other; they were supposed to care for one another and the Pack as a whole. And despite what had befallen him in his life, Cal still believed in those ideals. His commitment and respect for those ideals prompted him to ask Hunter if he could join his Pack back in OT. How would things have been different for him if his Pack truly embodied them rather than dismissing them when tragedy struck?

"What if..." Della spoke with quiet caution, "what if there was some way for Silas to atone?"

"I was thinking banishment, myself." Hunter rinsed his hands again. "It's kinder than what the rest of those bastards got, that's for damn sure. What did you have in mind?"

"He should replace the food that was lost." Della's voice swelled with confidence. "Give him a horse and let him go out and find work. He can trade his labor for food stores—dried goods, whatever he can get his hands on. Once he's collected a sufficient amount, then he can return."

Cal grinned at his mate as his chest gripped tightly with pride and appreciation.

If Silas chose not to accept the task, then he'd effectively banish himself by his own choice, not by the Pack's judgment. If he chose to accept the task, he would have time to contemplate his life choices as he worked to replace what was lost. Returning with food would demonstrate his recommitment to the Pack and help the Pack forgive someone who had so dangerously betrayed them. It was the perfect solution: creative, merciful, practical, and fair.

"Won't be easy to replace all that was lost," Hunter muttered.

"It's not supposed to be easy," Della countered, her conviction growing. "He was responsible for a lot of destruction, so he bears an outsized responsibility for the reconstruction. It's a *chance* for redemption, not a guarantee."

"It might be good for him to spend some time away from the Pack," Hunter said thoughtfully. "He'll be persona non grata around here for some time."

"He made a mistake." Della leveled Hunter with a somber look. "Maybe it was maliciously intended, maybe not, but it would hurt you and the Pack to harm someone you considered a brother, and the settlement has already had enough violence. It's time to move forward." Her attention shifted to Cal. "What do you think?"

Was it possible for a heart to explode from too much feeling? If his abused organ tried to contain any more love for this woman, Hunter would need to return to sew the overtaxed muscle back together.

"I think y'all should listen to my Omega." Cal pulled Della down to his lap with an unexpected tug on her hips, laughing at her surprised yelp. Her hair wisped soft and fragrant over his face as he planted a kiss on her cheek. He shot a glance to Hunter, who appeared to be slowly backing his way to the door.

The bond trilled a sweet, happy note as Della's emotions flooded out from her and into him. Craving recognition or deference would never be Della's prerogative, but that didn't mean she didn't deserve to be appreciated for all she did for Morris Hill. Too humble and modest to demand it for herself, Cal made it his personal mission to garner more respect for Della from the Alphas who fancied themselves in charge of it. One foot or no, the next Alpha who derisively referred to her as "mommy" in his earshot would be very sorry they did.

"Will do." Hunter disappeared out the door, not lingering over a goodbye, which Cal suspected was both his style and a nod to their need for some imminent alone time. He hooked a lock of Della's hair behind her ear, peppering her cheek and jawline with kisses.

"Is he gone?" he purred in her ear, his hand finding its way under her shirttail and grazing the underside of her breast. It wouldn't take much to pick up where they'd left off earlier.

Della hummed an answer, the vibration snaking its way from low in her throat directly to his groin. Angling her head in a clear invitation to continue the amorous attention he was paying to her neck, her throaty voice whispered, "Do you want to talk about it?"

Cal growled against her skin. "'Bout what?"

Her shoulders quaked with a small laugh, and he pulled back to her elegantly concerned face. She rasped the pads of her fingers over bristles of his beard growth. "Your foot. Hunter's apology. The Pack. The future. Anything. Everything."

"Y'know..." Snatching her hand, he brought her palm to his lips, kissing it before laying it against his heart where it belonged. "I've spent too much of my life punishing myself for mistakes and being punished by others for the same. For too long, I've been living in the past." Cal drew in a deep breath against the expanding love for his mate. "You're my present and my future, darlin', and that's the only place I want to be."

Eyes overflowing with affection, Della heaved a sigh that brought her shoulders down from her ears. "Okay. As long as you can be happy here."

Grinning, he palmed her chin and dragged her lips to his, reassuring her in the best way he knew how. Between softly frantic kisses, he whispered against her lips, "Don't you know? I already am."

EPILOGUE

Cal

Two months later

"Time for a refill?"

Cal reluctantly tore his attention away from the sight of his mate, laughing with a small group of Omegas across the fire. She'd gone to fetch another helping of roast pig and, as usual, had been waylaid by people wanting to tell her something or ask her questions or advice. Not that he minded, not in the least. No longer holding herself back, no longer on the outside looking in, it warmed his soul to see her embrace and be embraced by the community in this way. It was everything she deserved and nothing less.

The last two months in the settlement had been busy and difficult but ultimately reparative. The Alphas made a point to reach out with friendly offers and invitations, and the topic of potential prosthetic designs was frequent around the campfire. Matteo teased him frequently about his future as a "peg-leg cowboy," but he didn't care, laughing it off and grateful for every morning he awoke to Della nestled beside him.

The Pack had launched into the rebuilding effort as soon as the wreckage stopped smoking, clearing it out and framing a new and improved mess hall within the week. The damage, while significant, was far from catastrophic, and everyone understood whom they owed for that. Once Cal could move about with the aid of crutches, he'd thrown himself into the efforts as much as possible: sawing, planing wood, hammering, or debating proposed design plans. It was such a relief after weeks of inactivity that he didn't mind the additional discomfort in the healing stump or the fatigue that had him crashing in bed before the sun set most nights. Apparently, recovering from a traumatic amputation really took it out of you.

The recovery efforts proceeded so well that Hunter announced the evening's pig roast and bonfire in celebration of the mess hall's completion. Next, they would start on the Omega bunkhouse, finally fulfilling Della's vision. As a nod to his mate's new position of respect in the Pack, Cal had made sure everyone involved understood it was Della's project to spearhead, and no one dared object, not even the Alpha loitering to his left.

Colt, brows raised, held an outstretched pitcher of beer. "Refill?"

Wrestling down his surprise, Cal drained his cup and held it out. "Thank you, brother," he said, tone studiously bland.

Cup refilled, Colt took a seat, nursing his cup as a cautious silence permeated the air. Since the night of the attack, Cal had seen Colt plenty around the settlement, but their interactions, when necessary, remained brief, to the point, and superficial. Of all the Alphas, Colt had been the one to hang back in extending the olive branch, which always struck Cal as not an accident. But he couldn't dwell on it. By unspoken agreement, he'd buried all of their unresolved history in a shallow grave Cal fully intended to ignore.

He examined the younger Alpha with a critical side-eye. As a general rule, Alphas flourished under exertion. With the effort required to rebuild the mess hall and erect the new Omega bunkhouse, muscles grew and honed and hardened day by day. Even Cal's injury recovery was aided by diving into the hard work as much as he could, and despite the nightly fatigue, his leg strengthened and body healed at a pace that never failed to keep Della in constant awe.

Colt, though Cal frequently saw him in the thick of the reconstruction, appeared exhausted and weakened, a far cry from the confident Alpha Cal had fought at the beginning of summer for entry into the Pack. But they were not close—far from it—so Cal had kept his observations to himself.

Tipping his head back, Colt poured at least half a cup of the alcohol down his throat, pounding a fist against his chest to choke it down before giving a final cough to declare his mastery over the mouthful. "I owe you an apology," he said, voice strained and gravelly.

Shock locked Cal's body in place; any response to this revelation held tight inside as reactions stampeded through his mind. Colt, the one who possessed the key to the shackles that could've set Cal free with the simple flick of a wrist rather than an impromptu hacking surgery, most certainly owed him far more than an apology. Responses like, "*oh, you fucking think so*" and "*what took you so goddamn long?*" and "*how about apologizing to Della for putting her in a position where she almost died and then had to cut off her mate's foot?*" danced on his tongue.

But he didn't say any of that. Instead, he turned his face toward him before blandly asking, "Is that so?"

The Second's eyes squeezed shut, lines carving their way into his forehead. "I shouldn't have kept the key." He swallowed thickly. "That night. I should've given it to someone else to hold—one of the younger pups, someone who could've freed you when I didn't remember."

Cal lowered his brows. "You. Didn't. *Remember*?"

A shake of his head rustled Colt's shaggy hair over his shoulders. "Not until it was too late. Not until the first half of the building collapsed. I got wrapped up fighting off the attackers, but..." His chest deflated inward. "That's not the whole of it. There..." He cleared his throat as if dislodging something sticky. "There were reasons I may have been inclined to forget... reasons I may have wanted you dead but was too cowardly to even admit to myself."

Belly filled with solidifying ice, Cal stared into the fire. "Go on. Not that I give a shit, but seems like you got a need to get this off your chest."

The younger Alpha released a long, unhappy sigh. "When you joined up and brought your friends along with you, I started to notice some things. Simon and Matteo were your friends, but they respected you and deferred to your judgment, and in the time we traveled from OT back here, a few of the others started to do the same. You helped Hunt save Kess, and everyone admired you for that. It... uh... got into my head."

The realization smacked him in the face. "You thought I would take your place as Second." After everything that had happened, Cal could barely remember the journey Colt referenced. Perhaps a few of the younger Alphas gave him some additional respect, but supplanting Colt as Second was the furthest thing from Cal's mind then, as it was now.

Colt's head drooped miserably. "When you chose me for the initiation fight, I took it as a challenge."

"I had to choose someone, so why not you?" Cal asked with quiet menace. "And if you thought that was the case, then why not take it up with me directly?"

"I know. It's just..." He speared a hand into his hair. "Some things had happened before you joined up, and I already had guilt for not protecting Hunter's Omega better. And then you came along and helped Hunt get her back and. . ." He stared down at his hands, anguish written in every line of his face. "Hunter is like a brother and a father to me and... I felt like I'd let him down."

Cal's brows hiked up his forehead. "All that has fuck all to do with me."

"I know that now." Colt poured himself another cup from the pitcher. "It sounds weak to admit being envious of you, but there it is."

The implications sprouted in front of him like pictures in a pop-up children's book. It all made so much more sense: Colt's open hostility toward him, especially after the initiation fight and then even more once they arrived in Morris Hill, his exuberant condemnation of Cal in that initial conflict with Silas, Colt practically encouraging him to leave the settlement, and Colt's fury when he'd returned.

As if he could feel the weight of Cal's judgment, Colt's head sunk farther toward his chest, shame rolling off him in waves. "I'm sorry... I... I'm so sorry."

"Oh, well, that makes it all right," Cal said with a heavy dose of sarcasm. A fat lot of good it did for the asshole to be sorry *now*, now that everyone survived and he didn't have to live minus one foot.

Resentment poisoning his blood, Cal sought the silver strands of Della's hair glittering in the reflected firelight. Seeing his mate, he felt his irritation surface even more. "But what about the apology you owe her?" he demanded. "For what your actions forced her to do? Did you know her husband died in a fire? Your actions forced her to run headfirst into another one," he snarled.

Colt stared across the fire at Della, and a thick swallow bobbed in his throat. "I'll make it up to her. I'll make it up to both of you, I promise."

Cal sucked down a long, thoughtful gulp, feeling the alcohol work to hamper his temper before it exploded into full-on rage. Huffing angry gusts, he cast a sidelong glance at Colt, noting that deep bags had taken up residence under Colt's eyes and that his normally thick, shiny hair hung limp and dull over his slouched and hunched shoulders. The Second suffered under the weight of this. Whether or not it was even possible for him to make anything up to them, wisdom told Cal that taking this refreshed anger out on Colt wouldn't actually alter anything about their current circumstance.

Although younger than Colt when the bridge collapsed, he knew what it was to be haunted by remorse, to live with the angst of being forever forsaken with no path toward forgiveness, your every decision tainted and corrupted by fear and dread. There was no value in cursing Colt to perpetual penance. Perhaps he would curse himself, Cal couldn't change that, but for himself, he wanted no responsibility for that pronouncement.

Sighing, Cal dropped his chin in a move toward sufferance. "You made a mistake," Cal said, fishing for the words like moving about in a pitch-black room. "For what it's worth, I appreciate the apology."

Colt's shoulders deflated even farther, his expression one of weary wretchedness. "Thank you."

"A piece of advice"—Cal shifted on the log where he sat, bending his footless leg a few times at the knee to shake off some stiffness—"more important than making it up to me and Della, you need to find a way to forgive yourself."

Colt nodded slowly and stared into the fire, giving no indication of the merit of the advice. Slapping a palm on the Alpha's shoulder, Cal levered himself to his working foot before bending to retrieve his crutches.

He'd had enough Alpha heart-to-hearts for the evening, and now he needed his Omega.

*

Della

A strong arm hooked around her middle and hauled her against a broad, firm chest. Delighted, Della tried and failed to suppress a laugh. A deep voice purred in her ear, making her toes curl, "Are you finished networking and schmoozing?"

To her regret, she'd introduced Cal to some of the more tedious terms and idioms of her former life, which, unsurprisingly, he now used to tease her with whenever possible. She swung a guilty glance toward the Omegas she'd been talking with, two of the new additions that had been held captive by the rogue attackers. As Hunter had described, the new Omegas were indeed a bedraggled group, fearful and bordering on paranoid after their ordeal. Della hadn't managed to get the full story out of them, but the hints and rumors she'd gleaned were grim enough. The question whether they'd choose to stay in Morris Hill or move along on their own lingered, unasked and unanswered by everyone. Della hoped with the impending construction of the Omega bunkhouse, they could be enticed to stay, if only for their well-being and safety. But, then again, contrary to the more forceful Alpha opinions, she understood it had to be their choice.

"I suppose I'm leaving," she said to the Omegas, reaching up to pat Cal on the cheek. "This poor invalid needs his beauty rest."

A rumbling growl cascaded down her spine, putting every erogenous zone on high alert. "Woman," his drawl accented with another deep growl, "don't test me."

"Good night, girls," she laughed before spinning in Cal's hold to wrap her arms around his neck and take in a deep, greedy lungful of his coffee-cinnamon scent. Seasoned over the long day with the tang of sweat, the bitter hint of beer, and the savory note of roasted pork, it made her senses twirl like an exuberant child spinning around till sick. "Hmmm," she hummed against his skin, "what kind of test are you proposing?"

She grinned up at him. A smile flirted on Cal's lips, and he bent to brush his lips over her cheek, then her jaw, and the sensitive spot behind her ear, making Della's shoulder shoot up in response. "Let's take a walk," he whispered, sliding a hand down to take a firm hold of her bottom.

They skirted several groups of Alphas who tried to entice them to stay with offerings of food and drink. Cal had become a minor celebrity around the growing village, and plenty of crude comments followed his polite declines, which only made Della laugh and shake her head in embarrassment. Undaunted, he powered through the party and charged into the dark, away from the fire's glow, with a determined step and swing of the crutches. At times like these, memories of her mate's easy, fluid, two-footed walk drifted to the surface of her mind, bringing with them a sad wistfulness for the loss of his sexy swagger. A small price to pay for surviving that night with their lives and their bond intact, but a price nonetheless.

Away from the party, their feet crunched along the gravel path, loud in the tranquil still of early night when only the scurry of a small animal in the underbrush or the distant hoot of an owl touched the wind. The dark, once able to send her heart rate skittering through the roof, now only elicited a dull wariness. She'd never be totally comfortable in this new wilderness, but the tether to Cal, with its shining warmth and connection, chased away the desolate fear of abandonment.

Notably, they were not taking a direct route back to their cabin and instead diverted by the newly restored mess hall. Cal's wide back, his pale shirt visible in the low light, disappeared around the corner. Della hastened her steps to catch up, amazed at how quick he managed to be, crutches notwithstanding.

She turned the corner into inky-black night, and an arm shot out and spun her body till her back pressed against the side of the new building. Rough, hard boards scratched at the bare backs of her arms, and the fresh, cut wood scent blended with Cal's musk and filled her lungs.

"There you are," spoke a voice in the darkness, repeating the first words he ever spoke to her. Only this time, instead of a mysterious stranger with an intriguing twang tripping her out of her staid, lonely routine, the words came from her beloved mate and lit her up from the inside.

Her hands found their way around his waist, nudging his shirt aside to seek the solid, anchoring feel of his skin. Slightly tacky in the humid night, where the air hung thick with moisture and expectation, her palms tingled at the contact. "Here I am," she whispered back, her unerring lips finding his in the darkness. She sighed into the familiar taste and feel of his sensual mouth, breathing him in, drinking him in, lapping him up, and loving him so, so much. Large, Alpha hands roved over her body, hot and hasty, teasing her breasts through the thin fabric of her sundress, kneading the dip of her waist, rounding the swell of her ass, and dragging her dress up her thighs. Communicating, beyond a shadow of a doubt, his intent for this little pit stop.

Cool air whisked over her legs, and Della arched into his touch, instantly awake, instantly alert, and instantly ready. Her lips fell away from his, and she tasted the line of his strong jaw and the divot in his chin, his salty tang exploding on her tongue. A broad knee worked its way into her crotch, bold and insistent and adding a tempting pressure for her to grind against. "Let's finish what we started that first night," he whispered in her ear as he fiddled with his belt.

Despite her cranking arousal, Della couldn't contain a small outburst. "Here? Now?"

Snatching her hand in his own, he brought it to meet his newly freed cock, and she circled him by both instinct and desire. "Yes, *now*," he said, exerting pressure on her hand, the unspoken signal to grip him tight and stroke the way he liked. Because she knew that now, reveling in the knowledge as she drew a grunt from his bobbing throat. "Best be quick before the party breaks up. Unless you want them to watch?"

His face was a shifting patchwork of shadows beneath the waning moon, but she heard the devil in his voice and upped the ante. "Good thing I didn't wear underwear," she said against his lips and then swallowed his groan like a glutton, his cock growing impossibly thicker in her palm.

She noted the crutches propped against the building, and a question popped out even as her legs spread wider. "You sure this is a good idea?"

With a frustrated groan, Cal adjusted his stance, planting the footless knee against the building for support. "Worst-case scenario? I fall over, and we finish on the ground."

Della snorted. "Worst-case scenario, I end up with splinters in my ass."

Cal chuckled against her neck, his teeth nipping at the scar of her mating bite. "And I will lovingly remove every single one. With my teeth."

A big, impatient hand hiked her leg to his hip, the scratch of his jeans thrilling and illicit under her bare thigh. It opened her damp sex to the night air and sent another anticipatory shiver down her spine as she continued to pump his dick. Hot and swollen, she guided it to her core, rubbing the velvety head over her expectant clit.

Cal's chest rumbled with an ardent growl, the sound vibrating against her hardened nipples and skittering pleasurable lightning down between her legs. Slick burst from her core, coating the petals of her sex and the tops of her thighs. Della moaned. Response to the Alpha growl was probably her favorite Omega trait. Even after two months, the growl always affected her thus, like a tether that yanked her arousal several rungs up the ladder. Not one to waste his gifts, Cal deployed it with a measured skill that kept her permanently on edge and always needing more.

"Slip it inside, and I'll do it again," he promised and goaded with a sensual purr that ignited her like a reflex. It was a wonder the bond, now crackling with hot, sexual electricity, didn't light *her* up like a glow bug from the inside out.

Hands clumsy, Della made the connection, tilting her hips to notch him in place. Cal reached down, gripping her naked ass cheek for support as he drove inside. Della's head fell back, a dull, hollow thud against the building as her body stretched around the delicious impaling. His hips levered back and punched forward again, gliding through the slick with wet, squelching noises, filling her again and again.

Cal licked up her neck, open-mouthed and hungry. "So fucking hot," he breathed, "your pussy is so hot for me." He squeezed his hand on her ass tighter, pulling her cheeks apart and dragging her pelvis onto his cock. "You want more, Omega? You want my growl?"

He plunged inside, fast and rough, hitting a spot that shot fireworks off in her belly. "Yes," she said, all semblance of dignity and reserve incinerated in the detonation. She did want it. She wanted all of it: his cock, his growl, his hands, his voice, his purr, his knot, his body, his smile, his heart. All the things she'd run from that first night, the things she'd convinced herself she didn't want, things that would only bring her pain, now she wanted them all. She wanted all of *him*, now and forever, and to that end, there was one more thing she needed to do.

Desperate fingers scraped a path along his prickly chin and clenched in the scruff of his neck, hauling his throat to her mouth so she could breathe him in and savor the promised sound against her lips. "Give it to me. Give me your Alpha growl. *Please, Alpha.*"

The plea put him over the edge, and he unleashed his thrusts, pumping so hard her teeth rattled together, and she clung to his body to climb the crest of her pleasure. A growl charged out of him. Long and low and thick with feeling, it danced across her lips, buzzed her nipples, and sent her sex into tight, hot spasms around his invading cock.

Words left her tongue, strings of incomprehensible vulgarity, and her teeth found their way to his shoulder, where mid-second climax, they pierced his salty, fragrant skin. Cal's back seized up, his rhythm ceasing for a split second before redoubling in efforts. Della held on, sinking her teeth in so there would be no question, no mistake as to the intent and purpose. She had delayed delivering this final gift, waiting for the right time, but beneath the moon on a night that felt both old and new, she had no doubt the moment had arrived.

His body a coiled spring, Cal thrust a final time, and hot, iron-rich blood oozed over her lips. Riding the crest, Della lapped it up, tasting his pleasure in every swipe of her tongue. She released his flesh, feeling the shock and astonished joy flood the bond, the ecstasy of his climax taking a back seat to this new development. "Della, my darlin'," Cal panted with reverence and awe.

A single beam of moonlight stretched across his face and burnished his beloved golden eyes a wolfish silver. His knot filled her entrance, and their bond exploded in a shower of dazzling white-light shards, buzzing with glittery, snapping electricity.

Della ghosted her lips over his and whispered, "There *you* are."

THE END

If you want more of the AfterEnd Omegaverse sign up for my newsletter at **www.marloweroy.com** for bonus epilogues, character artwork and more.

Want to see what I'm up to next? Come join me on Instagram and say hi!
https://www.instagram.com/marloweroyauthor

xo, Marlowe.

Acknowledgments

To my fellow authors and beta readers, Deena, Liz, and Jocelyn, thank you for your support and feedback. You made this book immeasurably better.

I'm forever grateful to Merel and the Reticent Desires team for ongoing cheerleading and enthusiasm for my writing. It honestly kept me going this last year.

Special thanks to my readers and everyone who has been cheering me on and patiently (or not so patiently!) awaiting this story. A particular shout out to Barbara J., who sent me some very creative dirty talk for inspiration, and to Kim R. who helped me with Rue's French-Canadianisms. Don't worry, Rue will get her story, too.

As always, thanks to Dawn who not only did another bang-up developmental edit, but sent me the greatest one-line email I've ever received. It said: SHE CUT OFF HIS FOOT?!?!?!?!?!?!!

Speaking of which, many thanks to Dr. Sean and Dr. Elsa for exchanging truly unhinged text messages with me while I tried to figure out this amputation scene. For the record, Sean, you didn't have to remind me there are two bones in the lower leg, but I appreciate it all the same. However, I do *not* appreciate learning what a Gigli saw is and I advise anyone reading this to *never* google that.

Big hugs to my real-life friends, Mary, Allison, and Diana, who buy my books and gift them to people and guard my secret identity. Y'all are the best; let's go celebrate.

Lastly, I couldn't do any of this without the support of my own hero husband and my very loud, but very adorable, children. Please know that I love you and I'm sorry for all the times I yelled "Leave me alone, I'm writing!" XO.

Marlowe Roy

Marlowe Roy is a Midwestern transplant living in the beautiful Pacific Northwest. Her husband describes her dystopian omegaverse stories as "punchy and unboring." She writes late at night and on weekends and does not want to go for a hike.